D0919745

THE WAILING MOUNTAIN

MIHAILO LALIĆ

The Wailing Mountain

Translated from the Serbo-Croat by Drenka Willen

HARCOURT, BRACE & WORLD, INC. ⊞ **NEW YORK**

CONTENTS

There Was Darkness . . .

Men's chests have grown cold,
freedom has died in them
as light dies on the mountain
when the sun goes down into the sea . . .

       —NJEGOŠ

FOG

YESTERDAY THERE WERE meadows here, and a forest. On the other side of the valley, if I remember correctly, there was a rutted plateau. Now everything seems different. Fog lies across the wrecked land, gradually dissolving it. Of the forest I have nothing but memories: it vanishes like an apparition, only to reappear somewhere else. It comes back to me in the form of an unusually long dream. At times a cliff appears, attacked by fog, the transformed remnant of a flooded shore. Then for a long while there's nothing except us, deprived of our own shadows, diving into this vague, vacuous softness, without bottom and without sky.

I don't really know where we are and I don't want to think about it. Let Vasil think, or Ivan, if they want to. I'm all right the way I am. I walk through caves of branches arching overhead, along winding corridors, rising and falling. Subterranean halls open up, along with the secret world of one's imagination. If only I could go back to such things, where everything was created from nothing, and to no purpose . . . ! There was an odd sort of passion in it which still touches me occasionally. I should like to find it and grab onto it, but I don't know how. It's slipping away from me, into a vacuum. It has already slipped away.

And, as in a dream when the scene changes—you're chasing a butterfly and find yourself face to face with some monster—I recognize myself as I am: bearded, louse-ridden, a heap of rags. . . . Under my arms impetigo is spreading, and it torments me. A patch on my trousers irritates me constantly; it flaps behind me like raindrops, sometimes like footsteps—a man approaching breathlessly to take a shot at us. I was

3

fooled like that twice, but it won't happen again. I cut the patch off with a knife. I look at it—a strange object: it's as though it belonged to someone else or to no one at all.

I am reminded of Niko, the cave, and the apples at Gubavche.

I listen to the rain, remembering Anya as she ripped open the lice-infested seams of an old overcoat with her white, delicate fingers. Her face was pale, her mouth compressed. She cut off a piece of cloth and pondered a long time: where should this patch go? She was having difficulty threading the thick wool yarn. I close my eyes and ask myself if there was anything between her and Niko. I feel myself envying him and think that envy, like poverty and nakedness, ought to be covered up by a patch of some kind.

"What are you doing, Lado?" Vasil asked me. "Why are you staring at the patch?"

"I'm shedding the past," I said, and tossed the patch away.

"Don't be ridiculous. You'll have nothing left."

"I have the impetigo."

And what has he got, I thought? He's making a face. Something's bothering him. Or is he drowsy and trying to keep himself awake by being mean? I feel much the same. Since I've become invisible, I should like at least to hear myself. So the two of us quarreled. But Ivan would have none of it.

"Why are you squabbling like children? Be still. This is a damned good day for traveling."

"Day!" said Vasil, bewildered. "What day? This is simply . . . fog."

Ivan fell silent and hurried on to hide his laughter. He was all good spirits. And why not? What could be more natural? He had suddenly found himself in his element. I've always suspected it: he is not like Vasil and myself, superficial beings given to noise and vanity. He is one of those who quietly gather strength in the darkness, preparing for some sort of permanent role. Sometimes such men are successful. When they are not, they go back into the darkness as though nothing had ever happened, to prepare themselves once more.

A pine, felled in distant times, glistened like the skeleton of a sea monster that had been picked clean. There were pine-woods all about; one sank into the needles up to one's knees. Juniper branches like apparitions were everywhere. The long, indecisive dawn that was our day began to retire penitently, fading into darkness. The forest obliterated our path. The three of us sat down at the roots of a juniper tree, whose high invisible branches were spinning raindrops from the fog. The resin smell, softened and muted, surrounded us like a regret for some indefinite thing that had once been beautiful.

Vasil collected dry twigs and made a fire. This is clearly his greatest pleasure: warming his feet by a fire and lighting a cigarette with its coals. He can have his pleasure today: the smoke will not be seen. The fire is already crackling, the flames jumping after one another like red squirrels. Around us is a fresh smell of bark and pith. A whole new world is being created: the juniper above is our roof, and for walls we have logs overgrown with moss. The fire has miraculously improved everything, even the past. Perhaps we haven't lost as much as we think, perhaps ours is merely a momentary loss. We'll muster those who are left, give them new life, and where now there is but one man, there will be a whole army. . . .

Ivan spotted something nearby. He tapped me with his hand and motioned to the right. I turned around: a rabbit was squatting, looking at us, rubbing his eyes with his paw. I felt like stroking his head, but that would have frightened him away. I preferred just watching him and his small twitching nose. He looked a trifle surprised: as a rule he was hunted by everyone, yet here no one even bothered him. Vasil suddenly started and swung about. His gun was lying across his lap; he raised it slightly and fired. A fluff of gray hair dispersed and blew away into the fog.

"Why did you do that?" Ivan asked.

"He was sniffing about like a spy."

"If you'd let Lado shoot, at least we'd have had some dinner."

Instead we had to go; the shot had betrayed our presence. We were hesitant about leaving: we had enjoyed ourselves under the juniper. Ivan scattered the coals, pushed them down into the earth. The coals hissed in defiance, revenging themselves with a wrathful smoke. That was the end of that. We stumbled on something that felt like a path and followed it. The light was uneven—in the clearings the sun was coming up, under the trees it was still pitch dark. Finally we reached a mountain that looked like the Devil's Table. For a while I thought it was the Table. One cliff made me think it was, but then I saw that my cliff was built of fog and fantasy. The spring wasn't where it was supposed to be. The road turned uphill instead of down. This wasn't it.

Nor did I know what hill it was. We crossed it anyway, following a straight path that stretched like a beam toward an infinity beyond this earth. Finally the path ended in a knoll scabby with rocks. Vasil wanted to climb to the top. So did I. Perhaps the sun was up there somewhere. But not Ivan.

"I don't think you know where we are," he said to Vasil.

"No. Do you?"

"You should have spoken up earlier."

What difference would that have made? We have to move on even though we've no idea where we are. Does anyone know where he is under this rotten sky? Not our men, certainly, who are isolated islands and lighthouses, nor the others, who would like to put them out. But it'll be dangerous to enter the Kolashin Mountains. It's easy enough to get lost there, even without fog. A guide's no help—you could never be sure whose side he was on.

We descended into a small valley. A stream was roaring and clamoring nearby. We washed our faces and dried them on our sleeves. We were plodding slowly across the hillside in large open arcs. That's the best way—the less ground you cover, the less risk you run of getting lost. Night would come soon, and tomorrow—better luck! Vasil bent down and picked up something from the ground.

"The same damned spot again," he said. "This is the patch you threw away to get rid of your past, Lado."

At first I thought he must be joking. His eyes were playing a trick on him. How did the patch get here? Who brought it here? My head was spinning. Ivan didn't believe it either. He felt the patch as doubting Thomas felt the wounds: there was the same broken thread. No two ways about it: we were going in circles.

At any rate, we do know where we are. We can go on, but it's dusk and the fog's grown thicker. Soon there'll be no light at all. The scraps of the past no longer exist, nor do the memories of its solidity. Those branchy caves have merged into one, into softness and despair. Everything that's happened and that's about to happen grows more pliant. The subterranean halls have melted away. Only the fine porous substance of time and space remains, not as yet molded, to rock in this vast cradle.

YABLAN, THE FOUNTAIN AND THE GIRL

I FELT SUDDENLY worried and oppressed with foreboding. I stopped for a moment to think why, but by then the feeling had gone. The faint hint of it that still clung to me led me back into my childhood—the snows and clanging mornings filled with fear.

Those mornings were crowded with wild congregations of

some canine religion. Mountain dogs as big as bulls came
down to establish the true faith and to wring the necks of all
the heretics in the valley. They would start their sermons off
in deep bass voices, without passion or excitement. It was the
sins they enumerated, heavy and growing heavier, that finally
worked them into a rage. Then the slaughter began. Their
victims would let out shrill squeals and dying sobs, their
spines broken, their throats torn, their intestines spread out
on the snow.

The crows fled from the fields and hid in the bare alders.
Men were astride their horses, noisily brandishing their clubs
in defense. Those who didn't have horses clustered together
for greater safety. Everyone was terrified of those dogs and
thought of nothing but how to save his own skin. I knew
the best way: not to go out of the house! However, one had to
go to school, and all night long I would think of my lonely
hazardous journey through that slaughter in which everything
within reach was torn to pieces.

A faint sound, more an echo than a voice, encroached upon
my hearing, breaking this chain of memories. Down the hillside and under the coil of fog, someone had coughed perhaps,
or a dog had barked in the snow. The same uneasiness came
over me again. For a long time now I had thought I was free
of fear; yet the anxiety was still there, caused not by dogs, but
by people. Encounters with people were tiring and required
constant vigilance: one had to uncover their deceptions, figure
out why they wanted to deceive you in the first place, lie to
them in turn, and make certain they didn't find out who you
were or where you were going. . . .

The fog left only broken tails in the valley, resembling
scraps of a polyp torn to shreds—the blind pieces drifting in
search of each other. Their wriggling and shifting made the
mountain surge—green hillsides and ribs of grassy ridges
emerged, sunlit cliffs appeared and then sank away again.
Everything was uncertain except danger, and danger concealed itself carefully.

Even in the *katuns* there was no safety. Often these clusters of herdsmen's huts high on the mountain slopes were left empty. The Italians rarely gave our people permission to graze their cattle on those high summer pastures. When they did, it was only to lure us up there and seize us.

We finally reached *katun* Yablan, which belonged to Velko Plechovich. We were supposed to look for Velko. But how? From a distance we could be any group of men with rifles; there was no way he could tell us from his enemies. Only luck could bring us to him, but luck hadn't been with us for a long time.

Between us and the next patch of forest lay a meadow—an unavoidable open space that we hesitated to cross. In the meadow, spring water poured from a pipe into a hollow log trough beneath. On the slopes above one could see the cluster of huts called Yablan. I went out to scout the area. Two children were splashing each other with water from the trough. Soon they started to quarrel, and ran off, yelling at each other. This might be a good time to cross unnoticed.

I was about to signal my companions to move up when a girl appeared, carrying two pails. Even from a distance she struck me as being quite beautiful. Then I realized that she was also quite young. She put down her pails and peered about to see if anyone was around. Then, cautiously, she lifted her long knitted skirt up above her knees and let a stream of water from the fountain pour down over her sunburned leg and trickle off her ankle. I stared at her as this scene unfolded, like a secret, and for a few moments I forgot that I existed. I moved toward her, frantically searching for something to say. She was startled and turned pale.

"Don't be afraid," I said. "I don't eat people. How are you?"

She mumbled a few words, glancing nervously up at my beard, and then at the crossed bones on my cap.

"Are there any Partisans hiding around here?" I asked.

"No," she said. "There are no more Partisans."

"Come now! What about Velko Plechovich? You are hiding

him, and keeping him for seed. But I'll find him. With this knife, see, I'll cut his throat!"

She looked at me in astonishment, her eyes resting on the endless array of rags and patches that made up my trousers.

"I have a new pair of trousers at home," I said. "But, tell me, girl, when are you going to get married?"

"There's time enough for that," she replied, and bent down to scoop up water with her pail.

"Listen, I like you! Let's get married! How would you like that? Your eyes are just right, and your legs too, by God!"

She picked up the pails and started off from the trough. As she left she turned and said:

"Not with that beard, not if you were the only man left in the world!"

"I can shave it off," I protested. "I would shave it off to please you. Even if it were made of gold. Right now, if you want. Look!"

But she didn't want to look. She was running toward the huts, the water from the pails splashing over the grass by the road. Before she could raise an alarm we hurried across the meadow. In the woods we sat down to rest. Yablan could be seen through the foliage—four huts with smoke rising from them, and a fifth in ruins. Two children were climbing in the trees like monkeys. Everything was calm, except that Vasil and Ivan were giving me a long sermon: how stupid it was for me to have exposed myself by the trough. They are right; why did I have to speak, I thought. But I felt no remorse. In fact, I was not really thinking about it at all, but, rather, lying in wait to catch another glimpse of the girl. Soon she appeared on a narrow path, carrying a pile of leafy branches for the steers. I envied the steers. My God, sweet must be the leaves that her hand offers . . . !

We were about to push on when Velko Plechovich turned up. Ruddy, round-cheeked, he was wearing a cap of rabbit fur. He must have been watching us from some sheltered spot, waiting for a good moment to surprise us.

"You're a bunch of gypsies," he said. "Without those rifles you could pass for beggars. Everyone would pity you, and you'd get a bowl of soup to boot."

"You sniffed us out all right," said Vasil.

"A spy network, comrade! No one gets through my territory without my knowing it."

"Is there anything to eat in your territory?" asked Ivan.

"We'll find something," he said, as though it were a simple matter.

He led us to a wooded spot that commanded a good view of the approaches. From a hollow tree trunk covered with leaves he took out a bucket of milk and a basket of bread. Real bread! True, there was cabbage in it, but that kept it soft; there was carob bark in it, but that made it smell like chocolate. Ivan patted it fondly with his hand; Vasil sniffed it. I reached for my knife, and Velko said:

"Is that the knife you cut throats with? You frightened the daylights out of my niece. And you can all go to hell!"

"A nice girl, your niece. Put in a good word for me," I said.

"This area is swarming with my relatives."

"That's why you are so ruddy," said Vasil. "You've rooted yourself here like an oak. You don't stir, by God."

There is indeed something oaklike about Velko: his joints resemble knots and he seems to have more of them than nature requires. His hands are thin and small, almost childlike, but nothing short of iron can resist them. He is solid and slow, and has that indifference to time and external danger that is common to all the Plechovichi. Even when they don't want to be honest, they tell the truth, because they don't know any better. Their women are highly valued because they bear healthy, beautiful children. As a result the Plechovichi have always had rich and influential friends.

"We are going to set up base near here," said Ivan, "and later you can join us."

"Your menu is not exactly inviting," replied Velko. "So why

in God's name should I join you? I am of some use here, but
what would I do out there? Just one more hungry man."

"You've got a love-nest here," said Vasil, "so why join the
hermits? I wouldn't either."

Ivan disagreed; it was much better to be in company than
alone. The habit of indoctrination was strong with Ivan, but
Velko resisted with the self-sufficiency of an island. It didn't
do him much good. When Ivan has something on his mind,
there is no room for common sense; he attacks with boring
and deadly persistence. I turned away so as not to listen to
that steady rainfall, each drop of which could pierce a rock.
I glanced up at the village, where three or four steers were
sporting with each other. One of them charged into the fence,
whirled around and paused as if to think about what had
hit him.

As though on purpose the girl didn't appear again. I grew
tired of waiting. I rested my head on a rock—I'll surprise her
when she thinks I am not looking. . . . In fact, she's not
Velko's niece at all, but my Vidra! I had taken it into my head
that Vidra had been killed, but she hadn't been, really. She
had recovered at a hospital and was sent here by the Party,
disguised as a peasant. She still bears me a grudge for having
left her in ruined Belgrade, and that's why I haven't heard
from her. Perhaps she doesn't even know that I was pushed off
the truck. After all, she was unconscious. That doesn't matter
now: she's alive. The mere thought that she exists fills me with
a painful, sobbing pleasure. Perhaps she will hear some news
of me. Perhaps she will forgive me someday.

GRASS AND WATER

THEY SAY THAT if you dream about someone and you want that person to dream about you, all you have to do is turn your pillow over on awakening. I turned over a rock. It is not because I am superstitious, but, rather, because it is a man's duty to do what he can. If under this stony pillow, or anywhere else for that matter, there is even a trace of that soul which visited me in my sleep, let it be released. And, indeed, I feel that her soul is accompanying me now. A childlike joy shines through the bearded forest above the path and the clearings.

There is something young, silly, and unfathomable in this dream, sparkling with unfamiliar colors and transforming the pine trees, the hills and people. The world has suddenly become amusing. Velko Plechovich struts about, bearing himself as befits the master of the house. This is his territory, and it covers a whole series of feudal possessions, of forests and pastures, reaching all the way to Niko's land. While other men were falling dead and perishing, those two stood like oaks whose deep roots protect the land around them from erosion. It is a good thing there are strong men around. Without them this country would be bare and foreign.

At last the time came for Velko to turn back.

"Watch out," Ivan repeated for the tenth time. "You think everyone is as honest as you are. A price has been set on your head; and someone will pay it."

"Probably. But how will I recognize him?"

"Don't trust anyone."

"What the hell! You have to die sometime, or you'll be a hundred years old before you know it. And that's too old."

We shook hands. Now we were alone again. Suddenly it grew gray and cold. I could no longer remember a single image from my dream. Everything goes to waste, a dream more quickly than anything else. It is strange that I was able to pay it any attention at all. The radiant dream had been replaced by the usual slag of sorrow and anxiety. A breeze I hadn't noticed before blew the leaves wrong side up, and the late summer flowers were closing as though the sun had set. I turned to look at Velko—he too had gone down. I didn't understand how he could have disappeared so quickly.

All around there was the dull, slow surging of mountains. The sky was overcast and a steady cold rain filtered through the patches in our clothes. We took off our shoes; it was easier to walk barefoot. From the north a huge cloudburst was moving in like a massive wall of soot. It was still far away, but I heard its roar interrupted by occasional thunder. Its progress was uneven: it paused a while when it crossed a valley invisible from here, then suddenly leaped across a whole mountain range, erasing it from view. Vasil grew angry: he cursed God, the only means of punishing Him for His many betrayals.

Ivan was indifferent. He didn't give a damn about all the noise and clatter. He spotted a hut whose roof had fallen in, and that, he said, was just what we needed. A dozen boards were still standing; the ground under them was dry and inviting. Through the cracks in the beams we had a good view of the nearby meadow. And no one could creep up on us unnoticed.

It grew dark, and a heavy rain rattled against the boards and into the puddles which were forming everywhere. Hail was crackling against twigs in the forest. The storm subsided, then it swelled again. So it went. A gust of wind jolted the roof, then the rain turned to pour in at an angle that caught us as we squatted against the planks.

Finally the storm blew over. The rain kept up; drops glistened in the light. Ivan motioned to me to look through a crack in the planks. What could it be? A rabbit or a bear . . . ? Neither. It was an even greater miracle—a man. How the devil did he get here? I was scared: perhaps he had seen us. . . . But then why would he be standing there, shoeless and hatless, with a hoe in his hand? He was up to his knees in water, and still he didn't seem to have enough of it. He was channeling water into a ditch, distributing it through the field. He seemed to find great pleasure in his work—he was one of those prehistoric cattle breeders who since time immemorial have worshipped water and grass. It is their inheritance and their lifeblood.

Still it would be better if he didn't see us. The news would spread. Let's hope he doesn't. He seemed absorbed in what he was doing. Then, for a minute, he vanished. My fear was replaced by sadness. What have we come to that after all our glories we should fear this wet, miserable lout of a shepherd? Everyone has turned against us; everything imperils us. We raised our heads: the sound of footsteps in front of the hut. The shepherd put down his hoe and, stooping, entered the hut. Instantly, he straightened up, bracing himself against the door. Vasil grabbed him by the sleeve and pulled him inside.

"Lie down there," he shouted. "Why are you flooding this meadow anyway, if God himself is watering it from above?"

"I am a poor man, brother, so I do what I can. We just went through a winter without hay."

"You're no pauper, and don't lie—because I know everything! How many sheep do you have?"

"I swear to you by Saint Petka I sold my last twenty for grain."

"Twenty! Nonsense! Don't try to deceive me! You're Mirko, aren't you? See, I know! You swear by Saint Petka, but your patron saint is Archangel Michael; you never mention him when you're telling a lie."

It turned out, of course, that he had sold only eight sheep, and not for wheat either, but for a piece of meadow. However, he was set on complaining and annoying us anyway. I interrupted him, and I combed my beard in order to attract his attention to this distinguishing mark.

"Are you afraid of the Partisans?"

"I'm afraid of everyone, brother, I swear to God! Everyone is stronger than me. You can see how feeble I am, can't you?"

"When you steal hay," said Vasil, "you're not feeble, and you can lift a hundred pounds in one try."

He hates Communism, he said, because under Communism they all eat from the same pot and their women are passed around so that no one knows to whom the children belong. They managed to fill his head with this; no harm done really. The only thing that distinguishes him from his ancestors is that they were unfamiliar with such matters. What a difference! No wonder he hates us. We want to drag him through time into some sort of a kolkhoz in which he will be deprived of his lice.

"Old man, would you kill Niko? We'd pay you well. You'd get a hundred thousand lire."

"Niko Saykov? No, by God: how would I do it?"

"We'll give you a rifle. Here, take it."

"It's no good. He'd get me first anyway. They're fast, that family. His father was the same—quick to kill!"

"All right, if you won't do it, we'll do it ourselves. But, not a word, old man! You'll lose your head if anyone hears that you've seen us."

We left him seated alone inside the hut. He was not likely to leave much before dark. All the same Ivan wanted us to go through the forest, where we would leave no trace. The earth was covered up to our ankles with leaves and twigs, and we sank deep into its soft swampy mass. The distant hills looked familiar to me. We were getting close. The trees were still wet, and it was beginning to rain again, so that the mountains were concealed and we were again lost. The gods had intervened to upset our plans once more. But when we came to the spring I recognized the landscape and the road that led into the valley.

Barking came from around the huts and a sheep's bell echoed in the damp air. It was dusk; sheep were being milked, fires lit. People were shouting. It sounded like a quarrel, but that's only the way they talk. We turned in behind the hill and we could no longer hear their chatter. The Leper's Cave was on the other side of the low valley, but the forest was thick and dark: thick enough to scratch our eyes out should we enter it. I remembered a hut concealed behind a nearby slope. I found it from memory, proving I was the same man I had been before. Yes, the same!

We entered the hut. The air was dry and stale. I lit a match: the bed made of boards had not changed. Vasil brought in some wood.

"I wouldn't make a fire," Ivan said. "We don't know who may be around."

"If I don't get these rags dry," replied Vasil, "I'll catch pneumonia for sure."

"All right, have it your way. But we'll have to put it out soon."

Vasil took out kindling from his knapsack—he always carried some to disguise the emptiness of his bag. He lit one piece and let me hold it. I have been his apprentice in these matters for a long time now. But he would never let me do the job myself. No, not so long as his hands were healthy. He liked to awaken the first flame personally, to feel its shy warmth and see its flickering. When it started crackling, he rubbed his hands with pleasure and clapped his knees for joy, and his face broke into a wide smile. Sometimes it seemed almost a sexual pleasure for him. Or perhaps it evoked some clandestine remembrance that even he had forgotten.

Using branches as prongs we hung our coats over the fire to dry. They looked like scarecrows laughing at each other. We removed the boards from the bed, so each one of us had something to stretch out on. Creeping around the hut, Ivan removed two slats from each window. If the door were blocked, we could escape that way.

Now everything is neat and orderly. Shadows play on the planks, as in childhood, when Dana made pancakes and Branko and I stole them from the platter as quickly as she made them. We had a long stick, pointed at the end, and with it we picked up the pancakes when her back was turned. She would look at the dish in surprise—it wasn't getting any fuller! Then suddenly she saw what was happening. "You little devils," she laughed, "what will you do next?" In fact—that was all we did.

SAVE YOUR OWN SKIN

FROM THE OTHER side of the valley, as through a porous wall, a shapeless sound arose. At first I listened to it indifferently, not knowing whether it was the wind or the fog. But then it separated itself from nothingness, penetrated the surface with two syllables: la . . . do, and hovered in the dark. As it got closer I realized that the two syllables were my name. Someone was calling me, and I was not at all pleased. Someone who didn't know where I was and hoped to find me. It sounded like a man drowning, desperately wanting me to give him a hand. It was dark. What could I do? I had no idea where this man was. Suddenly I was wide awake, and sat up waiting to hear the voice again. Disturbed by my commotion, Vasil sprang to his feet.

"What is it, Lado?"

"I thought I heard someone calling me."

He listened. "It's a dream. I hear the same thing myself now and then."

"Should I put out the fire?"

"Let it be. It'll go out by itself," he said, and fell asleep instantly.

The rain had stopped. Water was dripping steadily from the trees, each drop making a separate sound. Nothing else existed in this wasteland. Those cries had indeed been a dream. All the same I could not forget them. They awakened anxieties and fears that had been dormant for a long time. Then I heard a cry in the distance: a whiff of air, curdled with pain, was hurled toward me. Perhaps it's Iva and her child: but that isn't a woman's voice; it's a man's, hoarse and distorted by pain. . . .

He is calling me in vain. It's no good thinking about my own family all the time. Others are suffering too. The shadows are playing on the planks. Ivan is asleep. He must have been unusually exhausted, because he fell asleep while the fire was still going. One coal is still holding its own, wounded all over: the flames, like butterflies, are hovering above it in swarms—some golden, others purple. They snatch at each other, then wander off into the darkness and die. They are dwindling in number. There's plenty of heavy smoke left. It's not true that smoke is the excrement of fire, as some say; it is, rather, her weeping, twofold: once at birth, once at death.

I fell asleep again and soon found myself with the sheep at Gluv. The autumn, the leaves, the shepherds' fires . . . They draw out a heap of baked potatoes from under the ashes. Their smell excites me and I cannot wait to begin eating. The neighborhood girls are around me, but they don't care much for food. They are ripe for marriage and they seek a man's strong grasp. So they wave their kerchiefs and twitter like birds. Their breasts rise under their blouses and their bare legs glisten under their whirling skirts. They are dancing a reel around the fire with increased speed and intensity, disappearing one after another as in a game of hide-and-seek.

Now the girls are in the blackberry bushes; their song has died down. I am left alone. But a stranger is standing at the door. I am simply unable to open my eyes to see who it is. There is really no need to open my eyes. I can see him any-way: he's holding a rifle and looking down at me. I should figure out my next move before he realizes that I am awake. I reach for my rifle, but it's too heavy. Something is pressing on it, I cannot lift it for the life of me. How would it be if I simply jumped up and fled . . . ? But he has me in his power, and is merely waiting to make his final move. My only chance is to play for time.

I simply cannot understand how I managed to fall into a trap like this. All around there is a chaotic region of valleys and hills, and in the distance a door. Vasil and Ivan have gotten away. They must have escaped through the windows, leaving me behind. Who knows why? Perhaps they thought I had already gone. I am not surprised. Under such circum-stances you think of nothing but saving your own skin. But then again, who cares? When this rascal flattens me on the ground—there goes my skin.

I raised my head slightly: the door was ajar. I was cold. There was fear in the pit of my stomach. My body, which had been calm, gave way to trembling. Tears came to my eyes, not from the smoke, but from sadness and some sort of mocking self-pity. I felt sick, ready to vomit, softened and dizzy. The feeling of falling through space! You cannot stand upright any more and the world is at a permanent tilt. All the same, let me fall on something hard at long last, reach some bottom. . . . I turned over quickly and unfastened my holster. The man at the door said:

"Who are you?"

Perhaps he really doesn't know who we are. His voice is not at all unpleasant; underneath the coarseness there is a gentle quality. I could swear that we had once talked together.

"Come on, my doves," he mocked us. "I won't harm you, on my Partisan word of honor!"

He must be stupid, I thought, to try this old trick on us. There was a time, during the winter and spring, when we fell for it, but not any more. I brought the pistol up to my cheek. All I had to do was to slip a bullet into the barrel. . . .

"Don't move," he cried harshly. "You'll get shot uselessly, so don't move, I repeat."

"I'll move, by God, even if your teeth are made of steel," said Vasil, rattling his rifle.

"Ah Vasil! You're the one I'm looking for! Didn't you recognize my voice . . . ?"

"I was scared, you madman. To hell with your voice and everything else."

It must be one of our men. It's Niko Saykov! I quickly let go of the pistol, or I would have shot him, I was so tense. I should be happy to see him, and, like Vasil, jump up in pleasure. But no! I was humiliated by my fear. Real danger would have been preferable. As it was, I felt cheated, my anger repressed; and I lacked the courage to laugh at myself. I got up, but I could hardly stand on my feet. I offered him my hand: it was trembling. He will know that I was frightened. No, he suspected nothing—he grabbed my hand and shook it heartily.

I withdrew my hand. His heartiness was too much for me. Shabbier than I, he resembled a loose rock that teeters in the dark and threatens to drag me down along with it. Ivan was also peevish.

"What would have happened, Niko, if you had run into a Chetnik patrol instead of us?"

"That had just occurred to me," he replied. "We would have cursed each other. Good practice for my tongue."

"And is that wise?"

"Perhaps it isn't," he said, and paused. Suddenly he was agitated. "But is it wise for me to be hanging about here like some damned Robinson Crusoe? What point is there in this stupid life, cut off from everything? What's the point? What's so wise about that?" He waited for a reply and then continued: "I fought! I carried out orders even when I didn't like them, and now you've entombed me here, and I have to hide from my child, my wife, and God knows how many patrols, as if I were a leper. I have no idea why I am here. I feel I am being punished. . . ."

Perhaps he's right, I thought. Two months ago we should have gathered everyone together and joined a regular unit. That would have saved us, and I would now be somewhere else, and things would be better. But Martich brandished his directive like a sword and delivered that exasperating tirade about how Bolsheviks were buried alive by Russian peasants and how the Party sent replacements to follow them into the ground—all in order to maintain our ties with the people! We had been silent, and Martich reprimanded Niko, saying that he didn't have a speck of Communist spirit. As for Martich, he didn't wait for the peasants to bury him, dead or alive. He gave himself up and now sits quietly at home. And Niko is doing penance here.

I don't feel sorry for Niko. He doesn't want pity anyway. On the contrary, he likes to appear tougher and sharper than is humanly possible. He is really like a stone, and it never occurs to anyone to pity a stone until it starts rolling into an abyss. And now, in the light of the fire that Vasil has revived, his face seems chiseled out of clashing straight lines.

Ivan yielded the point instantly. He had an inborn sense of knowing how to give way the moment he was wrong. He smiled, looking a little guilty, and offered Niko some tobacco. Niko hesitated, but finally rolled himself a cigarette, lit it with a coal, and inhaled passionately, as if he hadn't smoked in days. Perhaps he hadn't. Who would have given him tobacco? I felt a stab of pity, but then I remembered how he had frightened me. I changed my mind. The pain in the pit of my stomach was a barrier between us. I knew that he hadn't wanted to wound me, but that didn't lessen the pain.

"I didn't know that was how matters stood," said Ivan. "Velko hasn't complained."

"Why should he?" said Niko. "He has his clan; they're protecting him. Even our enemies protect him. After all, the situation may change and he may be of use to them. They are all the same: for protection you put one of your men in each party. Velko has a position and that's something. But I have nothing. To them I'm a foreigner, as my father was before me, and if they lose someone, they resent my survival. Sometimes they'll offer me food, but they aren't happy about it. And they say: 'Don't call on us again, we have nothing, but if you should see Velko, or Ivan, tell them to come see us.'"

His voice creaks as though two grindstones are rubbing hard against each other. Sometimes a spark flies, and then again a bitter tear. I am afraid he'll start crying, and then I will too.

A TEETERING ROCK

I AM LYING in the sun, under the skies, in the scent of the juniper trees. Hunger is getting to me, but that's nothing new. I can think of other things and amuse myself while watching the River Lim flow by. The river left its bed during the night and started wandering in the groves. Along the way it wiped out the gypsy encampments, dug ditches in the meadows, built up dams of tree trunks and rocks. It cannot get along without some sort of mischief

A lark whistled by like a bullet and chirruped high up.

"Some joy that is!" Ivan sneered. "She had an impulse to fly; so what? What is there to be joyful about up there? The air, the skies, empty . . ."

"We get impulses too," said Niko.

"What, for example?"

"I should like to hear the whistle of a train again."

Vasil raised his head and looked over at Niko: he must be joking. No, he is tired of silence, he says—there is too much of it here. As for me, it's just the opposite: I find it too noisy, too much empty talk. I should prefer to sit in silence and watch the village across the Lim. A wall is still standing where the house of my father, Yoko the Sly, once stood. The spot below the road, that's a well, and there are plum trees around it. I think of how much time I spent there, running around barefoot as wedding parties and armies passed by. And now it is coldly staring at me as if it were a stranger. This indifference of the dead landscape angers me.

They are talking again, and they are telling stories. One is about some meadow or other, about a man who sold it, the last piece of land his father had left him. Actually someone sold it for him. He just gave his approval. And who should have bought it but the greedy Mikla? Now Mikla owes him a lot of money, and he has nothing to eat. Twice he has offered to forget the debt if she would only give him a sack of flour. She would get the meadow for next to nothing, but even so she didn't give in. I don't have any flour, she said. No one believed her, of course. Sue me, she said, knowing that he could never do such a thing. Her real hope was that he would be killed, and she would get the meadow for nothing at all.

"Tyranny," I said in sudden bitterness. "I know that kind. A wet rope for her . . ."

"What!" Ivan's reddish eyes almost popped out.

"Over her rear end. Twist her skirt around her head, and then beat her bare ass until it turns blue."

"The Chetniks would later ring all the church bells to adver-
tise her well-striped bottom," said Vasil.

"And you, Lado, you would be the first to demand my expulsion from the Party," added Niko.

Forgive me! I didn't realize we were talking about Niko. I
babbled without thinking, basing what I said on general
principles of justice. But since it concerns Niko, it's a different
matter. Of course, as a Communist he has no right of protest.
Let him suffer! No one forced him to become a Communist.
But since he is a Communist, his hands are tied! He must live
on air, on alms and ideology. Think of the reaction of the
masses if one of us were to whip Mikla. To say nothing of the
Eastern Front and Russian-Allied collaboration. Of course, I
agree, absolutely: no one owes us anything, and nothing is
ours if anyone else needs it. That is the essence of self-denial.
A sacrifice has to be made, and who can make one if not us?

"How is Luban?" I asked.

"I don't know," said Niko.

"Haven't you ever dropped in on him?"

"Yes, but his woman barred the door and said I would enter
over her dead body. Luban is not at home, she said, but I
knew he was, of course, crawling among the cattle. Anything
was better than talking to us. We saw him later busying himself around the house."

"And Vanya?"

"As always."

"You mean like Luban?"

"No, worse. Vanya actually stinks of fear. Like a skunk, he
spreads his smell around the whole region."

Niko would like to stop talking. This whole matter is
boring. But Ivan will not let him. Ivan is pursuing it as far as
he can, as if there were some special pleasure in rummaging
through this stench. We knew that Vanya had actually arranged his own surrender to the Chetniks, and allowed his
father-in-law to disarm him. And now he sits and rots at

home. There were several similar cases of prearranged
capture. Ivan wants to know everything in detail; he is even
taking notes. It so happens that a man was captured along
with Vanya, and this man had borrowed Niko's rifle—so all
Niko had left in the way of arms was a hand grenade. But
that had been Vanya's. The following day Vanya sent his
mother to beg for it.

"You didn't give it up, did you?" asked Vasil in astonishment.

"I did. It made me sick. One can sometimes go mad out of
pure disgust, and then a man doesn't know what he is doing."

And so Niko reached us at Moykovats without anything. He
was mocked behind his back for having let the Chetniks disarm him.

"You haven't seen Vanya since?" asked Ivan.

"Yes, I have, and do you know what he said? 'I plead with
you in the name of Saint John to leave my house! I plead with
you in the name of God not to call on me again!' And it was
all like that."

Niko laughed miserably. Ivan watched him with a frozen
face and had no further questions. The situation was worse
than he had realized. That was why he was silent. And all this
was caused by one miscalculation: when we returned from
Moykovats we decided that the peasants among us should
resume their lives as peasants again. Niko had warned us then
not to go back, that we'd be ruined, that our longing for bread
was too great. But that was too rational, or honorable, or what
have you. People are more attracted by what's comfortable. In
fact, the commandant turned out to be a traitor, the commis-
sar an opportunist. The silly theory of a "link with the people"
was concocted in a split second and blown up like a balloon.
These foul valleys. We felt a terrible longing for them; we
thought that they felt a longing for us too, that they wanted to
. . . bury us.

I closed my eyes in order to recall that night. A column
pushed up the hill in the snow softened by the south winds.

The snow was dirty. The birches glistened. There were no
stars. Niko broke from the column and sat by the road. He
stretched himself out full length. He must have been ill—but
no one leaned over to ask him anything or to try to help him.
Not even men from his own village. They blamed him for
suggesting that we abandon the River Lim and our homeland.
He wants to stay there, I thought, and later he'll join some
other battalion. Let him be! He is a stranger among us anyway.

"Why didn't you stay behind?" I asked him. "You could
have joined the Donyokraiski battalion."

"I could have, but it wouldn't have done me any good. They
were also sent back eventually."

"I wouldn't be here either," said Vasil, "but when the devil
takes hold of a man . . ."

It's useless talking about it now, because here we are! The
stunted juniper bushes, with their intricate low branches, form
a wall protecting us from surprise. We are sunning ourselves.
When we've had enough of the sun, we'll bury our heads in
the shade, exposing only our backs to the warmth. Niko has
gone looking for food—that explains why it's so quiet. Pa-
tiently I roast my impetigo, feeling its tentacles as they penetrate my flesh.

From time to time a hoarse bell is heard in a distant
pasture. Along the road a truck with soldiers buzzes by like a
swollen insect. Branches crackle in the thicket as Niko returns.
An odor precedes him, an odor already familiar to us: bread
made of carob. Food for mules. But since it has happened on
occasion that a mule has died from this food, the Italian quar-
termasters gladly swap carob for hay, pound for pound. It
appears that our people have strong stomachs, and one cannot
help but see a stroke of providence in it. True enough, some
have fallen ill, but no one has as yet died of it.

The first mouthfuls are not bad, with a sweet taste that
gradually becomes sickening. Ivan frowns, tastes it, and then
gives up. Niko has given up too. Vasil claims that there's some

mineral in it, some clay. I feel the same inorganic substance, but my stomach is empty and this emptiness is called hunger. I must fill it with something. The carob tastes increasingly like clay. I have filled my stomach with clay. My head aches, and my throat as well. I should very much like to throw it all up. The pain makes me see darkness. Objects close to me seem shaky; distance I can measure only by memory. The valley is like a well. In the well the dull blows of shooting echo.

"It's an attack on the Ramovichi," said Niko, whose face was pale.

"How did the Chetniks get there?"

"In search of bread. They're not accustomed to hunger. Or else some of our men have got into trouble."

"Nothing of the kind," said Vasil. "It's some Chetnik celebration."

"Celebration indeed! In honor of our flesh."

Niko's voice seemed to invite disaster. It was so unpleasant that it forced me to open my eyes and to stare, along with Vasil, at this gray face made of stone. What's the matter with you, man? Couldn't you give up this ominous color for a moment? Why always anticipate the worst? Even if you're right, who wants to know? Again a veil drops in front of my eyes and I can barely see Niko through it.

OUR UNJUST JUSTICE

I AM WALKING, but my legs feel like wool or straw. Soft, unsteady, disobedient. I am looking at them, touching them, but it doesn't help. The controlling mechanism seems to have been paralyzed. I experienced this sensation once before. It was right after the uprising; we were without any salt and lived off rice plundered from an Italian warehouse. We suspected that the food was poisoned or stale. Perhaps it's also true of carob, yet Niko doesn't seem to be bothered by it. No one else is bothered by it, except me. The men are walking and glancing back, and I am dragging myself and trotting and struggling after them. I have no time to recover my breath, and yet I am not catching up with them either.

They seem to be deliberately hurrying. They have secrets which they don't want me to share. It's not really that, I know, but I must find an object for my anger. I lower myself to the ground. I cannot move another step. Let them go! They seem to have their minds set on it anyway. Leaves swivel and whisper anxiously on a nearby branch. I can hear birds singing. I should go. I am a stranger here. I don't know which way to turn. I let go a long whistle and finally Vasil replies. He recognizes it after all. I am tottering slowly and pausing to rest. Niko comes back looking for me.

"What possessed you to whistle, anyway?" he said.

"Were you afraid I'd scare the birds?" I asked.

"Their damned ambushes, that's what it is."

He bores me with his caution and the fact that he is again right. We walk along a piece of the road. From time to time my strength returns, but not for long. I lean against the trees and reach for the branches to steady myself. I just barely make it to Ivan. I sit down, covering my eyes with my hands. I am silent. Now they'll start guessing what's wrong with me and suggesting this or that. I am waiting. They don't say anything. I don't like that either. We are bored with each other; we've become hardened and insensitive, like trees and stones.

Ivan is talking with Niko, giving him instructions.

"What about that teacher, the one who lost his hand? Why don't you try to get in touch with him?"

"A waste of time. His only thought is to avoid contact," said Niko.

"But we've got to find someone. We can't simply give up, and lose village after village."

"I'm afraid, Ivan, at the rate we're going, you're going to lose both the village and me."

These are accursed times. Sunspots or some unknown sorcery corrupts our people, destroys their nerves. Niko is disheartened. He is looking at me with sad eyes, imploring me to help him. I hesitate. I don't know how to begin, what to say. Then the opposite current sweeps over me: I refuse to torment myself with this nonsense! I don't like entreaties: a shabby form of bribery to divert attention from the correct path.

I know that teacher with no hand. He is scared. Even if he wanted to help he would not dare, because of his wife. But if we are ordered to do so, why not try anyway? We are all carrying out hopeless orders. . . .

"In a week's time we'll send someone to bring you back here."

"There's no need to send anyone since I don't have to go in the first place," said Niko.

"You don't believe we'll send someone, do you?" asked Ivan.

"You may send someone, but it'll make no difference."

"Don't talk nonsense."

Nonsense indeed. Comrade Niko is hypersensitive. He cannot endure for a few weeks what his father endured for years. Men seem to grow perceptibly weaker from generation to generation. And what's he complaining about? Loneliness, of course. Personally, I accept it. It's not that bad: alone, what of it . . . ? Your time is your own: you don't have to put up with empty chatter, and you don't have to obey or to protest. Nothing. You stretch yourself out on the ground and look at the skies and know the truth.

"Come on, Niko," I said, "if you could tolerate being alone for three months, you can make it for eight days!"

"This'll be more difficult."

"Why? What's bothering you?"

"Nothing, but I'll go crazy here."

We shook hands, and again that strange look, as though in warning and reproach. He was sure we'd betray him. For a moment I felt sorry for him. I should console him with something, with a word I could not find. Then a cold current came over me: why do we have to go on bargaining like this? He is no child! What can I do? I am not leaving him here, nor will I prevent him from coming with us. As though I didn't have enough trouble! It would be easier for me if he stayed. He walks fast and pulls the rest of them along, leaving me to my own pace.

We set off. Below us was a sunlit valley from which a two-story tower of rock jutted out. On the rock there was a ledge, like a balcony, covered with a rug of moss. I turned around: Niko was standing, stooped, frozen. His eyes were nervously following us. I was scared. He'll scream and we'll never be able to forget it. My hand rose involuntarily in a gesture of farewell. He did not respond.

"Why don't you ask him to come with us?" Vasil asked.

"Someone has to work in the valley with the people," replied Ivan. "Didn't you hear? He has a job to do."

"But he's frightened. That's serious."

If I had supported Vasil in this argument, Ivan might have given way. I could have pointed out that the teacher was of no use to us anyway, but my head ached and I felt that same nausea I always feel when I have to act decisively. I felt there was a curse on Niko. What could I do against such a fate? Then again he may regain his self-confidence and perhaps, when it's all over, he'll be grateful to us. We turned behind a hill and now I could freely look back: Niko couldn't be seen. He was not there.

"Why were you so anxious to get Velko to join us," Vasil asked Ivan, "and yet you sent Niko away?"

"Someone will fool Velko, but I think Niko can hold his own."

"The truth is you need Velko because he has a clan and influence, and is not a loner like this one."

"That never occurred to me."

"I know, that comes by itself, without thinking."

Ivan is silent. His eyes are lowered, withdrawn. It is quiet except for the rustling of the leaves on the ground.

MASNIK: A SNAKE OR A CAMEL

WE WADED THROUGH a swamp, through an open gate, and burst into a fortress made of juniper trees. It was dark and fragrant inside and everything that was visible suggested something else that did not exist. Hollows between trees resembled deserted sentry boxes, dry fir trees looked like minarets. Hallucinations arose as in a dream or an illness. Moss-covered rocks were the tents of the devil's army. At times a disheveled face peeped out, not in malice, simply in curiosity. What seemed to be a bog turned out to be a clearing; the grass had swallowed the paths across it.

The green fog of the forest thickened again. I pictured castles of vacationing coal miners, lakes, boats, and swans, instantly created and dissolved. Suddenly a neat pile of logs, left to dry in the field, dazzled us with their whiteness; they stood resolutely and did not vanish like the other visions. I rubbed my eyes, but the image persisted, its fresh whiteness inviting us to approach. We had not seen so innocent a creation in a long time.

"If I were allowed to choose a life for myself," said Vasil, "this is what I would do. Lumber, wood. This must have been cut today. Perhaps yesterday."

He picked up a splinter, and from behind the piled logs emerged the pointed, mustached head of Nedo Masnik. His face was flushed with sleep and his two disturbed eyes blinked fast and jerked like gray mice trying to run away from one another. Their jerks made Masnik's cheeks twitch. His jaw, as if forgotten, had dropped completely. The expression on his face alternated between terror and confusion, followed by a false affability which evolved slowly into a dubious joy. His arms, thrust forward in defense, went through the motion of an embrace. Finally, he regained his voice.

"Vasil, old man, what in God's name brought you people here today?"

"Fast legs, Masnik."

"You are our pride. In the name of God, is that Lado with the beard?"

"Yes, that is our pride with the beard. Did you miss him?"

"I did, more than you think! Ah, welcome, my friends!"

Masnik is huge and bent, his long neck grooved by the loads he carries in the rain and in the sun. He is dressed in a grayish sweater, and, in some strange way, he reminds me of a camel. In the winter he carries loads of hay and leaves from the mountain. In the summer he brings wheat and green peppers from Pech. In the autumn he pushes barrels of diluted plum brandy to Savnik and Zhablak. In the spring one can see him spreading manure across the fields.

"And who's that?" he asked. "Ah, Ivan, you've lost a lot of weight!"

"He is lucky to have kept his skin," said Vasil.

"There were rumors that he was killed, and some people even said they have seen his grave. But he is holding his own. How are you, Ivan?"

A happy thought struck Masnik: to show us his hut. We may find it useful some day. He walked some dozen paces in front of us, looking this way and that, closely scrutinizing the terrain. Was he afraid of an ambush? At times I felt that he intentionally exaggerated the danger. As we approached the cottage, he pointed to it with pride. He asked us to wait and went inside.

"He took part in the uprising, didn't he?" said Ivan.

"And he fought damned well, too, but now look at him: buying land, trading cattle . . ."

"But what's he doing in there? Sending someone to inform on us?"

We looked—there was nothing coming out of the hut except the smoke between the boards of the roof. New rugs were draped over the fence. In the silence the buzzing of flies was heard above the straw mattresses under the eaves. In one enclosure there were lush green potato plants; cabbage in the other. Horse and ox skulls glistened on the picket fence: to scare away rabbits and badgers. A small field of barley was swaying in the breeze. The orderly peasant life, which we have rejected in favor of a more dangerous existence, was taunting us. At last Masnik arrived in an odor of warm hominy, yellow as gold. He didn't forget the brandy either, and it was strong and burned its way through.

"A bad year, this. Hunger is killing us," remarked Ivan.

"If it weren't for the Italian supplies, it would be even worse. We're perishing as it is, and our bellies are bloated with cabbage."

He gave us a long account of who gets salt from the Italians for nothing, who is allowed to buy it for money, and who gets none at all.

"Do you ever see Niko?" Ivan interrupted him.

"Niko?" He started for some reason. "Not very often. When he is really hungry. If he survives until autumn, you can cut my throat!"

"What makes you say that?"

"His paths are known," said Masnik, "where he visits and sleeps. They are constantly after him, lying in wait. Niko is like a lone fish in a shallow pool of water. I can't figure out why they haven't done away with him already. They could have done it a dozen times."

I am tired of listening. I don't see a camel any more. I see a
snake. A long winding snake, hunchbacked from the loot it
has swallowed, squatting in ambush, waiting for the lone persecuted rabbit to appear.

YASHA—ALONE

TODAY IS SUNDAY, that is to say boredom, praying, bell-ringing,
people sitting in their living rooms, reading their newspapers
and interpreting their dreams. This room-world of theirs is
incomprehensible to me. I can only picture it as something
turned upside down; chairs suspended from the ceiling like
bats, their occupants groaning, desperately hanging onto their
seats. It seems like a very difficult way to spend a Sunday. But
I don't really pity them. We are better off: we hear no bells,
newspapers are not delivered at our doorstep. Black goats are
scattered across the fields; in fact, they are not goats at all,
they are people picking mountain cabbage and nettle. Mountain cabbage ripens later in the season than valley cabbage,
which is scorched and nibbled to the root. That's why it's
juicier up here.

"Let's walk over," said Vasil, "and see if any of our people
are there."

"Let's wait a while," I added quickly, fearful that Iva
and the child might be there among them.

We crossed the Labuditsa meadow in silence. The tall ugly
grass was up to our waists. No sheep bells were ringing, no
dogs barking, not even the sound of oxen. The mountains
were bare, and not as beautiful as they appeared from afar.

Beauty has flown over to Turiya and the distant Belasitsa—it always flies away like that, not allowing itself to be approached. The tombstone of Oto Pometenik glistens in the sun.

Somewhere below us is the invisible scource of the River Buchnitsa, marking the beginning of the Donyokraiske regions. But they are deserted too. The silence, which had not bothered me before, has become oppressive. The fields offer a momentary hope. But they too are bare.

We walked down the road a while, and then we stopped dead in our tracks, watching the smoke rise from the upper edge of the forest. Not a heavy smoke, but quite straight, reminding me of the Dogheads, a strange forest people no longer in existence—cleaned out by our ancestors in conquering the mountains.

"Who could that be?" asked Ivan.

"Let me see," replied Vasil. He darted off into the woods.

There was nothing for us to do but to follow him, our rifles in position. We found a man all shaggy with hair and rags, cooking a meal over a fire, stirring it with a wooden ladle. He noticed us but paid us no attention. He was more interested in his broth. His nose and his forehead were dirty with soot from the cauldron. At last he put aside the ladle, wiped his beard off with his sleeve, and looked at us indifferently.

"Do you know him?" asked Vasil.

"No," said Ivan, "unless it's Yasha. What's the matter with you, Yasha? What's happened? You look terrible."

"You aren't exactly spotless," retorted Yasha.

"At least we've washed our faces."

"I'll wash my face too; there's plenty of time."

Again he reached for the ladle: his defense against our sudden intrusion. As I watched him, forgotten faces and names arose from the abyss.

"How are you, Yasha?" I asked.

"Well, I've got flour and salt."

"You don't need anything else?"

"I don't need anything else."

He pulled out of his pocket a wad that looked like a tobacco pouch and untied it with trembling fingers. It was not tobacco, but dirty yellow-black salt mixed with hairs and crumbs. He measured out a little salt and looked sadly at what was left him. Perhaps he is a miser, I thought. He put some salt in the cauldron and took the cauldron off the fire. Picking up the ladle, he headed for the brook. We followed him with our eyes and waited. The Buchnitsa was roaring. Finally he reappeared, his face washed, his hair smoothed down. He looked a little more like himself.

He offered us food. No, we were not hungry. Indeed, we were terribly full. Not of food, but of misery. He shrugged his shoulders, and looked at me askance, almost spitefully—perhaps you've had something better. Then he turned aside. He found our concentration on him embarrassing. His overcoat was torn right below the collar, and through the opening one could see a shirt made of sailcloth. He must be cold at night, but apparently he can endure everything.

"Yasha, this smoke will betray you," Ivan commented finally. "Up here we never make fires in the daytime."

"Protecting oneself is a bore."

"If you don't, you won't last very long," Ivan persisted.

"I've lasted too long as it is."

Ivan put out the fire. He sprinkled it with earth and erased its traces with his foot. Yasha watched in surprise and shook his head. But he didn't really care. He had some books with him, he remarked, he could give them to us; he knew them by heart, and was tired of dragging them around. One was an English Grammar, which I took, I don't for the life of me know why. He had nothing else to offer us, nor had we anything to offer him. Except Vasil's tobacco, which Yasha took and sniffed. He would love to have a smoke, he said at last, but it was better not to. He was already used to being without tobacco. He knew nothing about the Ramovichi, or about any of the others, or about the shooting we heard from Kletye.

The shooting was continuous, he said, but he paid it no attention. His only link with the world was his grandmother, who supplied him with a little flour. She was deaf and knew nothing of what was happening.

"We are on our way to Lom to see your people," said Vasil. "Come along."

"I've been looking for them long enough, let them look for me. Besides, I don't need anyone. What I am doing now, I can do alone."

We sit in silence. It would be better to sleep, or to go. One thinks less when walking. And what is there to think about? The man had removed himself from the world and withdrawn into himself. Something must have offended him. The silence overwhelms us again. I wait impatiently for something to break it: a shot, a cry, anything—except that human voice that teaches, instructs, explains, bores. In the depth of the silence the hoarse humming of the Buchnitsa is heard, that tributary of the River Lim which is not recorded on any map.

BAYTO WITH AN EYE ON THE NAPE OF HIS NECK

THE PEOPLE OF Lom knew exactly what we needed. They brought us a pail of salty potatoes, and then left us alone to stuff ourselves. Now I am thirsty, but this type of thirst is a fine pleasure known only to those who have experienced hunger. Nor am I crazy enough to disrupt this pleasure with water. There is enough food left for this evening and for tomorrow. I am full of admiration for their riches and their foresight. That's the way they have always been: not like us—seeking new exploits. They appreciate those small things necessary to survival.

They even have a pharmacy. A big word for two knapsacks of bandages and two bottles of iodine, but words are not important. They found an ointment with which to treat my impetigo. I don't think it will help me, but it has a powerful smell. The lice will sneeze themselves to death. I hid behind some bushes, threw off my rags, and spread the ointment over my body from head to toe. If I could get rid of this damnation, I would be born again. I put on my shirt and trousers. In my armpits the impetigo was burning and crawling as though an anthill had been disturbed. From somewhere a man suddenly appeared—Bayto. Standing on his thin legs, he surveyed me from a distance.

"Are you sun-bathing there?" he asked in his strict mocking voice.

"No, I am putting ointment on my impetigo," I said.

"If you'd been more cautious, you would never have developed it."

"If a man knew he was going to be killed, he would not go into battle."

He walked over, his joints cracking like a goat's. I had known him in Belgrade when he was not yet a functionary, and in those days he spoke in a different tone of voice. He wore a good coat. During the scuffles with the police he always managed to find an open door through which to flee. His coat and his hat were his salvation. And a scarf! Now something had changed.

"So it's you," he said, regretting that he had recognized me. But he extended his hand.

"I don't shake hands; I have a bad case of impetigo."

He quickly buried his hand in his pocket. "The men from Moracha haven't arrived yet. They're always late, as if on principle."

"It's a long way for them," I said.

"The distance is known, so one must simply leave earlier."

For men like Bayto everything has been reduced to *ought* and *must*. Perhaps there is a special school for them, I thought, where they constantly repeated *ought* and *must*, forgetting the rest of our language in the process. I looked at him and I listened to him; I am no longer certain he is the same person I used to know. He has erased all mutual memories, pushed them aside, and coldly ignored my attempts to revive them. His coat and his scarf have been forgotten.

I don't feel envy, but, rather, that sort of uneasiness which precedes it. Somehow or other he has skillfully jumped across the barriers and found a place for himself here. Why the Party had to send him baffles me. Wasn't there anyone else? How can he lead me? I know him and everything he knows. I have more merits, if it comes to that. I was jabbed in the ribs, and fought back with bricks and rocks. If it is envy, it has certainly disguised itself well, assuming the shape of some vague concern for the general cause. They always send us these characters when they don't know what else to do with them. That Goyan, for example, was a gluttonous animal, and stupid besides. And they are surprised that our peasants join the Chetniks! What can they do if such people represent the Party?

"I'm fed up," said Bayto, "trying to teach them how to protect their heads!"

"You've had plenty of experience in the art of self-protection," I said.

"You're just like them. If a man takes care of himself, he's a coward. We have to be careful. They're hitting hard."

They are hitting hard, by God, and they feel no pity for us. Moreover, they believe in themselves. Their men are good shots and hunters, and they are always at us before we get away. And money does its share, and glory, and the medals sent from London. If autumn finds us here, and the war is not over before the year ends, our seed will be extinguished. After that there won't be a soul left—not even someone to call out our names from time to time. Those who must, let them think about it. Like this Bayto.

On the hill, in a trench overgrown with grass, sat the remnants of the local party hierarchy. Some were still dressed well—they happened to pass a warehouse, and these clothes were imposed on them. Each wore a different cap; but hunger, fear, and traveling by night had rendered the faces under them uniform in appearance. The thinness of their faces made their noses seem more prominent, longer and sharper, their lips swollen, their eyeteeth fiercer. An observer might mistake them for brothers: some cursed breed which can find no repose, an ugly cast of bones and skin, fleshless, bloodless, with mocking eyes fixed on this miserable Bayto, who was delivering a sermon. Subject: Caution.

"Under these circumstances," he was saying, "everyone should have an eye on the nape of his neck."

"That's just what we need," Vasil mumbled. "We are handsome enough without that."

"When two men are traveling together," Bayto elaborated, "they must each look in a different direction."

"Should the last one walk backward, Bayto, like a crab?"

"You laugh, Vasil, but men are falling, one after another, and none ever rise again. Not one of those down there is smiling."

He motioned toward the valley stretched like a huge winding tomb between Plav and Tifran. It's full of the dead, but you cannot tell. The grass is growing, the sheep are grazing. One must get along without those who are no longer around. Our men are not welcome any more, even in cemeteries. Some have been dug up and tossed into a ditch where drowned bastards and dead horses are buried. And while the women are driven wild by corpses that are already rotting, their neighbors gather along the road to scoff and mock them in song: the Partisans, those black horses to whom black days have come. I turned around: to whom will they sing next . . . ? I recalled the gunfire in the valley.

"I don't see a single Ramovich here," I said to Bayto.

"They've surrendered."

"My God!"

He shook his head and pouted his lips. No harm done really, he said. A struggle among the clans might even turn out to be advantageous for us. The Ramovichi are up in arms, and the Lipovichi, those bloodthirsty drunkards, are now agitated too.

"Perhaps we should incite them further," I suggested.

"Impossible. They'd instantly see our hand in it."

True enough, I thought. The two clans would join forces and turn against us. The Party blames the Ramovichi for having surrendered and we are figuring out how we can turn it to our advantage. I go along with that. It's as though these two clans were merely bones to be tossed to the dogs to fight over.

SIMPLY UNDER THE TREES

I THOUGHT A good deal about the Ramovichi; but it no longer mattered. It was all over. As the sun rose, their bodies could be seen stretched out in a field which hungry gypsy horses had long since stripped of grass. Nearby, under a steep slope, the Lim howled like a dog that foretold disaster and invited death. That's how the Lim took leave of the Ramovichi. They were later buried in three fresh graves. I know for sure that they've been buried, and yet I cannot believe that they are dead.

The things that should have saved them—the merits of their ancestors and the power of their rich clan, influential in Chetnik circles—only hastened their end. So long as they lived the danger of strife and a mutual settling of accounts threatened everyone. So one night the Italians took them out of the Chetnik prison and at dawn shot them. They conducted themselves steadfastly and proudly, as though they scorned everything. I can well imagine it; they have always been proud.

Bayto firmly believed that the example of the Ramovichi would end the voluntary surrenders to the Chetniks. If *they* could not be saved, what hope was there for the rest? On the other hand, the fear of death is not the only thing that undermines courage. There are moments when we feel like damned fools, mocked by the whole universe, betrayed by our youth, and by comrades from above. Some have left with the brigades for Bosnia, others sleep in their own beds and send patrols out after us. They have all found a place for themselves, leaving us to stumble about in the mountains. God knows why.

The lice, the impetigo, the rags, the rain, all conspire to play cruel games with us. When we dream, we fly too high; when we observe, we've fallen too low. Our bookish prophecies of freedom have grown so obsolete that even children laugh at us. They have twisted our songs and are singing them inside out. We are miserable, unwashed; we are beggars. In our misery we crawl into a badger's lair, and we come out when hunger drives us insane.

Little by little our ranks grow thinner. We are recruiting no one to our side. We have lost all touch.

Ivan does not agree. We have not lost the people. According to him, in fact, we cannot lose them. We listened to this statement, dumfounded. Even Bayto looked at Ivan with bulging eyes. If I had sputtered out such nonsense, I would have turned dumb with shame. However, Ivan didn't notice a thing. He summarized his argument slowly and boringly: in every village there remain about ten families loyal to us. Even if they want to go over to the other side, they cannot do so. The Chetniks will not allow it, because in every society there must be an oppressed class. Who would make up this class if not these families? Each family has relatives—godfathers and the like—who cannot be of help now, but who will later compensate for what they have neglected to do. . . .

His logic was superb. If we had been strangers, we would have accepted his arguments instantly. As it was, we simply listened as he droned on: out of desperation many have gone over to the other side, to feed their children on the flour and salt that the Italians offer. When this hunger is gone, they will come back to us.

In the meantime we must preserve our ranks, in caves and under trees, in groups of two or three. We should think of the future: happy cities and crystal ships of humanity. I have already had this experience. I know what it's like when a man is hungry, wet, and picking lice from the seams of a ragged shirt. The dreams wilt away, the castles vanish, the lamps and suns are extinguished. I recall the time, only last autumn, when we sent exuberant messages to our enemies warning them that there was no hole left for them to hide in. Now we are the ones with no hole or lair in which to shelter our own heads. Come to think of it, who wants to go underground anyway? I prefer a comfortable spot under the trees: the air is clean, the heavens are above.

All the same, Bayto was not satisfied. He was convinced that we were an impossible kind of Communist, given to extremes. Many have lost their will to live: they are overcome by lice and wretchedness, they are indifferent, dozing, virtually asleep. Soon they will lose their heads. Equally untrustworthy are those who display a dangerous vivacity. Some have stolen sheep; others, it is said, have ravaged a small field of onions. One group broke into a Chetnik home, beat up the master of the house when he refused to feed them, and then helped themselves. It never occurred to them that this was a case of simple plunder.

Vasil cleared his throat. "What you are saying, if I follow you, is that now even the fascists are to be spared."

"You've understood correctly."

"What about that bastard Yanko? If he should pop up in front of my gun, can't I let him have it?"

"Not even Yanko. Except in self-defense, of course. A decision's a decision; you cannot equivocate."

Vasil paused and finally said:

"Then the best thing is to go to sleep."

Bayto grew increasingly agitated. He thrashed about with his arms and legs, sprinkled us with saliva, and accused us once again of being wild, stubborn, indeed as bad as the Chetniks themselves, capable of any crime. I am no longer listening to him. Let him say what he likes. That's his duty. But I would take revenge all the same. Evil cannot recognize itself until it is hit on the head. I would start off with Mikla, who deceived Niko. I would beat her on the behind with a wet rope. Ah, if only it could be done secretly! And Vanya—I would punish him because he is a coward. There are many; each one deserves a form of punishment suitable to his crime. I wandered off into these daydreams and didn't even realize that Bayto's tirade had ended.

"Come on, Lado, let's go," said Ivan.

"Where to? I'd rather stay here."

"Then stay, if this meadow pleases you."

It is not that this meadow pleases me. I simply don't want to go into the mountains again. I am sick of both the mountains and this meadow. On my way to Lom, I had hoped (on the sly, as it were) for some news, for some change for the better. And since we arrived I've been waiting for something to happen. Now it is time to go. There is nothing. I should not have deceived myself; what possibility was there? We shall return to what we have come from, only now we are without hope. Dilapidated, tough, and callous, we shall be running in circles again, gnawing at each other.

The path we ascend is no longer new to us, nor does it hold for us any longer those secrets which momentarily deceive the eyes with dream-world images. At times the path looks like a spit spanning two rocks. The same scenery, but now it is turned the other way around. The hills are chunks of greenish meat being broiled on a slow fire for a gluttonous great eternity. At first it was amusing, but now it has been transformed into a raving fever which infuriates me. I would have preferred to have seen nothing. I wish the fog would descend, never to rise again. The fog would keep secret and unknown all those places where we walked, sowed salt, and hoped in vain.

Alone

Damned land, how low you have come!
Your name is wickedness, your name is terror. If
I have a young knight, you
snatch him in his prime: if
I have a young man in the pride of his manhood,
you take him before his time.

—NJEGOŠ

A RIFLE FULL OF LICE

IT MUST BE acknowledged at last: we have become tramps! This first occurred to me some ten days ago, and I've had repeated proof of it since. As soon as we came back from Lom, with the usual sores on our feet, we began looking for a new base. There were lots of suitable places, but we always found fault with them. Either water was too far away or a road was too close. If we found no fault at all, it was automatically excluded: for that is exacly where the peasants would expect to find us. So we went on, dragging ourselves to exhaustion, convinced that in this expanse of forest and cliffs some perfect spot existed, set aside just for us.

Finally we agreed on a place called the Desert. It was not exactly right, but it had certain unusual qualities. Seen from a distance, the Desert resembled the belly of a woman. Everything around was smooth and white. Two streams met on a nearby slope. The Desert itself was spacious and open, untrampled for many years, thick with fern and hawthorn. It had a spring and many birds. There was no path through it, and not a single tree had been touched by an ax.

We stole some shovels and for three days we dug a trench for ourselves under the low branches. Two men dug while the third kept guard. We waited for the sun to go down before throwing the earth into the ravine. We spread handfuls of dried leaves over the traces of our work. We roofed over our trench with boards we had brought from a distant hut. We concealed the roof with moss and pieces of bark. The result was a pleasant den. The interior could stand certain improvements, but we did nothing more for fear of spoiling it. The

49

entrance was imperceptible, especially when a pile of branches was drawn over it.

The den was for use in case of rain. But we continued sleeping under the trees; when one man snored the others had room to move away. Ivan wanted us to institute a guard system, but he finally agreed that it was unnecessary. In the daytime no one could approach us unnoticed; at night they would have broken their legs and ribs before finding us. We dug out a radio receiver. It seemed in good condition and would have enabled us to hear what was going on in the world. However, there was no electricity. Laka was the only one who knew where the batteries were buried, but no one knew where Laka was.

We were proud of the Desert, the forest and the ravine, as if we had created them ourselves. We discovered that it was possible to make fires in the ravine that no one could detect. The stream was also convenient for quick retreat should we be surrounded by Chetniks. I wanted to boast to someone of our good fortune, and I thought of Niko. We had planned to pick him up on our way back from Lom, but the Chetnik patrol diverted us from our route. So he was alone once again. The Mitrovichi had offered to lead him to us, but there was no sign of them. Or of Niko.

"They should have been here long ago," said Vasil.

"They are a slow lot," said Ivan.

In fact, two weeks had passed. Out of boredom we had already begun quarreling, natural for people who spend any time under the same roof. The roof was wide, a whole sky, but that didn't alter the case. We were members of the same household, and argument was the major family entertainment. Everything bothered Vasil. He began reading *Faust*, but he couldn't stand apparitions and choruses. The English Grammar didn't fare any better; they invented this confused spelling, declared Vasil, as a barrier against the lower classes. He seemed to feel that Ivan and I were to be blamed for it. Nor were the two of us as composed as we used to be. We were ready to argue and quarrel at the slightest provocation.

I grew tired of this round of arguments and reconciliations. I set out to find this Laka who knew where the batteries were hidden. A solitary shepherd lived nearby. He pretended to be sometimes deaf, sometimes crazy. He had no dealings with the authorities, and the laws of the valley did not apply to him. With his club and his hood and his sheepskin coat, he smelled of animal life, and when I asked him a question he squirted saliva through an opening between his teeth, and aimed the point of his club at the spot to which it had squirted. He knew nothing of Laka, he explained, but he remembered his companion, Goyan.

"A fat one, ruddy, yes. He wants you to send him some flour and lard."

"You tell him we want him to send us a whole battalion, never mind the lard," I replied.

"You mean a battalion of lice," said the shepherd. "He has enough of them."

"Sure. Since people stopped bringing him spies and riffraff to shoot, he's had plenty of time to acquire lice; even his rifle is infected."

I really shouldn't have said it in front of this idiot. Damaging to the Party's prestige. I had blown up in anger. Too late now. The shepherd was grinning, with a cagey expression on his face, pleased to have caught me. Then the look tapered off, along with the smile—he would not get mixed up in our business, and he would not take messages or look for anyone. He buttoned up his sheepskin coat, covered himself up with the hood. Everything was closed and bolted. One couldn't drag another word out of him, not even with pincers.

I returned to the Desert, hoping to find that Niko had shown up. But everything was as before. The underground den had lost its charm. We paid no attention to it. How childish! All our work in vain. The radio was a deadly bore. Per-

haps we'll give it to the crows for a nesting place. Our sole
recreation was watching the brook fall capriciously over the
rocks. A little farther down it dropped, wailing, over a precipice. We grew dizzy watching it. Ivan became agitated.

"I am going to find the Mitrovichi. I want to know what
they are doing."

"They are taking a rest, of course," said Vasil.

"Ask about batteries," I said. "Tell them to get some at Plav,
if that's possible."

"Why not?" Vasil was teasing me. "There's a lot of industry
at Plav."

The truth, of course, is that in Plav they may not even know
what batteries are. But a man must do what he can. I am
pleased that Ivan is going. At the very least it means a change
and news from the outside world. When my father went to
visit my uncle in prison, he would always come back with
something new to tell us. Invariably he would bring me candy
money or fresh bread that melted in my mouth. Sometimes he
would be late, and I waited up for him by the window.

Even now there remains some of the sharp pleasure of waiting. It draws a line between the immediate future and the
infinite chaos that lies ahead. Since Ivan left, Vasil and I have
hardly said a word to one another. Each to his own business.
He leaves early for the forests, making sure to cross the crags
before dawn. He comes back at night. We eat in silence. I
don't ask him where he has been, nor does he tell me. Perhaps
he is looking for rare stones, or collecting herbs. (In his knapsack there is only the usual store of kindling.) More likely, he
starts up a fire somewhere and sits by it, warming his heels all
day long. Why not? I have no objections so long as he does
not make his fires here.

Once he brought a rabbit back with him. He must have
killed it some distance from here. I didn't even hear the shot.
We skinned it, and buried the skin in the mud by the stream.
We washed the meat in the water a long time, then we cooked

it. We left a few choice pieces for Ivan and Niko. But before
the sun was up we had eaten those too.

Like Vasil, I tried to kill time with *Faust*. It's out of date by
now. I am not enjoying it. The archangels are vying with each
other in flattering God; they're sickening and odious. God
struts about, pleased with himself, clucking like an old wedding guest, or like Boyo Mumlo when he boasts about his
property. Nothing better could be expected from such creatures. The devil could have been better developed. I don't
know why Goethe involved him in so much bargaining and
speculation. I would have done it differently. My devil would
not have been a bargainer. I would have seen to it that he
appeared a little nobler than God. That must be closer to the
truth.

Yesterday a squirrel came by. We looked at each other for
several seconds before he waved at me with his tail and vanished into the darkness of the trees. There are no other animals around. Even snakes have run away. They don't like
tobacco. Vasil has come across some alpine goats; he has followed them, and they are luring him farther and farther into
the mountains. For some reason these creatures assume we are
dangerous, and don't trust us. Perhaps our bad smell trails
behind us; that's why everything is empty and quiet where-
ever we go. The birds too have moved away, and those that
have stayed are silent.

I bathe myself in the brook three times a day. The impetigo
has disappeared. There is an anthill in a rotted oak; I keep
feeding it with lice, so their numbers have diminished too. But
there is still plenty of time left, and it's boring. A man is not a
tree to be standing in one place all the time, looking at the
skies. He is not a tree, I keep repeating to myself, searching
for some reason to start on my way. But I don't know where to
go or why.

A WAILING MOUNTAIN FULL OF SNAKES

LAST NIGHT IVAN arrived. It was immediately evident that he did not bring good news. Nothing terrible, he said, but he was angry with the Mitrovichi. They had not raised a finger to help Niko. Nor did they intend to. We cannot count on them. They stink of opportunism and shallow selfishness. You cannot recognize them any longer. They would like to hibernate like bears and sleep through the war and all the troubles.

They are squabbling among themselves. That I can imagine. We are doing the same thing. They are breaking down into little groups, busily defending themselves from all responsibilities. And left to themselves they stink like a bog. They didn't bring Niko over, they said, because they couldn't wade across the Lim.

"Don't worry," said Vasil. "Tomorrow Lado and I will go and get him."

"I'll go too," said Ivan. "After all, it's my fault that he's in this mess."

"So it is."

As I listened to them I decided that Niko's plight was really my responsibility. I had wanted to help him out and I don't know why I didn't. I felt remorse, but that didn't alter the situation. So I stopped feeling remorse.

Before the sun was up we crossed the crags and reached the forest. It is pleasant here: the legs are walking, but the head is not thinking. The waiting is over, and the torment that goes with it. Soon we ought to reach the Plechovichi land. Perhaps we can stop at one of the huts for a while. I may see that girl by the fountain again. Nothing will come of it, and yet I don't want her to forget me, because in some way that equals death.

I fetched some water from the brook and Vasil made a fire by an oak tree. We put some hominy on to cook. The sun was warm. A sack of flour, hanging from a branch, rocked in the wind. Something rustled in the oak tree and frightened us: an enormous rat, attracted by the smell of flour, was creeping up to the bag. We hurled live coals from the fire at him—let him pay for being a rat, for having scared us, and also for running away! We hit him, repeatedly, but he was a tough rat. He squealed and tried to bite us. Finally he fell dead, his little paws clenched.

"One of these days the Chetniks will do the same thing to you," said Vasil, looking at me.

"They won't exactly caress you either," I replied.

"I don't ask them to caress me."

"Now, now, you aren't children," Ivan pontificated.

"We aren't children at all. We're scorpions, I think."

In the shouting we forgot to put salt in the food, but we gobbled it down all the same. We descended into the valley and crossed the road. In a willow thicket we removed our shoes and trousers. The Lim did not even reach our waists and was not much trouble. We waded across and climbed the hill. We crossed the clearing in a slow stride, occasionally pausing. A few Chetniks watched us from the other side, probably thinking that we were their men. We had a good view. The grain in the fields was still green. The summer was late in arriving, making the hungry year longer, making those who are waiting for new bread wait to the bitter end.

It's long past noon. We've been sitting for some time and we're tired and thirsty. Below us, in a clearing, there is a hut. A swarm of flies is buzzing in front of the door, indicating that there are people inside.

"If only we had some milk," said Ivan.

"Maybe they'll sell us some."

"They probably would, but it's risky to show our faces."

"We'll pay and run! They'll never know who we are."

"No, we can't risk anything for our stomachs."

"Have it your way." I shrugged. "I'm not all that hungry anyway."

I lied to show off, but in fact I was as hungry as a big fish about to gobble up a small one. Vasil was quiet. I turned around; he was no longer there. Gone looking for mountain goats, I sneered to myself. Tonight we'll have hominy again, but this time we'll remember to put some salt in it. We could have pinched some onions during the night, but we always forget to do that. Onions are ripe now and they're juicy. Damned good in small doses. If Velko's niece—I don't even know her name—cooked something for me to eat, I'd gobble it down with no salt and no onions.

Vasil returned. He had not found any game, but he'd picked some blueberries for us. Not really blueberries, they were larger and they looked like those dog grapes we used to make ink from. He offered me some. They were edible, he said, he'd already tasted them. I chewed two or three to start with. They were sweetish and full of juice thick as blood. I put a few more berries in my mouth, and I wondered why the peasants had not picked the fields clean, since they were so good. Vasil offered a handful to Ivan, and he started as though a dead mouse had fallen into the palm of his hand. He fixed his eyes on the berries and squeezed one between his fingers.

"Do you know what this is?"

"It's sweet," said Vasil. "Taste it, you'll see."

With a grim face Ivan turned to me and noticed that I was about to swallow the last few.

"Spit them out," he yelled. "They're poison!"

"I've eaten more than a pound," said Vasil. "See, nothing happened to me."

"Watch this madman, Lado. I am going to look for milk. Shove a belt in his throat to make him throw up!"

Ivan dashed off, downhill toward the hut. With his eyes

Vasil followed him. He was still smiling. His smile froze before it had time to disappear and its traces, suddenly monstrous, remained on his frightened, contorted face. He unbuckled his belt and shoved it in his wide-open mouth. He couldn't stand the sudden cramps, and fell on his hands and knees. I put my hand on his forehead, which instantly grew slippery from the perspiration. Finally he threw up a red lump, like a piece of meat, and, weakened, fell face down in it. I wiped his face clean and forced the belt a little deeper, but that no longer helped. His eyes were blood red and terrible in the dew of perspiration and tears. He pushed me aside, smiling with his stiff face, trying to catch his breath.

"A witch," he said, "impossible, but it must be. . . . The reactionary forces . . ." He rested his head on his knees and hands, and in a changed voice he began enumerating: "I am purifying you with incense, I am washing you with water, I am cutting you with an ax. I am burning you with fire. This is no place for you! Away with you, devil! Away! Go to the Wailing Mountain, disappear over the Hill of No Return, where bells don't ring, the reel doesn't dance, girls don't comb their hair, horses don't neigh, roosters don't crow. There is no one to see, no one to hear, no one to be confused . . . They have blighted us with fire and with incense and with axes. We are now on the Wailing Mountain, where only devils are hatched. And snakes. Here, my stomach is full of snakes; they are butchering one another. . . ."

"Take some milk," said Ivan, who had just returned. "You'll feel better right away."

"I don't want it," he yelled in a drowning voice.

"Just taste it. You don't have to finish it if you don't like it."

"That's lye, and you've made this mixture yourself to poison me."

"You take some too, Lado."

"I am a man," said Vasil, "and I have my own orientation. Step back! We are being eliminated!"

The rest was completely incoherent. I drank a few gulps

and hoped that somehow everything would get better. Ivan crept up behind Vasil and twisted his right arm behind his back. I subdued his left arm and tightened a belt around his elbows. We bound his legs to a young oak tree which shook hard from his convulsions. Finally, exhausted, he stiffened. We could just barely pry open his jaw. While I pressed his chin to his chest, Ivan poured a thin stream of milk into the dirty, bluish pit of his mouth. My hands were dripping with milk which had fallen in great puddles on the ground.

Vasil was choking. We let him catch his breath again and he muttered something about the Wailing Mountain. Broken fragments of hallucinations, in themselves incoherent, began making sense in an odd way, and it seemed to me that, consciously and persistently, he was reminding me of something both familiar and forgotten.

ON AND ON

THE LEAVES ARE STILL, the birds are in hiding. Alone in an abyss of silence our voices rise, fall, and clash together like lunatics. We look at one another—perhaps someone is eavesdropping—and we fall silent. The trees are not on our side either; if they conceal us from our enemies they also conceal our enemies from us. One can sense something diabolical in the air. Knives are being sharpened for our skins. But even if we caught them at it, they would swear that they were preparing this doom for someone else.

Here and there we had killed a few petty spies. But that was like extinguishing a fire with straw. I don't know what

made us place any hope in intimidation, in wrapping ourselves
up in its mist like dragons. Our newspapers published the
names of those we executed. The idea appealed to me at first
—an open matter and rather naïve—but later on I found it
quite distasteful. Dangerous characters understood the warning and concealed themselves behind paid guns and wild
clans. The situation quickly changed. For half a year they
have been killing us off, and will continue to do so, but they
are not mad enough to make their lists public.

"Was there anyone in the hut?" I asked Ivan.

"No one; it was empty."

"I hope you didn't leave money for the milk."

"No, they'd know it was us right away."

"Good. Honesty has cost us dearly."

Vasil silently thrust his head into the shadow. That reddish
broth had roared out of him, ripping up his intestines in the
process. He must feel relieved. His shoes were spattered with
the broth and there were stinking traces on his rags, which I
would have to wash out somehow. We untied him. He felt his
sore spots and opened his eyes. He recognized us reluctantly
—he'd seen us somewhere before, we tortured him in some
way. We had something in common. It was all unclear to him.
He continuously rolled the troubled whites of his eyes like a
vampire, and shook his head.

"How are your guts, Vaso?"

"Quiet," he mumbled.

"Can you stand up? We've been here a long time."

We walked along the hillside. Vasil thought that one of his
legs was shorter than the other. He swayed to the right, constantly losing his balance. Going uphill he found a little easier.
His head felt rotten, he said; something was being ripped
apart under his skull. At times he paused and sighed, striking
the ground hard with his foot, as though he would like to fly
off. As we got to higher ground the forest thinned out. Vasil
was convinced that only the mountain air and wind could
clean him out. We held him back at the crag—if we went any

farther we might be noticed. I offered him a lump of resin to inhale; perhaps it might help.

"This Niko, he's jinxed," said Ivan.

"Should we forget about him?" I asked.

"No, but we have a choice: either you go or I do. . . ."

"I will; you stay with Vasil."

"All right, but don't get too close to the huts, and don't take short cuts."

I promised him, of course, to stay clear of the huts, but that was merely to get him off my back. I'm not too fond of going in circles. I could barely wait until I got out of Ivan's sight before I took my first short cut. Now I'm on my own. I am responsible only for myself, and I'll go wherever I want to. I was seized by a crazy excitement, the sort of excitement that comes suddenly and without cause after long days of boredom. Perhaps it is caused by loneliness, or freedom. I can quicken my pace when I want to and leap ditches. A rabbit dashed across the clearing, convinced that I was chasing him.

If my feet hold out, I thought, I'll reach Yablan, Velko's parish, in daylight. It would be pleasant to arrive at the fountain when the girl comes for water. Dusk would be best, when she cannot see my patches too clearly. She'll recognize my voice instantly and will remember. There is still something childlike in me, and that child needs a glittering object to follow—a star, even if deceptive, to guide him on cold nights. This girl is such a star, to be glimpsed from time to time. That's not asking much, nor will it harm anyone. Others get more; why can't I have that? The sun is setting too quickly. I am competing with it and, as I'm racing over the mountains, I think that I shall get there. Later some valleys I had altogether forgotten blocked my way, wore me out, and stole my time.

At sundown I still had hope, but the forest spread out as though to spite me. It was already dark when I arrived. Two fires glistened in the huts. I could hear voices. I drank some water and lay in the meadow to watch the stars. Suddenly I was seized again by the same zest: why shouldn't I see her immediately, why should I deprive myself of anything? I approached the hut and peeked in—some other woman was scraping the tubs and rinsing them. The girl was not there. Had I invented her? I turned toward the forest, but I couldn't go any farther. I took three steps forward, and then three backward. I was at the cottage again. I knocked on the door.

"Good evening," I said. "There was a girl here. Your sister, I believe."

"Yes, Maga," and she frowned. "What do you want?"

"I'd like to see her, to ask her something."

"How can you see her if she's in prison? Your men took her away."

"In prison? Why?"

"Who knows what you do with people. Jailing us, killing us, robbing. What are you up to now?"

She scanned my beard. I felt that she wanted to spit at it. What do I do now? She hasn't asked me to sit down; she's holding a knife in her hand. She'll chase me away like any intruder. I stood there, awkward and superfluous. I edged toward the door, ready to scramble off with my tail between my legs. This woman is her sister; if Maga is anything like this, no wonder they jailed her. This one is older, but they look a lot alike. The hut was stuffy, the air close from the smell of milk and cheese. I am no longer accustomed to such smells. That's why I am so confused.

"I wanted to ask Maga something. . . ."

"She isn't here! See, she isn't here!"

"I was here once before, and I got in touch with Velko Plechovich through her."

"So?"

"That's what I'd like to do now. I can't find him myself. You see, I'm a Partisan; I am Tayovich from Meda, my name is Lado."

Thus at the first opportunity I spilled out everything about myself. Now I am, as it were, naked; only the beard remains.

And I'll shave that off as soon as I come across a razor. Worst of all is the tone of voice in which I said it; sticky, soft, unconvincing, with a touch of fear. It is only natural that such a tone of voice and such a confession cannot be believed. She looked at me wide-eyed with astonishment. She glanced at my rags and my miserable battered rifle.

"Velko was killed, you poor devil," she said, and the words roared in my ears.

"What do you mean, killed?" I yelled in a completely changed voice, rushing toward her.

"They buried Velko a week ago."

"Impossible!"

"That's what people will do these days for canned food. I hope to God they pay with their blood!"

I lowered myself onto the stool and listened. First they took Maga to prison. A few days later, when Velko was sitting and sunning himself below the forest, someone spotted him. A little later soldiers appeared. They surrounded Velko, and there was no one to give him any warning. He noticed them only after they had already blocked off every route of escape. When he rose to break away they cut him down with a machine gun.

I asked for a glass of water. She brought some milk. The milk was thick and sluggish, and I couldn't get it down. I wondered who was next: Niko or I? Perhaps Yasha, if he is not dead already. There are always fewer of us than we think. Life is now like a book: everything is written down, but one doesn't have time to finish reading it. I felt stifled under the roof, among those beams whose shadows danced a black reel. Without saying good-by I left for the darkness full of brambles and ditches.

THE RUINS

In the distance, in the silence of the valley, a lone ax is heard, as though laying the foundations of a different life—a warmer world with windows and a balcony. The instrument must be enormous, wielded by a person of gigantic muscle. As I move along, the sound changes. In the mountain it is clear and all steel; but when I descend into the valley and walk in the shade by the river the sound is muffled and dull, as though a coffin were being nailed down. At times the sound stops altogether, as if the last man on earth, alone and shattered, has dropped his tools and fallen to the ground. But he pulls himself together and advances once again.

I approached and peered out from behind a tree: it was Taslach from Sleme. Childhood images were instantly awakened. They used to say he was a vagabond, but that only meant that he had no land. He was a large man, who carried a pistol and a harmonica and wore his cap tilted to one side. At weddings he would get drunk and he would kiss the women one by one during the reel. And they liked it. Only Dana refused; she grabbed an empty bottle and told him to keep his hands off. That same evening on the threshing floor he was given a beating from which he barely recovered. And that was the end. He sold his harmonica, got married, and made his home at Sleme.

"Are you building a house?" I yelled to interrupt him.

"Yes . . ."

"Why isn't anyone helping you?"

"Who'd give me a hand? Better men than I are alone these days. Our people have gone to the devil."

He shook his head indifferently. Since the beating with a pitchfork on that threshing floor, he had turned his back on everything that was not his own. When he fell to the ground they jumped on him as they would have trodden the clay from which bricks were made, yelling wildly. A few local people were present who later acted as witnesses at the trial. They said that Taslach had provoked the quarrel and that he should pay all expenses.

"Does Niko ever call on you?" I asked him.

"Well, I wouldn't say so. Not since Sunday, at any rate."

"Has he been here since then?"

"Well, he hasn't been here for a few days. Since Sunday, or, rather, Saturday."

I offered him some tobacco. He rolled a cigarette and lit it. Something was on his mind. He pointed to a bag of potatoes, and to a cauldron. He would boil some for me if I felt like eating. He had nothing else to offer. No salt either. Someone had taken his ration. The potatoes were still covered with dirt; he had dug them out that morning. I washed them in the brook and put them on the fire.

"I wanted to tell Niko something," he said, lowering his voice. "He must watch out for Masnik."

"Masnik's not dangerous."

"He knows how to caress with one hand and slaughter with the other."

Taslach picked up a pointed twig and pricked the biggest potato in the cauldron. "It's soft," he said, "it's done." He poured out the boiling water and placed the potatoes on a leveled stump as if it were a dining table. The hot steam rose, but he did not wait for it to cool. No time. He was hungrier than I, wanted to eat as much as he could, and had his own peculiar way of doing it. He stuffed his mouth full of potatoes, skin and all, as though they were plums, and then loudly spat out one part of the skin, pressed tight and hard as a bullet, and the rest he swallowed. And so it went.

We finished our meal, had another smoke, and parted. I don't want to sit at the same table with him again: I'm not fast enough. His stories about Masnik were probably nothing but petty local gripes. I turned around a hill, but still heard the sound of the ax. As the path wound up and down, the sound alternated—now it built a house, now it nailed a coffin down. The sound was the only sign of human activity in this area, except for the shabby path itself. Then this too disappeared. Only the trees, the bushes, and an odd anthill remained. A pebble rolled down from the heights. I was overjoyed: it must be Niko! And he had noticed me first. I ran up the hill, but there was nothing there except a pile of rocks which glared at me.

It was the Leper's Cave, gaping wide open like a house abandoned in disorder. Traces of life were visible, but how old they were it was hard to determine. Perhaps a week, perhaps a month. There was a passage inside leading to a smaller cave, quite dark and damp; and from there to several narrow corridors where skunks go to bear their young. It smelled of skunks; they probably moved in again as soon as human life disappeared. It stank like a tomb. I hurried outside. My head began to ache from the smell.

I looked everywhere. There was no sign of Niko. Perhaps he had been ambushed, but there was no sign of an ambush either. If the Chetniks were anywhere around, they would have appeared; it was all the same to them, him or me. The trees on the mountainside, lit at an angle by the setting sun, glistened like white teeth, long, thin teeth, a gigantic palate somewhat tilted and jagged. Finally I grew tired of this wasteland and began to find the sound of my own voice disgusting. I thought of Masnik's woodpile and I quietly started in that direction. There he was, sawing and singing, but his voice was not pleasant either. He lifted his head and laid his tools aside. I noticed instantly that he was not pleased to see me.

"You're looking for Niko?" he said. "Don't bother, he's finished."

"Dead?"

"Not exactly, but he's not too well."

"Wounded, you mean. Badly?"

"He's not wounded either," and he could barely mutter it: "He gave himself up."

The forest, the ditches, and the valley with the invisible river below grew hazy before my eyes, as though it were I, and not Niko, who had fallen into an abyss. A cloud of white lime dust and smoke arose. I saw Masnik's face in it. He was the man who had driven the cart through Belgrade filled with bits of flesh and corpses . . . ! It was he who had pushed me off that cart. I ought to kill him on the spot!

"Sit down!" I yelled. "And let's have it from the beginning."

"I told you not to leave him."

"I've come here to take him away."

"Three days ago you would have found him! But he thought you'd taken off for Bosnia."

"He must have been out of his mind."

Masnik took out his tobacco pouch, as if to give us a breathing spell. Niko hadn't quite gone crazy: he had some strange idiosyncrasies, he would jump unexpectedly and things like that. In fact, he was too soft for this kind of life. He had to go.

"Who in hell told him that we'd left for Bosnia?"

"Maybe it was his own idea."

"He should have killed himself."

We were silent a while. Masnik said that it was better like this. If the man had killed himself, people would have said it was an admission of guilt, that he'd lost hope. This way, he can tell them off to their faces and not be ashamed. Nor do we know what will happen; the trial won't be for some time.

It occurred to me that Masnik may have given Niko this very same speech. And in this manner he stole Niko's soul. Now he wants mine. I ought to kill him. I looked at him over my rifle. He's as ugly as ever. I haven't killed anyone in a long time; in fact, I'm not sure that those I shot at were really killed. But I will kill him. He seemed to have sensed my thought, and his heels sank into the ground as though into soft snow. He was searching for a firm footing from which he could take off. I waited for him to start running, but he knew that it was too late. He grew limp, his jaw fell, his eyes became glassy, as though he were already dead. Not good to shoot a dead man, I thought; no warm red blood, only green saliva. It's bad, it'd stink, I won't do it. I put my rifle away.

THEY KILLED AND FLED

IN THE CLEARING there are a host of small shadows, each squatting under its own bush or stump; gradually they grow in size. Now they disappear, leaving only a few streaks of dark. Now they steal upon one another and devour each other like fish. Their bellies are elastic, they expand according to need and take in everything they come across. The assaulted shadows do not defend themselves. They may wriggle at times and try to escape, but that only prolongs their torment.

I was carried away by these images and felt as though I were on the shore of a ghostly lake. There were reflections there too, but not of the skies and the clouds or of the rock-flecked mountainsides and the trees, but something altogether different. I was not even sure what it was—perhaps time, perhaps eternity. The past was looking for repose in the depths; the future was in pursuit, devouring the rotted past as it went. Elongated necks floated by, and beaks and claws and toothy jaws; the circular pursuit never ceased.

"I kept telling you—" Masnik coughed as if throwing a rock into this black water—"to get him out of here."

"I know, I know."

"Why blame me then?"

"Who's blaming you?"

"I gave him bread whenever he came by."

"I know."

"My door was open to him at all times."

"I know that too."

He began feeling sorry for himself, and his eyes filled with tears. He left enough time for me to see that the tears were genuine, then wiped them off with the rusty palms of his hands. Finally he was silent, and that was a relief. Below us, in the gully, the river was heard: water as black as liquid coals. It is going, it is falling. I should be going, and falling, but I don't feel like getting up again. I don't know where to start. There is some sort of a balance on this earth, in the air, and with my first move I shall tip it to my disadvantage.

"Come inside," said Masnik. "We'll find something to eat."

"No. I am full today."

"I've got some good rakiya."

"I don't want any rakiya either."

I rose. If I had had a load on my back, I could have removed it and would have felt better instantly. As it was, however, the burden was everywhere and could not be removed. I didn't feel like going uphill. Everything was pulling me down! I started downhill, following the heavy shadows, and that felt better. It was now my turn, but I would go about it in a somewhat different manner. I didn't know where to go, but it would be in the direction opposite to that Niko took. I could see the River Lim below; perhaps the Lim was luring me down. I would wade across it. The water would refresh me, and my luck might change when I was on the other side.

In the shallows near the village of Ravan the river had overflowed its banks, as if quarreling with itself. I listened for some time, and I could clearly recognize the sounds of its tributaries, some gurgling softly, others tingling with a sharp sound.

I passed through the groves and approached our old house. Uncle Luka used to come here, and it was from here that they took my father away. I could get no closer; people were standing by the well, talking. They wouldn't even let me have my memories. I crossed over to the forest path leading to the village of Meda. There were no guards on the roads. There was no Niko. The valley was calm. I should call on Iva to see how my brother's son, little Tayo, was coming along. I crossed the river again. The light was on at Boyo Mumlo's; he must have gasoline. Trobuck's light was on too. It was not for nothing that he was a permanent Chetnik entitled to a monthly stipend. Finally I arrived at Iva's house; no light was on. I raised my hand to knock, and then paused. Today was a day of evil news; it would be better not to call on them. And I went on.

Was this the same lovely valley, with its beautiful autumns and fancy plums, for which I had once dreamed of silver bridges and concrete dams? No, I guess not. The valley gaped wide open, like a monster's mouth. The peaks in the starry skies were jaws which would shut tight as soon as I was inside. I knew what lured me down: the Lim, the old house, and little Tayo. I didn't know what lured Niko; some trick perhaps. I grew frightened: in these deserted parts a man is full of the devil.

Around midnight I reached Volunik and I lay there dozing until the sun came up. The nearby valleys resembled open boxes lined with green cloth. They were of various shapes, with indentations on both sides and clasps of tarnished silver overhead. Their hinges were at the rivers, and in some places the glistening metal was clearly visible. Now the valleys lay wide open, but when a hand pushed down the lid they would shut tight. Everything that happened to be inside would be doomed to a long-drawn-out death in the stale air. That's why I am not going to go down into the valleys. Those who are in a hurry, let them go; I feel more secure among the tall peaks of the mountains.

At sunset a long column of Chetniks crossed the ridge below me, going in my direction, but lower down. I waited for them to get ahead of me. This was their first appearance here. I had no idea what they were looking for. They disappeared in the valley and I didn't see them anywhere. Near the crags of Pustara and Zhenski Trbuh I paused again and waited for the coming of darkness. Fatigue and hunger had brought me farther down into the valley than I realized. As I was clambering over the brook I thought of how I was going to describe everything to Ivan and Vasil: I climbed up the ravine and found them at the first clearing. They were snoring. I nudged Vasil.

"Is there anything for me to eat?"

"What?" the man grunted loudly. "You woke me up, you swine!"

"Who are you?" I asked.

"Don't you know me?" he said, and he looked at me in surprise.

I stepped back and lifted my rifle. Perhaps it was the Mitrovichi.

"Are you a Mitrovich?" I asked.

"Yes, I am." He was pawing the ground. "Don't you know me?"

"What are you looking for?" I asked. He was looking for his rifle, and he found it.

A thought flashed through my mind: I cannot wait. And I fired first, into the midst of the black mass. I heard his groan mixed with an echo of the shot. I am to blame, I said to myself. I backed into the bushes and sank downward into a pit. For a moment I lost my breath. I felt fine earth on my lips. My rifle broke loose and reached the ground before me. I grabbed it and clutched it tightly so as not to lose it again. Roots scratched me, and pebbles buried themselves in my flesh. Still no sound from above. I felt like screaming. I had killed one of our men! Then gunfire was heard and sounds.

"He's dead."

"Where did they run?"

"Over there."

"Where are the guards, damn them!"

There were at least ten men up there. They were not our men either. I was relieved. I was pleased that they didn't realize I was alone. But where were Vasil and Ivan?

I heard Masnik's voice.

"Down the stream, men, I could swear," he yelled.

"They wouldn't be able to get away even if they had wings!"

I should like to hear Masnik's voice once again, to make sure, but I had no time. In the growing din nothing was too clear to me. They couldn't hear each other and they didn't know whether they were being ordered to shoot or not shoot. They were cursing, asking questions, howling, some in soft tones, others harshly. They were like the Lim, I thought, remembering how the river broke into many pieces in the shallows. Perhaps that voice was Masnik's, that snake! How could he have gotten here before me? Perhaps he crawled through holes in the ground. Or was it just someone with a voice like his? It didn't matter. The most important thing was that I was on my feet.

I moved away. The voices receded. Two shots rang out one after another. The cliffs over the brook turned into a greenish deep-sea landscape. Where was I? In what depths? I hid behind the stones and closed my eyes so as not to be blinded. Then it grew dark. I rumbled through a forest of panicky birds. In the pasture behind the village I found a horse, mounted it, and rode for an hour, at a trot, across meadows and wheat fields. I crossed the Lim and let the animal loose in a cornfield on the other side—let them quarrel among themselves tomorrow when they see what has happened.

DEVIL WOMAN

I MISTOOK A tree trunk for the leg of an old elephant. I didn't know where I was. Two pools of sun lay ahead: they were creeping toward me like coils of golden scorpions. An anthill cropped up in front of me, looking like a sponge, thin streams trickling from its holes. That's why my fingers are damp. Still lying down, I broke off a twig and drove it into this porous heap, down to the lowest floors. I waited for a few moments for the "ant honey" to stick to the bark of the twig. I refreshed my mouth with it. I repeated this performance several times, until I felt the acid gnawing at my empty intestines, and then I threw away the twig.

I watched the ants fussing about in astonishment. I felt sad that I'd destroyed their house. It looked like open intestines, with a myriad of fine sinews and tubes from which these wounded, trampled creatures were desperately trying to flee. They emerged, and ran off, then remembered something and returned. They ran into each other, collided, rolled over, and forgot where they were going. Pausing to consider their situation, others rushed at them and annihilated them. They were in a daze.

I grew tired of watching this dumb spectacle—a living mirror of my inner self, where everything is crawling about. I started off again in search of some better spot. But I could hardly drag myself on. I found a place free of anthills, and stretched out. It didn't matter what position I took; something always ached. To say nothing of the scratches on my back.

Then everything grew confused and went numb. This is a better spot: the earth is soft. The trees are swaying, and from under one branch Niko is painfully extricating himself. His legs seem to be broken. He looks as if he has two knees on one leg; he is trying to stand up, but he can't. One split bone of the shin has broken through the bandages and protrudes at an angle.

"Niko, old man, what have they done to you?" I called out.

"I did it myself," he said.

"Why, Niko?"

"Out of spite, that's why. Off you went to Spain, leaving me to beg here."

"You can see that we haven't gone, can't you? I am here."

He spread his arms like two broken branches and sank to the ground. He was crying, but he didn't want me to see his tears. He curled up and stopped sobbing. Soon he was calm again, and gray like a stone. There were holes all over his back: some from bullets, others from knives. From them frantic ants were emerging, carrying larvae on their backs like white sacks. Niko turned around; his face was full of scratches. He had no upper lip, and his naked teeth grinned in a continuous smile. One ant entered through a space between the upper teeth, and quickly fled in terror.

"You know they've killed the Ramovichi?" I asked him.

"Yes, and they killed Velko too. Surely, there was nothing I could do."

"Not now, at any rate, not in the abyss."

I am not going to fall! I must protect myself. Every opening is in fact a gorge of stinking acids which will digest and absorb you in no time. You can laugh as much as you like. I tell you one thing: They will not get me alive! I will go mad and kill myself, but I will not endure capture, because I am soft and haven't got enough courage, and I am wild, and without Christian piety. That's why I'm not going to get trapped in a cave, or in the deep valleys, or under roofs. Nor will I allow sleep to cheat me. One can do without sleep.

"I killed someone," I said to cheer myself up.

"If you killed ten, it would make no difference."

"That Masnik is a bastard!"

"There're lots of bastards in the world."

"You're not Niko Saykov," I said to the bloody hulk standing in front of me. "You are a plague in disguise. You're a sickness of the will."

He nodded and grew dejected. That infuriated me. "In fact, you are an oaf, a devil; you've come here from the Wailing Mountain, haven't you?"

He again nodded. I was surprised. "You assumed Niko's shape in order to approach me and poison me. But that won't do, because I'm a Communist, and such things make no impression on me. And now get out of here." I spat at him. He hid behind a ghostly smile and vanished.

I reached for him: a rock with a hat of moss and a gray smile. I really grew frightened. I had no recollection of the rock. Had the devil transformed himself into a rock or concealed himself under it? Nonsense, I said, but my lips were trembling. What day was it? I must find someone to ask. I thought instantly of Maga, and her sister. I must find out what day it was. I had no idea where I was, but at the thought of these two women the world's four corners came into focus again. Instinctively I determined the exact direction. I arrived after dark, peeked in, and gently nudged the door. The sister was inside. She looked up and quickly motioned me away. Later she came out.

"Obrad's in there, my father-in-law," she said. "He's asleep. He was in action today."

"Was anyone killed?"

"Yes, one man. He was hit in the belly and there's no hope for him."

"And what of our men?"

"They ran away after the attack."

I asked for a glass of milk, and she got it. She told me that Ivan and Vasil got away in time. They had seen the Chetniks approaching, and had gone down along the stream. That cheered me up a little. This smell of human life, of cattle, of smoke—there is a splendor in it without which it's hard to live. The sudden loneliness is destroying us and has already carried off most of our men. If it got Niko, it could get me. I must find something, even if it is only this woman who is now coming out of the shack.

"I could easily have killed your father-in-law, you know," I said.

"What do you mean?"

"There was no attack. Just me. I was looking for Vasil and Ivan and I stumbled on them while they were asleep."

Vasil and Ivan will surely not go back to that place. They will look for a better spot. If I look for them aimlessly, I shall be ambushed. I'm in the same position from which Niko tried to escape. He wanted to find shelter and he's found it. I am his heir and that is my punishment. Yet I must find some other way, some other solution.

"I don't know where to go," I said.

"I'm sure you haven't eaten anything today."

"No, nor yesterday."

"Wait, I'll find something."

"Don't bother, just another glass of milk, if you will . . ."

My voice was thin, soft, whimpering like a child's, or as if coming from the throat of a beggar, like the voice of that beggar who used to kneel at the corner near the Law School. He may still be kneeling there, whining at the students, if bombs haven't finished him off. But why have I now assumed his voice and how did it come to me all by itself? Is this inevitable in such a disaster? What was my real concern? Neda. I don't want to lose her. This woman, Neda, is the only thing I've got.

She brought some pie and a chunk of cheese wrapped in green leaves. Something was bothering her too; she was silent. I should speak; it isn't good to eat in silence. Her father-in-law coughed. I wished he would choke. She vanished, leaving only

the sound of the door closing behind her. She didn't even say good-by. Apparently she didn't want to see my rags again, my beard, or my gluttony. Her abrupt departure was intentional, I thought. It is common knowledge no one asks a beggar to come back again; he'll come back anyway.

Her father-in-law is to be blamed for everything. He can't be that old, the beast, if he can still drag himself into action. And now he's resting comfortably in bed, and breathing the same air she breathes, and perhaps sinning with her. He doesn't have to sit out in a meadow like a beggar. I should be going, but I don't move a muscle. I doze off, resting my head in my hand. I shan't find a better spot for a nap anywhere under the stars. The meadow is soft as a mattress, and when I turn over, it's still soft. Then the clouded eye of day appears and chases me back into the mountains.

FOREST PRISON

LAST NIGHT I went down into the valley, to look for the teacher without the hand, to see if Niko had got in touch with him. I surprised him, so he had no time to slip away. At first he thought I was an apparition which would vanish of its own accord. Then he gave in and offered a ransom for his soul: a sack of flour, a pack of Albanian tobacco in a blue wrapper, plus matches. He would have given me America if he had by some chance had it with him—just to get rid of me.

On my way back I finally remembered to dig up some onions. I washed them in the brook. As I was shaking them off, I felt that something had changed in me for the better: I've grown sharp and I can attend to a variety of matters at one and the same time. Possibly I exaggerate, and yet there is some truth in it. You should have seen how skillfully I caught that teacher, and how quietly I crept along the fences, surprising the foxes. With this experience I could become a professional hunter, and make a lot of money selling hides. After the war.

Now I am the master of the house. I dug myself a nice hole to use as a hearth, and out of two flat slabs of stone I constructed a rack of the type used to support a vat of brandy. Instead of a vat, my little pot sits up there, and in it the hominy is boiling and bubbling, and I myself am sitting on a stump trying to make a pipe out of a tree root. It isn't much of a pipe; in fact, I've already ruined it. But the second or third time I am sure to succeed and then I'll no longer have to use my English Grammar for rolling cigarettes. A chip of wood jumped out and fell into the pot through a cloud of hot steam. Never mind, I shall find it later and discover what it was doing there.

In connection with the pipe a thought struck me: How would it be if in my idleness I invented something—a new machine gun, say, that would spit out simple rocks in place of bullets. I liked the thought. It would solve a problem I've been thinking about quite a bit. All our defeats, beginning with Spain, were chiefly caused by the lack of ammunition. This contraption of mine would be a really democratic one. We would no longer have to cringe like cowards or run away out of fear. . . .

After pondering the question a while, I concluded that I was on the right track as far as the basic principles went. I didn't want to tire myself with minor details, or get involved in the actual design until the underlying principles were settled. I let my fancy rest and stirred the hominy. It was salty and hot, just as it should be, and when the onions were dipped into the salt . . . an excellent combination! I put the fire out so it would not smoke needlessly, and covered the

hearth with twigs to keep the smoke down. Next time I come
to this mountain, the scene of my invention, I shall seek out
this pleasant spot: three paces northeast of that hollow beech
over there.

I had a drink of water from the stream, and then again I
remembered Niko. He was really a limited person, I said to
myself, and unimaginative. He couldn't stand loneliness, and
that implies a lack of certain higher values. Someone possess-
ing imagination and inner fire, as I do, will not be bothered
much by loneliness. On the contrary, it will spur him on to
unprecedented discoveries and will enrich the treasure of human invention. When I've completed my machine gun and
carefully tested it, I shall invent other instruments of equal
importance. First of all, I will occupy myself with problems of
aviation. The present type, which depends on gasoline, is almost useless. . . .

Hurriedly looking for a piece of paper, I ransacked everything in my bag. I found an empty sheet: the last page of
Faust. On it I drew a basket for rocks, an accelerator, a lever,
cogwheels, and a barrel. It resembled a strange catapult, and I
immediately understood that there were problems. If I am to
achieve a certain degree of precision, I thought, the rocks for
my machine must be of approximately the same size and
shape. They will have to be prepared in advance and that, of
course, alters the whole concept. I pondered the drawings for
another hour or so. I grew tired and leaned back to doze off
for a while.

It doesn't matter whether I fall asleep or not, I thought. The
solution to my problem—the initial move as well as the general course—could just as well come to me in my sleep. Such
decisive things, which cannot be accomplished with work, generally come about when one is not looking for them at all. The
branches begin to sway and the leaves are losing their color,
their shape. The trees themselves disappear and the uncer-
tainty as well. Fear melts away, and in the great silent oblivion which is like a wasteland, differences are erased; there

are no boundaries, no night, no day; everything is mist and thaw in which the mountain rocks like a green cradle.

A spider descended from a branch and played around my ear. I scratched myself, but he managed to get away and stubbornly went on with his work. At last I woke up and wiped the sweat off my forehead. The shadows had moved, the trees had altered their appearance, and the forest looked altogether different. The spider frowned, enveloped in itself and perfidious. I felt that I had momentarily interrupted it in some dark conspiracy. My leg had gone to sleep, my cap had rolled away. My knapsack lay next to a tree speckled with moss. It looked like the wrinkled remains of a corpse. My rifle had slipped down to my knees, as though someone had tried to make off with it.

Perhaps someone did, I thought, and my eyes were wide open. He might still be around, hidden behind a tree, waiting to catch me alive. Now he was looking at me and he was ready. I dodged to one side to avoid the blow, then I grabbed my rifle, pretending that I saw him too. I growled like a beast, and it seemed to me that my growls were mixed with his. I aimed to the right, then to the left, but he would not be provoked or intimidated. I turned a little farther to the left. He rustled a twig. I rushed straight at him, but there was nothing there; I merely bruised my hip against a tree stump. The roots of an uprooted beech were looking at me like the head of a snake.

Leaving my cap and knapsack behind, I hurried away from the besieged area. If they are here, I thought, they'll shoot before I get to that hollow beech; if they miss me, I am not going to miss them, I am sure to get at least one of them. I got to the beech too soon, and so assumed it was not the right one. The boundaries of danger had expanded. I went on, bent forward and sharp as a point, with the vague hope that my wild appearance would confuse and intimidate my enemies. I imagined that I had actually scared them and that they were pulling back from tree to tree. They know I never miss.

The pleasant sensation of victory soon distorted my face into a smile. Then I realized the forest was empty. Otherwise they would not have given me so much time to get away. I went back to pick up my cap and my knapsack, and kept seeing things along the way. The cap and knapsack were still there, dismal in their unrequited loyalty. They will look equally dismal when I'm no longer around and someone else takes them. Let them! They're filthy. I'm sick of them! I just keep lugging them back and forth, and I don't know why or where to.

Among the shadows there were surfaces, struck by the sun, that mocked me along with the lizards that suddenly crossed my path and disturbed my precarious peace of mind. I put the knapsack on my back. A ghostly place, I thought, and started downhill. The forest resembled the bars of a prison, a series of bars, one after another, all the way to eternity. I merely imagined that I was free. In fact, I was inside, behind the bars, waiting to be dragged to the scaffold.

Now and then I came across a clearing. In one of them I sat down. To amuse myself, I studied the drawings of my rock-sprinkler. I was surprised: my earlier enthusiasm vanished without a trace. There must have been another piece of paper here, I thought, and started looking for it. In vain. It doesn't exist, I finally admitted to myself, and it never did! I had created only a wretched skeleton of an idea; the rest was the sick embellishments of my diseased imagination. In short, I was mad.

I took my head in my hands, and ran my fingers along its sides. My head is here, and it hasn't changed much. This isn't the first time it's gone crazy and imagined things. If I could anticipate these whims I wouldn't worry so much. Besides, there's no one here to tell me whether I am mad. No one even to say good day to me or ask me what I'm doing. And it's always like that. Those whom I've seen in the last few days eyed me suspiciously and shook their heads. They never said that I was crazy, but what point is there in telling such things to a lunatic anyway?

There was a rustling in the thicket, a crackling of twigs, but this time it was no lizard. I lowered myself to the ground and crawled to a sheltered spot. I looked down my gun; there were two women in knitted skirts. They were picking mushrooms, or perhaps out looking for herbs. They would pass some distance from me. It is better that way. Two women can make a lot of trouble: when they interrogate you, one asks questions and the other checks on you. They will get to know more about a man than he does himself. Suddenly a third woman emerged, spotted me, and ran for dear life, telling the other two what she had seen.

They gathered behind the beeches, and looked across at me. I called to them; I wanted to ask them if they had seen a Partisan prowling around the forest. They were silent. I started toward them, but they had run away. Only the pressed grass indicated that they had actually been there. One of the women had evidently slid down the slope on her rear end. Now they're probably figuring out what they will say once they get down to the village. How self-important they will be! Their story will doubtless be exaggerated, and later, after it's gone from mouth to mouth, it will turn out that they had encountered a black devil who tried to rape all three of them at once.

The shadows mingle and gradually merge into one; night is coming. I don't know whether to welcome the night or dread it. It's good that another day has passed, and that this one will never return. But I don't know how to abbreviate the endless hours of darkness. I've slept enough; there's nothing left for me to do now but chase badgers. I go to an open spot above the valley where the villagers can see me well. And I make a fire. Let them watch my fire to their heart's content! I have to move on tomorrow anyway. Do you see the fire? Do you see it? Ha! That's my fire; I am alive! I live out of spite. And later I shall hoot with the owls.

WHERE SHEEP DO NOT BLEAT THE AX
IS NOT HEARD

FOR THREE DAYS now I have been searching the Donyokraiske Forests, following Yasha's trail by the ashes of fires he left uncovered. It looks as though, like Vasil, he made a fire whenever he stopped to rest. I can tell that he has been hanging around Lom for a time, and there suddenly his traces vanish. In Lom it is quiet. From the fields below, as from a canyon, the cries of lone reapers are heard. Their voices are appealing. Something always quivers in me when I hear these sounds; I am overcome by a crazy desire to go down for a smoke and a talk. I know it would be suicidal, so I quicken my pace to get as far as possible from temptation.

Retreating, I approached the Rugovo Mountains. Then I came across last year's battlefields. The overgrown trenches were full of rusted shells and chargers. Here were the Italians; we were on the other side. Suddenly a sheep bleated, and I jumped as if a cannon had gone off. I hid, waited, then looked around: there were no shepherds, no cattle, no dogs, merely this one sheep, followed by a white lamb. She was running toward me as if she was out of her head, mad.

She arrived out of breath and—baah, like an old friend. She looked me straight in the eyes—baah, baaah—her voice had changed. She seemed to be trying to ingratiate herself, as if she were some cursed soul who had known how to speak quite well before she had been turned into a sheep. She came very close, anxiously licking my rags, seeking the palms of my hands, which I had hidden behind my back. For a second I thought of those mothers who took their kerchiefs from their heads and wrapped them around the feet of the tyrant on whose mighty word their salvation depended. Her lamb was more cautious, wanting to be close to its mother and far away from me at the same time. The lamb was running in circles around us and these circles were getting smaller and smaller.

I took out a handful of salt, and she licked it voraciously. A few grains spilled and she dropped her head to look for them. I ought to kill her, I thought, but how can I? It would have meant meat for three days. Yet that would have been a breach of faith. We have trained them to live in our midst and to place all their trust in us, and now—should we use that trust as bait? I gave her the salt. Let her go where she wants. I started to leave; she followed me, and the lamb followed her. Now there were three of us. It would be awkward to go on this way. If the Chetniks should get me, they would tell everyone that I had stolen sheep. I kept hoping that she wouldn't follow me any farther, that she would get bored trotting after me, and would soon leave me, like the rest of my friends.

She followed me all day, and we three spent the night together under the same tree. At dawn, when I awoke, she was already up and ready to go. Never mind, I said to myself, let her come along. We shall run across a herd of sheep on the way, and she will surely join them. She will be slaughtered immediately to destroy all trace of her existence; but that will no longer be my worry. In the distance I heard the muffled echo of Taslach's ax, and instantly I thought: I'll give it to him. He's bound to be pleased; no one has given him a damned thing in twenty years. I found him planing a beam. He looked at the sheep, then at the lamb, and then looked me up and down.

"Whose are they?"

"They belong to the Rugovo Mountains, I think. They must have gotten lost a long time ago. You can see that the lamb is wild."

"What are you going to do with them?"

"I'll trade."

"Unshorn . . . That means they have been lost since spring."

"Would you like them . . . as a gift?"

He was startled; it was too much for him. He frowned and shook his head. He had his own sheep. That was enough. He didn't want to take anybody else's. "Other people's things bring only sorrow," he said. His people had never taken anything from strangers, not even so much as the dirt under their fingernails; and yet they had lived, and he too lived, and asked nothing of anyone. He grew angry and finally began stammering and repeating himself. It took me some time to set matters straight. If he didn't want to accept the sheep, all right; someone else would take them and thank me for it too.

"Why don't you slaughter it?" he said.

"I can't."

"I will, if you are so soft. You wouldn't even know how."

"I don't want anyone to kill it."

"It isn't some holy animal now, is it?" he sneered.

"She is holy, yes, damn it, she is. Anyway, if I'm not going to slaughter her, no one else will."

I looked at the sheep browsing among the trees. She was hungry. She reached up for the leaves, but kept looking over to make sure I didn't get out of sight. It occurred to me that she was an omen of some transformation that was about to take place: one living soul followed me when all others had deserted. Taslach was quiet. In his eyes were signs of some vague understanding. I offered him tobacco and asked him:

"Have you heard of the Wailing Mountain?"

"I have."

"Is it one of those?" I asked.

"Perhaps several of them together."

"That's what I think too. They are together. And they are cursed."

I first heard about the Wailing Mountain when I was a child. From older people. Or was it from the village sorceress who extinguished coals to chase away illness? She used to whisper: "Go away illness, go away pain! Go to the Wailing Mountain!" She was not altogether expert in her craft, and perhaps she once made a false move and cursed me along with the devil. I turned to Taslach.

"Why won't you accept the sheep?"

"I can't. Down in the village they steal sheep from one another all the time."

"Who? The peasants?"

"Yes. But they say it's you, Lado."

"That's impossible. They don't even know I'm here."

"Perhaps they don't, but they have to pin the blame on someone. Before you, it was Niko."

Now I know why Niko hung on to us so desperately. We left him to suffer between that hell down there and the Wailing Mountain. It really is hell down there. They inherited that life and they are constantly perfecting it. They've lived that way a long time, they are accustomed to it, and they have sanctified it. If someone tries to improve anything they put the brand of the devil on him.

In the meantime Taslach had changed his mind. I don't know whether he felt pity for me or took a fancy to the sheep; at any rate, he agreed to accept her among his own sheep. It was like finding a bee in the forest—to take it is no sin. We had a smoke to honor the agreement and I started on my way. The sheep, like a shadow, followed right after me. She was gay and skipped around. I grabbed her by the scruff of her neck and furiously lifted her off the ground. I let her kick in the air for a few moments and shook her to bring her to her senses. What did she think she was doing? Why did she want to follow me? I've got enough trouble as it is!

I put her back on the ground. She looked at me in bewilderment. The lamb skipped across the brook and turned to look at us. Taslach handed me a rope, and I tied it around her neck and then to the tree. Again she tried to follow me. She bleated sadly. She went on bleating. The bleats were now longer and more sorrowful. Baah . . . baaaah . . . Hopelessly and as though warning me not to go on. At times I heard the lamb. Its voice was shrill and reminded me of children crying in church during holidays.

I am some distance away and can no longer hear them. The ax is finally silent. Only the brook, but that too is far off and unclear. This is the real Wailing Mountain: fallen tree trunks lying like corpses. Sprawled out. And rotting. Some resemble huge lizards with mushrooms growing on their backs like impetigo. Devils of different sizes jump from corpse to corpse and amuse themselves. This constant movement, in an air troubled with shadows and the smell of rot, causes a quiet commotion which is gradually growing. I approach a tree trunk, and the devils jump out like monkeys and disperse—some into the trees, others into the shadows. So they let me pass, and then return to their playground.

THE DAMNED DO NOT ENTER HOUSES

No AX, NO hand, has meddled here. No one has felled a single tree of the Wailing Mountain. I don't think men have restrained themselves out of fear, because men are aggressive animals and brigands to boot, but because they don't care to wear themselves out for nothing. Here all their work would be clearly in vain: no roads, no paths, not even a way of getting in or out. On both sides of the river there are steep slopes and it is almost impossible to find enough level ground to make a fire and sit by it. And when you do sit down, you feel the ground gradually slipping from under you toward the bottom of the ravine. Trees appear to stand at a slant, getting closer to one another through a slow shrinking of the ground, mixing branches and roots in a constant squabble.

Night caught me in this forest, and I went to sleep. The devils behaved with reserve—from which I concluded that here they too were timid. Around midnight a voice called from far off, the voice of an owl, and tried to get me involved in a complex debate on the purposes of the universe, the nature of light, and such matters. I turned over, and dropped into a university lecture hall at exactly the moment the professor of Roman law took his seat behind the lectern. Students were shouting and hitting him with paper wads; there was a demonstration. But he noticed nothing and continued jabbering. Behind his glasses his eyes were shut.

I spent the day on the Wailing Mountain. Nothing happened. On two or three occasions I thought: I've run out of flour. I should go down to the village. But a deep lethargy had come over me. Or was it the same old fear of the valley? At any rate, whenever I tried to decide which door to knock on, and to imagine what I would say, sleep would come and everything turned to mist. It wasn't until evening that I calmed down, and then I waited for the moon to light my way. In crossing the brook I got my shoes wet and the thin softened leather gradually disintegrated under my feet and curled up. If the steep slope had lasted any longer the soles of my feet would have turned inside out as well.

The valley, illuminated by the moon, gaped wide at my feet. I stood above it, the hated outlander, and I hesitated. I pressed forward, and immediately regretted it. I didn't know what village to go to, or what house; it was all the same to me. It was all foreign. Then I made up my mind: Meda was closer than the other villages, and in all of Meda the closest house was the one in which little Tayo, my brother's son, was now asleep. I crossed the river just before dawn, not wanting to be caught far from the mountain in daylight, down there in that pit which feeds the belly of the earth. But some force was constantly pushing me, preventing me from realizing that there were other roads than the one I had chosen.

The sky was overcast. A sullen dawn trailed across the

ridges. I knocked on the window and I saw Iva through the glass, like a shadow, her hair falling over her shoulders. She recognized me, slipped her dress on, and ran to open the door. Barefoot and pale, more frightened than pleased, she looked at me in disbelief. She had lost a lot of weight: her legs were thin, her hands warm. I was afraid it might be consumption, but I thought of even worse things. She is alone in this wasteland, and she is quite young and timid. Who knows what rascals and frauds are hanging around here, attracted by her fading beauty? Perhaps something has happened; such men are always successful with women.

"Are you all right?" I inquired first about the main thing.

"Yes, we are well. How are you, brother?"

"Where's the little one?"

"In the room asleep."

"I don't want to wake him up. I just want to see him. I missed him."

She pointed to a cradle. That surprised me. I had imagined him to be bigger, sleeping in a bed like a grown man. But he hasn't had time to grow up; after all, he is only a year old. For me that year has been fuller and emptier and longer than any ten normal years. So many changes have been crowded into it, men falling like leaves. I lifted the cover. The boy was sleeping as if nothing had happened. I looked at his eyebrows and his arrogant little nose. He was frowning; he didn't like being disturbed. He licked his lips; he must have been thinking of food. I forgot that I was inside four walls, under a roof, behind a closed door.

"Your shoes are just about done for," Iva said. "Take them off so I can mend them a bit."

"Do the neighbors suspect that I come here?"

"Trobuck knows. I told him that you come by often."

"What possessed you to tell him, Iva?"

"Nothing but fear would keep him away from me."

And since then he has kept away. He keeps his cattle off her fields and has stopped making rude remarks to her. Let's hope he hasn't picked this day to bring over a patrol. I climbed up into the attic; one has a better view from up there. Across the river, the mud houses of the Vukolichi glistened in fresh whiteness. Their windows faced this way, as if they were watching for me to show up. It started raining, and I detected a smell of soot. Iva passed up a small pot of boiled potatoes and milk. Later she brought a basketful of plums that were just beginning to ripen; they made my teeth numb. The little one woke up and howled. Iva brought him up to the attic. He enjoyed pulling my beard and looking out through the cracks. He cried when she took him down.

While I was falling asleep, a calf bellowed for a long time. Barefoot children clustered nearby, chasing each other with rocks. A dog whimpered in the rain, hungry probably. I guessed that he was chained, or locked up, and that that was why he was whining. I felt a certain anxiety, and I woke up in the sooty dripping of the attic. I looked at my hands. They were not bound. That's all I've got left, and the rifle next to me. The rest I've squandered in the most idiotic manner. I let the valley bait me and draw me into a tight airless coffin. Somewhere behind Kara gunfire was heard.

"Iva, do you hear that gunfire?"

"They entertain themselves like that quite often. They don't know what else to do with their ammunition."

"If they get near, you get out with the boy and put him somewhere safe."

"Why?"

"I'll have to defend myself. It's too late now to run away."

The shooting was getting closer and a broken cry was heard, which could be either a song or a wail. Some were approaching across the hill, others from down the valley. Someone apparently had noticed me. In the thicket of birch trees behind the house they were waiting for me to come out. Fear, like a ball of snakes, filled my intestines and began writhing. It was stifling my throat and deafening my ears with its screeching and humming. It was blinding my sight. I must calm down, and I screamed:

"Get out, Iva! Take the child!"

"I don't want to," she said. "I have outlived too many of you. Let them kill me first."

"For the child's sake, you fool! Go, I tell you! Do you want them to catch me alive because of you?"

She was silent, and stood there like a rock. She is with them, I thought, and the whole thing is a trap. I slipped down from the attic and pushed my way past her. I jumped over the fence and threw myself onto the wet grass. Now I am merely a rag in the grass, a heap of rags. To be exact, a scarecrow. I wonder why they aren't shooting. The situation is damned awkward: I am lying on my belly and my range of vision is quite limited. I am vulnerable on all sides, and yet I can defend myself only on one. Perhaps I should have stayed in the house. They wouldn't have figured out where I was shooting from. Before they could I would have picked off several of them.

From the woods above I heard a din of talk. Some ten yards away there was a hazel bush. It wasn't much, but it could serve as a cover for my retreat. I crossed the path and crawled over to the bush. And still I heard nothing. There were other bushes too, but now it was too late to search and fumble. I curled up like a hedgehog and edged my rifle out in front of me. The fear which gave me nausea in the attic seemed to have evaporated in the fresh air.

I heard the stamping of feet. They had Italian boots on. Not very good for our roads. I could see their heads through the branches, some young and hairy, others ashen gray. The gray-haired ones, they're the worst! When I shoot, I'll aim at one of them first. They set up their machine gun by the fence; they called out to Iva and asked her if there were anyone in the house. "Why don't you look?" she hollered back; "you wouldn't believe me anyway." I heard them enter the house. The child was crying. Because of me. I had no other gift to take to him. They climbed into the attic and stomped around, asking questions.

They fired a round from the machine gun to scare the hens and they laughed as a cloud of scattered feathers flew up. The child was crying again. I could hardly keep from shooting, I was so angered by the crying and laughter struggling in the air. Finally they went away. I heard them clumping down the road below me, talking loudly. They came quite close to me and, if it had not been for the branches and leaves, I could have recognized their faces. The last two were talking about Iva, her former beauty of which so little was now left. Hunger had emaciated her.

Silence set in and along with it a strange sort of fatigue. I am free, I am whole, nothing has happened. But my legs aren't holding me up any longer. I have just enough strength to drag myself to the doorstep, but how can I look that child in the eye? I am from up there, from the Wailing Mountain, a marked and cursed man, singled out to bring sorrow wherever I go. I shall no longer pay such visits, at least not to those whom I love. I must be patient. I lower myself to the wet, muddy ground and stretch myself out on it. I recall the tramping up and down in the yard and in the attic: now I feel it was on me they were trampling. They have trampled me well. I am lying dead, and the shaggy clouds, heavy with rain, pass through the sky above me.

A SNAKE'S BEAUTY

GROPING ABOUT, I scraped through a sponge of forest and darkness. The meadow opened up like the dawn: in the middle there was a rock, and juniper bushes grazed along the edges. A bush in front of me seemed to pull itself out by its own roots and fly off, low above the grass. I started from my slumber: it was either an apparition or another illusion in my eyes. I'm going crazy again. Now the rest of the brushwood will run off, and then the forest with all its trees as well. To forestall this flight, and crazy with fearful heroism, I rushed after the apparition. I reached it in three leaps and raised my arm to crush it. Like a shadow it curled up around my feet. It touched me with its hair. I felt its breath on my skin. I thought it would bite me.

Some miserable beast from underground! Not as big as it had appeared at first either. Everyone was pursuing it, so why should I kill it? I had let Trobuck live, and others too! It would be wrong to kill the weak. While I was reflecting, the beast slipped off and blew away. I waved my hand and laughed, and the forest wall suddenly bleated back an echo. Some enormous creature seems to be standing behind that wall, watching and mocking everything. I don't know whether it is God Himself or just some idiot.

There used to be a broken fence in the meadow. Finally I found it. I gathered a whole armful of twigs and lugged them to a sheltered spot. I made a fire, peeled the wet rags off my back and propped them up on forked branches to dry above the flame. There I was, naked by the fire! A passer-by would think I was mad. Let him! My bones felt much better. Sparks leaped like stars through the holes in my trousers. Some entered the pockets to light up an exit for the wet lice. Two branches had crossed like the Chetnik coat of arms. I separated them so they could never cross again.

My rags were dry before dawn and I put them on. The fire had gone out; there was no longer any smoke. I sat and waited for the sun to grow stronger and for the wind to lift the dew. At any rate, that's what I said to myself. In fact, I didn't feel like going to the mountain or into the water. I didn't want to go anywhere. I felt drowsy and my head swayed heavily to one side, then to the other. This was no place to sleep, I realized at last, and I staggered to my feet, as though from the dead, to look for a more suitable spot. I found some bushes along an overgrown path, and I crawled into them. I spread a blanket on the ground to keep out the dampness. There were insects and worms crawling under me. I could hear them as they fled.

I rested my head on my dusty knapsack and imagined that I was pushing down a long street which, like a snake, alternately curves and then straightens out. Its twisting is irregular and its course can never be anticipated. I cannot take two steps without being tossed back and forth against a long-decayed wall which bends like rubber. I am supposed to appear before an important person in the morning and I am afraid I'll be late. I don't know who the person is, but I do know that I am expected to bow before him and plead for mercy, or something like that. Suddenly the street makes an abrupt turn and catapults me forward. I see only a foot thrust out to receive a kiss, and I recognize a peasant's sandal: Taslach! I opened my eyes. He was standing over me.

"Are you ill?" he asked.

"No. I was asleep."

"Then you must be crazy. Why don't you take better care of yourself?"

"Tell me how."

"If someone else had come by, you'd be dead by now."

"I know. But it doesn't really matter."

He was holding his ax over his shoulder, and remained standing over me. I was a little afraid of the ax and I didn't like the glitter it made in the sun. I'd rather be in the churchyard, under the apple tree, throwing rocks in the air. My vision was hazy. First it was the apple tree, and then again Taslach. The sun and the dampness had made me feeble-minded, so I racked my brains to no purpose. There was no use fooling myself. I was on the ground; he was up there. He had only to strike once. I could not plead with him; that would not become me. Perhaps I should bite his foot! That would not improve my position, but at least it would put an end to his compassion and contempt.

"I could have taken your rifle," he said. "You'd never have noticed it."

"And what would you have done with it?"

"Are you serious? The Turks give a load of wheat for every rifle that's turned in."

"And you'd get ransom money too—a pretty penny."

"Ransom money is damned, but a man with a family needs wheat in a year like this."

"Yes, that's true. Why didn't you take it?"

He couldn't explain it himself. He licked his lips. Because he's crazy, he said. He has always been crazy and he will remain that way until the end. It's too late now to learn a lesson and to change his skin. Others grab whatever is at hand; they grab even what isn't at hand because they know where it is and they find it. And it shows. Not a single man who rides horses and wears expensive vests makes anything with his own hands. In these parts one's own hands aren't much help. This is a cursed earth; it hates men. One has to be tough to live here, never mind the soul. The soul only gets in the way.

It gets in my way too. That soul of his especially. I'd say he is overdoing the self-praise. I didn't ask him to spare me, and I don't want to owe him anything. Even if I am lying on the damp ground among worms and centipedes, stupid with sleep, he has no right to praise himself and to feel pity for me. I don't want it, I can't stand it, I am burdened by a crazy pride which refuses to plead or to owe. Doesn't he understand this? I am constantly underneath, wrapped up in a heap of burned patches and in the filthy wrapping of my own skin, but I'd rather he didn't boast of his spirituality or humiliate me with his charity. I could barely contain myself.

"Don't expect me to thank you for having pardoned my life."

"I didn't ask to be thanked."

"If you are sorry to have missed this opportunity, try and catch me next time. I frequently sleep like this during the day."

"You're really crazy. You won't last long."

"Go away and feel sorry for somebody else, not for me. Go tell others their destiny."

He seemed to be a man who once had some faint hope—gone now. He had reconciled himself to the loss, and was about to start on his way. I asked him to stay and have a smoke with me. He smokes only when he runs into me. We moved into the shade and sat down on the ground, as equals. Automatically this meant reconciliation. He told me about some ox which the Chetniks had picked up at Focha. On their way back the ox broke loose, and now it was rambling alone over the mountains. A big ox, strong and wild—it would be a shame if the wolves got it or the Chetniks recaptured it, while we were perishing of hunger.

"That's what I have against you," Taslach said, "because you're all soft, and you don't want to trouble anybody."

"There are tough ones among us too."

"I haven't met any. Niko never stopped at my house for fear of ruining me if he ate a piece of my bread. That's no way to live, don't you see? The honest ones go first."

I gave him enough tobacco to fill his pouch. One such lesson is worth more. We said good-by to each other and he started off, his ax over his shoulder. I stayed behind—alone with my thoughts. I was reminded of my scheme for combining catapults with machine guns. We had deceived ourselves. We thought that there was an honest solution to this problem. Our imagination had overtaxed itself. Neither the young nor the old had the slightest notion of what we were talking about.

So there it was: an honest man cannot survive in a time of thieves! This is an age of armed masses. The central question is: who will get hold of the masses—they or we? We set them in motion and gave them arms; they snatched them from us and are leading them off like a herd of cattle. We must wrest them back, but how? With what? There my thoughts stopped. We have no salt and no canned food, we don't know how to make macaroni or money. A wall of not having. There's one thing: we could show them that rascals sometimes suffer no less than honest men. . . .

I wanted to go into this more deeply, but a familiar noise interrupted me. I turned around: a handsome snake with a small head was shedding a whole length of silver and mother-of-pearl in its trail and was pulling it along. She looked at me, then continued, as though I were not there at all. She made no effort to hurry, but proceeded slowly, displaying her beauty. Perhaps she is the devil's mistress or one of his assistants. But not my problem. I hit her with a rock, ripping her back; it was only then that she began to hurry up. I showered her with more rocks, which forced her to curl up. She tried to bite the butt of my rifle, then hid her head under her belly and the torn shreds of flesh.

That didn't help her. I was determined to end her agony. I separated her head from her body and with strange pleasure pressed on it with the rifle butt until it turned into a thin, bloody piece of skin. Then I watched this hateful thing twisting, portion by portion, into convulsions and then death. Everything alive, here and below, is hard and resilient, like the waters and roots of the Wailing Mountain. Only the tough survive, the rest must perish. I am that way too. My end will not pass without convulsions. Those who witness it need not pity me or wail. I'd rather they hated me. I will make sure that they do.

With the Devil

Black Devil, Brother Mine
—RADOSAV LJUMOVIĆ

AN OLD APPARITION

It LOOKED as if it were going to rain. That was why I crossed into Gubavche, near the cave. The cave once belonged to Yevrem the Leper, and then to Niko. Now it's mine, but I don't feel like going in. The rain didn't amount to much; I slept through those few drops under a nearby beech. The air cleared before dawn and the sun rose in silence. Someone else is roaming through the forest; I don't hear anything, but I feel him approaching nevertheless. Two or three times I turned to look, and finally I spotted him: in a black business suit, limping and staggering from tree to tree. I was instantly reminded of Leonid Krestalevski, who taught us biology, chemistry, mathematics, and psychology. A thin, tall Tsarist colonel suffering from gout, he knew everything and remembered everything.

But he died before we graduated from high school. It's someone else. It must be Aga Vidrich from Meda. His son, the curator of a museum, once lived in Paris, and I used to write letters to him for the old man. I waved to Aga. He saw me and was frightened. His black suit lost its color and shape, and disappeared from sight. Then I recalled that Aga too was dead. This was some other devil. Perhaps it was *the* devil! There he was, by the tree. I beckoned to him and he limped over.

"You must be looking for a snake," I said. "It's gone!"

"You killed it," he snarled in his underground voice. "You shouldn't have done it."

"What made it come to me, anyway, when there's so much space around here?"

He vanished, and I thought: he's afraid I might kill him

too. But then he reappeared; he was sitting on a rock, that's why I didn't see him.

"I'm really pleased we've met," I said.

"Really?" He was surprised. "Why?"

"I'd like to sell you my soul."

"Someone's deceived you. I don't have any use for it."

Just my luck, I thought. Now that I've found the devil, he isn't interested in me. Perhaps that's how he shows his cunning. He wants to knock down the price of the goods I am offering him. In this he resembles Redo the Turk, who owned a butcher shop in Berane. In the spring, a lot of slaughtering was done in the village. I used to bring my bloody lamb hides to his shop. He always said he didn't need them, and not until I had left the shop would he angrily ask me to come back. Then he would find fault with each hide and bargain over every penny.

"How many devils do you have here?" I asked.

"I'm the only one."

"And how many at the Wailing Mountain?"

"This is the Wailing Mountain, as far as you can see. And I'm the only one here."

He's bragging, I thought, and that's a bad sign. When I asked the Turk a similar question, he said that he was the only butcher in town and that he handled the entire trade in hides. However, it was obvious there were others—hides could be seen hanging above every shop door. In that case, I should bargain with my new adversary.

"I don't ask much for my soul," I said. "Very little, in fact."

"I know: you'd like me to perfect your gun."

"Yes," I admitted readily.

He grew pensive and frowned. Finally he said:

"It would be just another popgun! Not worth the trouble."

"With a range of a thousand yards it could make every other gun obsolete and the ruling class along with it."

"So what? What would you accomplish? Only a more general extermination, isn't that so? You'd go completely mad, and choke one another to death. The lice would eat you, and these forests would too. And I'd have nothing to amuse myself with. I'd die of boredom."

"One can't really say that you hate men," I said.

"Why should I hate them? They're much more interesting than ants. Sometimes they get together and they build and build."

"And you destroy it all at once?"

"No, they do it themselves. They sing on their way to battle and they cry on the way back. I find them pretty amusing."

"All the same, they advance. . . ."

He looked at me in surprise. He started to say something, but he was seized with laughter. One couldn't exactly call it laughter. It was, rather, an inexpressibly wild mixture of choking and grinding, the sounds of a cave being warmed up by the sun. His rotten teeth were loose and dangling. It was as if everything inside of him were festered and putrid: a horrible odor of corpses and open bowels filled the air. I covered my nose, but that didn't help at all: his accelerated giggling constantly pumped out new waves of stink from within. It was going to suffocate me; I grew scared. I grabbed a handful of dirt and pebbles and threw it in his teeth. It went right through him, as through a shadow, and scattered over the dry leaves.

"Now what's the matter?" he asked.

"You smell like a whole butcher shop!"

"That's what it is, this progress of yours, a butcher shop."

And then, as if he had pressed a button, he released the stench of autumn billy goats, as thick and sticky as soot.

"I've had enough of your tricks," I screamed. "Go to hell and take them along."

"I only wanted to show you what I was."

"I can see what you are: an old, threadbare ghost and bastard, an accumulation of stenches, that's what you are!"

I was about to hit him with the butt of my rifle: I was really sick of him and my head ached from the stink. But suddenly he lost color, as though it had drained out of him and trickled into the earth. Only his outline remained, but that too grew thinner, merging with the lines of the dry leaves and twigs on the ground. In the end only the lines remained and one of them moved. I thought he had entered the ground at that spot and slipped away through an invisible tunnel. But I spotted him a few yards away, limping among the trees. I lost sight of him at times, but he kept reappearing.

I mulled over this encounter slowly and listlessly, as though with only half my strength, and saw nothing much in it. I looked around: I was sitting in front of the cave with a rifle in my hand. The knapsack was not there. I'd left it where I'd spent the night. That convinced me that he was really an apparition. Perhaps it had been the leper. He has lived alone for a long time and in his leisure has cooked up all kinds of strange things. Yet I don't know what possessed him to try to lure me into the cave. Good thing I didn't enter; I might never have come out.

GIVE ME BLOOD AND MEAT

It is generally known that young plums, like castor oil, contain certain ingredients which act without fail. They turn the stomach into a reed through which everything drips out. I swore once that I'd never eat them again. But even if I wanted to break my oath, how could I? Where would I find plums now, or anything else for that matter? Everything is far away. My feet are failing me, my eyes are no longer a safe guide. Perhaps someone will bring me some plums. But then, who comes my way these days?

I curled up to go to sleep. It was less uncomfortable that way. I have been told that there are snakes that bite their tails and rejuvenate themselves with their own poison. I ought to try that myself. There's enough poison in me for ten snakes, if only I knew where to inject it. I started biting my knees. They were the closest things to me, sticking up through my torn trousers. My teeth have grown sharp, they bite right down to the bone. "How did you ever become a Communist? And why did you allow them to defeat you? Why didn't you go to Bosnia? Why didn't you get killed earlier? It serves you right!" These words do not hurt, but the bitter fluid from my mouth inflames the bites like iodine.

Finally I grew tired of this game. What I really wanted was a piece of meat from a spit: the kind that burns the palm of the hand and then the tongue. I was dreaming about such a hunk of meat when I remembered the ox. Did someone tell me about it, or was it a dream? There was an ox who rebelled against the Chetniks and was roaming the mountains on his own. Perhaps the devil would lure him to me. I'd give my soul for such a mouthful; actually I'd give much more, only now I have nothing else. But come to think of it, even the devil would have trouble luring an ox into these forests.

How would it be if I started looking for him myself? Pretty hopeless, of course. If such an ox really existed, the Chetniks would not have let him live long. But if he had been seized by wolves, something would be left for me and I'd rip off a good-sized piece and roast it. It wouldn't matter that it had been bitten into. I'd wash it. Unwashed would do too. Fire cleans everything. And what was there to clean? My teeth or the wolves': it would be all the same. These thoughts, as persistent as flies, finally got me up on my feet. My knees were decidedly rejuvenated. I am looking at them: they are my own children, and I have let them perish of hunger. And my feet too. If I find the ox, I'll use some of the hide to shoe them properly.

I climbed the hill; as far as the eye could see there was

nothing on the peaks. Only the waves of green above and wind-swept whirls of grass in the valley below. The Italians still hadn't given these people mowing permits. Because of me, they were told. When I am gone they will get their hay. Once again I feel like curling up and going to sleep, but it's too late to lose hope. There is always the possibility somebody will come along. A lone Chetnik will come down the summer path. And in his bag there will be a can of meat which he has saved for his children. . . .

I was wandering up and down, searching carefully. Not a sign anywhere, not a single trace of blood. God has been against me for a long time, and the devil does not understand me too well either. That's why I have no luck. Across the marsh, down below the well, there were cattle hoofprints. At least a week old. Then my attention was drawn up to a clearing, like a slanting lake, on the other side of the valley. I spotted him there: a black devil of an ox. Could this be my ox? Why was he standing there like that? Why had the wolves spared him? Perhaps all of our wolves have fled to Europe to get away from the shooting. As for the Chetniks, they are too busy searching the forests to pay attention to the fields.

I descended through the thick pine wood to the bottom of the vale, waded across the river, and climbed up the steep slope on the other side faster than I had thought possible. I was seized by the fear that he would disappear right in front of my nose. He had not. Now the opposite fear: I wouldn't have the courage to attack. It was a trap: they were waiting for me in the forest. Perhaps Taslach, who told me about the ox, was one of them. Then the ox spotted me, blew through his nose and stiffened, ready to defend his life. I tumbled down the slope a dozen yards or so.

It wasn't a trap. He was the wild one. His senses were sharpened. I circled around him, watching him from a distance. Foam dripped from his mouth. He was very beautiful. His long neck thrust his head almost to the ground, the locks on his wide forehead glistened in the sun. How can a wretched creature such as I destroy such beauty? The sun was still high. It was too early to start closing in, and I was relieved to find a reason for stalling. I hoped for a while that the Chetniks would come by and stop me. Then I remembered Yevrem Srdich, who used to say: "When you aim at a man imagine him not to be a man but, rather, some evil beast, a dragon. . . ."

This is a dragon, I thought, and I will imagine that it is a man. I aimed at his forehead, then I lowered the gun a bit. My hands were shaking slightly, but less so now than before. He saw me as inevitable death. My eyes were clouded with tears, but I had no time to dry them. If I waited another moment, everything would give way, hands and all. I fired. His handsome head swayed as if bowing to the mountain and to the sun for the last time. He fell forward on his knees and buried one horn in the ground, down to the very root. I ran up to him to slit his throat. He looked at me with his large eye. I trembled: now he would start talking!

If there had been a way of reviving him, I would have done everything possible. But it was over and the blood was spurting out on the grass. I caught some blood in my hands and swallowed it, as Bele Trobuck used to do. It was not until I had gulped down a few handfuls that I realized it was tasteless, but not at all sickening, as I had imagined it to be. The smell of raw meat and deathly sweat excited me. It was as though all my great-grandfathers had risen up at once, stirred by the blood, and had crawled under my skin. What they had not taught me in their lifetime they were doing now by skillfully guiding my knife down the middle of the bull's belly.

My head was buzzing and I was vaguely aware that the sense of danger was gone. The softness of the hairy skin felt like a velvet skirt. It clung tight to the body and had to be ripped away before one could reach the hidden mysteries and sources of enjoyment. It could not be put off any longer: I was undressing her and she didn't even dream of defending herself. The knife was sharp. The cut was faultless, leaving two soft pieces of lace at its edges, just barely scratching the silky membrane which rustled like a petticoat under the touch and clung to the gentle forms.

The fine vapor of life drifted up from below. I was drugged. I came upon a foam of tallow, whiter than snow, in grated, perforated folds which melt in the mouth. I remembered that Trobuck always had something in his mouth when he was slaughtering, and he chewed and gulped continuously. Now I know what it was: I was following in his footsteps, and making a discovery. If I go on like this, I thought, not without bitterness, I might perhaps someday surpass him. I shrugged; let it be! Even that's better than being buried alive like Niko Saykov.

I skinned his belly, slit open his legs. With my left hand I gathered the skin and with the right I penetrated the solid flesh which was opening up and cooling slowly. I reached the spine—the best piece for the shoes. I would have to go slowly. It would be a shame to rip it. My hands were greasy and swollen. They were creeping along. My knife had grown blunt. My tattered knees ached. The sores smarted from the grass I knelt on. I was tired and I was slowly sobering up. What was I doing? I was so immersed in this butchery that I had forgotten everything else.

I retreated to the edge of the forest and lit a cigarette. The sun was still on the hills—yellowish patches constantly diminishing in size. Night was rising from the valley, and soon it would be falling from the skies too. I should yank off a leg of meat and get out of here. But something strange had happened. It was impossible for me to act reasonably. I'd been transformed. I was Bele Trobuck, who was in his own slaughterhouse and who listened to no reason. I sharpened my knife against the stone and continued to work. Who cared about the nightfall? The main thing was the meat. It would glisten in the dark.

I rolled the skin into a long cylinder wet with blood. I filled my knapsack with the tallow and long strips of meat. To protect my English Grammar and *Faust* I wrapped them up in leaves. If they should get greasy and bloody it won't matter— I'll throw them out anyway. It was a little harder to hack off the limbs and drag them through the forest and up into a fir tree. I was surprised by my patience and energy. Only a man who has been hungry for a long time could be so patient, so painstaking; in fact, he could not behave any other way. I took up everything into the tree that I could carry—to dry and rock in the wind. I covered it all with branches to protect it from the ravens.

I sat down to catch my breath. I was so tired that I no longer felt hungry. A headless trunk remained in the meadow, glistening like a tree without its bark. I was sorry to let it go. The wolves would have quite a feast. I should tell Taslach, but I was afraid he'd ask to share the whole thing with me. I didn't know, I'd think it over. For the time being I should get away from the meadow. I rolled the remains into the forest to keep it from rotting in the sun. And from a distance no one would be able to guess what had happened. Only the head was left behind; I preferred not to touch it. There was a horrible look in those eyes.

Still, I plucked up enough courage to glare at it: "It had to be that way, Great Head, because this is the Wailing Mountain. If I hadn't done it, someone else would have, and they are all worse than I am." I took the skin with me, but it was terribly heavy, and constantly unrolling, as if to spite me. Never mind, I'll roll it up again. Tomorrow I'll stretch it out to dry. I must find a nice spot near the cave, and far from the meat. If they find one, at least I'll have the other.

In the valley by the river my hunger returned. I made a fire. Here I could do it. The shadows waved their arms about and danced, but I paid no attention. I sharpened a juniper branch and cut the meat into thin slices. I salted each piece and then put it on the spit. Turning the spit above the flame, I listened to the murmuring of the stream. What a meal, I thought, as I took my first bite. No one in Europe could have such a feast!

Except Trobuck, who, in the meantime, has probably stolen another calf in my name. Now there are two of us. Two thieves. That's too many. One of us must go. I put out the fire and fell asleep right there. I dreamed all night that I was drinking water and getting thirsty again.

A BURGLARY AT BOYO MUMLO'S

THAT BLACK BULL must have had a lot of iron in his blood. I've absorbed a good deal of it, which is evident in a series of marked changes. I cannot say that I've become any wiser, but I'm stronger than ever and I'm only sorry that there's no one here to appreciate it. At the same time I've developed a keen practical sense: the way I stretched the oxhide on that steep rock and tightened it expertly with bolts of oak! My fear of apparitions is completely gone. A fine calm has come over me and I am quite pleased that I've outwitted luck.

I am going into the valley. My fear of the low places is now only a memory. The moon is up, and the road in front of me shimmers. The horses in the fields pause and wait for me to stroke them. Near the Grivichi threshing floor the wheat is standing in sheaves. The famine must have passed; otherwise no one would leave wheat out like that. I decided to take some grain for myself on the way back. I crossed Strmenti's field and changed the direction of the irrigation water toward our field. Let the old bastard fume a little! Soft clouds were reflected in the water, and young frogs jumped from the grass into the millpond and back out again. I wanted to stop at the

ruins where our house had been, but I was afraid to spoil my
good mood. I went on to Iva's and rapped on the window. Iva
opened the door.

"It's a good thing you came. I've got some flour for you."

"Did you get a lot?"

"You can get enough these days. We don't go hungry."

"And I brought you some tallow. You must give the little
one enough food to grow on."

"He's growing as fast as he can."

"He should grow faster. He must hurry."

I asked about Trobuck. She said that he had been impudent
again. A patrol came to look for me, and it was concluded that
I hadn't been there after all. Now it's the same old story: as
soon as Trobuck spots her, he jeers at her. That's how he
amuses the village. No one has ever done this to our family. I
thought of writing a note to Trobuck and placing it on his
doorstep; that should bring him to his senses. But I don't
really like the idea. It'll put him on the alert, and I won't be
able to catch him. Iva observed me with empty eyes. She felt
pity.

"You poor devil, your clothes are in shreds."

"They've lasted long enough."

"Take them off. I'll try and patch them together."

"Don't bother. I'm going to rob someone and get myself
some new clothes."

It's strange, I'd never thought of stealing as a means of
survival. But why not? If they don't catch me, they'll naturally
think it was Trobuck! An expert like Trobuck is never caught,
except on one of those rare occasions when he is innocent. I'd
confuse the hell out of him by such a stunt. And then, I'll send
him a note! It's time for me to get rid of these rags; they've
soaked up so much sweat, so much blood, they stink to high
heaven! I'll take a bath and then, in my new clothes, I'll call at
Yablan to see if Maga has been released from prison.

In the shadow of the plum tree I ate a piece of bread with

meat fried in tallow. I drank a dish of milk and talked quietly
with Iva. The thought of stealing, once conceived, stuck obsti-
nately in the back of my mind. What about our neighbors, the
Nastichi? No good; it's hard to get into their house. And they
always wear everything they own anyway. Then there are the
Yasikichi, up on the hill; they have good clothes, but they also
have a dog, which makes it impossible to approach the house.
Boyo Mumlo's house would be the best bet. His people are
away, up at the pasture with the cattle. Boyo himself is always
pottering about in the fields. Nothing has ever been stolen
from his house. I am sure he still keeps the suits of his two
dead sons, and their shirts too.

As I walked to the river and the cornfields, I carried this
idea along with me, a burden that kept pulling me backward.
There's nothing to steal in the mountains. How would it be if
I spent the day in the village? Out of sheer boredom I may
think of something. And why shouldn't I stay? I'll get a
glimpse of what's happening here. I crawled through a grove
of hazelwood and up onto a slope where only goats graze. I
fell asleep, and woke at noon, startled by loud shouting. Old
Savo was hurrying down the road. Someone must have died in
the next village: there'll be plenty of brandy! Savo was followed by a mob carrying sticks. They were calling Kacharanda, they were calling the town crier and finally Boyo
Mumlo himself.

"Come to the meeting! It's an order!"

"Ahan-huan-kakn-kuge" (or something like it), Boyo mumbled in his strong voice.

"Hurry up. We'll wait for you down by the pear tree."

"Ugangun-gagangaun-babun-babun," he replied.

"What did he say?"

"God knows!"

Boyo put on his coat and came out, followed by his son. He
looked at his house, as if to assure himself it was still there.
Then he started off. It's a good idea: these new gatherings at

which they vie for power. They all want to become accomplished orators. They need an audience to listen to them, and to praise them of course. So they get together each week to denounce Communism. They are divided into two parties: one side buys everybody drinks and makes a lot of noise, the other guzzles the brandy and shouts approval. They seem to like it, and I certainly have no objections. Boyo's house must be empty now.

To get there I had to follow the river for a while. It was bordered on both sides by old walls and was full of slippery rocks, horns, hoofs, and rotting intestines. I finally reached Mumlo's house. I peeked under the bridge: there was no one on the road, or on the porch, or in the garden. The bees under the apple tree were buzzing with an intensity that deepened the silence. I cleared my throat and waited for someone to appear at the window. I stepped up onto the porch and knocked on the door. The door was locked and the knocking echoed in the emptiness. I slipped down into the cellar, which was open. It smelled of fermented manure and in the corner there was a trough.

The trough reminded me of Mumlo's horse, Arab, and of that autumn when we had earth tremors almost daily. The house was nearly finished, and we used to gather to watch Boso the Muslim cutting an opening in the floor for a trap door. I looked for it in the ceiling; perhaps I could get into the house that way. I found it. I turned the trough upward at an angle, like a flight of stairs. I climbed up and pushed on the trap door with my head. It gave way. For a moment the cobwebs blinded and suffocated me. The room above was dim. Tsaga, Boyo's wife, was sitting there, waving her arms as though she were spinning. I had completely forgotten about her. They say she went out of her mind about a year ago. It seemed to be true.

"What are you doing, Tsaga?" I asked as I stood there, halfway between floors.

"I'd like to spin an undershirt for Dukan, but they've hidden my staff. They won't give me anything, not even a glass of brandy."

"Your Dukan has been dead for a long time. He doesn't need an undershirt, or even a shirt for that matter."

"Boyo is lying: bad Mumlo. Don't believe a word he says. Dukan is with the sheep at Sutivan."

"Is there anyone at home?"

"Boyo is out. He shoved his big balls in his trousers and he's out after women. It's always been like that."

Around the room lie several heavily carved wooden chests under piles of eiderdowns and mattresses. My loot must be in one of these chests. Having come this far I would be silly to leave without taking anything. If this madwoman squawks, I'll quiet her down with my fist. I no longer listened to her. I opened a chest filled with rolls of linen and a few wrinkled apples which gave off a pleasant smell. In another chest I found the shirts. I stuffed a half dozen in my knapsack. At the bottom of the chest I uncovered a brand-new pair of trousers. I grabbed them as if I had to fight for them. A shabby overcoat was hanging on the wall, thin at the elbows, but good enough for me. Tsaga fell silent and scrutinized me carefully. I was afraid that she might recover her senses.

"I'll take this to Dukan," I said. "And I'll give him your regards."

"Are you from Sutivan?"

"No, I am not. I am from the Wailing Mountain."

"Once a man came here from the Wailing Mountain. He was dark, dark, with a mustache, and his pants were unbuttoned and one could see everything. Is he a relative of yours?"

"No, just a partner."

"You don't say? And his penis fell out, long as a rolling pin, and nodded and nodded. . . . We died laughing. Damned women, they never have enough of it."

I hurried to get out of there and away from her, but the door was locked from the outside. I turned cold for a split second: I had fallen into a trap. I should return the clothing so that they find nothing on me when I am dead. Then I saw the trap door, still wide open, and I remembered how I had come in.

I lowered myself into the basement as fast as I could, and buried myself in the corn. For a few moments there was a powerful humming noise in my ears. I stood up. It stopped. Nothing moved. There was no one. With a heavy heart I reached the bridge and started down the brook between the old walls. In the distance the waterfall was pounding with a diminished power.

Now I am a thief, I thought, as I dipped my head to wash away the cobwebs. The water calmed me down a little, and an unfamiliar voice comforted me: "We are all thieves. It's always been like that. Why didn't you take that hat and those socks? Such opportunities don't come very often, you know."

A NIGHT FLIGHT

IN THE SAME brook and perhaps on the same spot where Yevrem the Leper used to wash and cool his leprous flesh, I am bathing and listening to the water change its voice as I turn over from my back to my stomach. My elbows and knees are sunburned; elsewhere, where my rags had protected it, my skin is still white. I lie in the sun for a long time, sprawled between two anthills, now and then catching odd ants to confuse them. Then I put on a fresh shirt and a shiver goes through my body. Lewd images and desires begin tickling me —so I quickly put on my trousers, vest, and coat.

I look at my rags, and they stare at me through their holes. I paused: what should I do with them? If I throw them into the river they will contaminate it; if I bury them in the ground they might drag me under as well. I pick them up with a long forked branch and trail them off to the cave, imagining that I am thus humiliating my past good behavior, fear and anxiety, sacrifice and self-denial. I enter the cave and, with a furious gesture, toss the whole bundle, lice and all, to the skunks.

I am warm and quite uncomfortable in my new outfit, but I know I look elegant. To reassure myself, I walk over to the only mirror around here: a pond in the forest over which a juniper tree has fallen headlong, as if wanting to reach its reflection in the water. I perch myself on the tree, and look at my image in the water. A fine figure. Everything seems all right, except for my beard. I sharpen my knife and, after finding a comfortable position on the tree, start scraping off my hair. As the fresh white skin comes through, I wince and see a new face which I almost like.

A sunlit rock is reflected in the water, like a living and friendly creature. Its eyes are green from the larch. The juniper trees have eyes too, hidden under tall hats, like those in a peacock's tail. They are all watching me. At the bottom of the pond is the blue sky in all its vaulted beauty.

I thought of Maga and her sister, Neda. I was soon on my way. I arrived at dusk. At the first sign of darkness I opened the door. Neda looked at me in surprise.

"You've changed a lot," she said when she recognized me. "Like a different man."

"Well, yes . . . no more beard."

"You look better without the beard, I think."

"Your sister said she wouldn't have me because of it."

"I always knew you liked her."

"Actually, I prefer you."

It was true. I realized it the minute I said it. What's Maga to me? A beautiful image and something quite childish and impossible. This woman, of course, is a different matter.

Maga has been released from prison, she said. But she is not allowed to come to the mountain. It's better for me that way, I thought. I am sitting on a chair; I'm free of lice and not afraid I'll leave a track behind me. And yet I feel uncomfortable. Perhaps it's the enclosed space, the illuminating fire and the shadows which hop on the logs as though in warning.

"How would it be if we went out to the field?"

"Why?"

"Your father-in-law may come by."

"No, he won't. He doesn't travel by night; he watches out for his skin."

"I remember the time you brought me supper in the field."

"You've grown accustomed to open spaces. All right, let's go."

I am walking on the grass, and unrest and fear and a hundred devils jump under my skin. I'd like to grab her and hold onto her, but I'm afraid. It's too early. From time to time my neck spins out and my head reaches above her ear, then, terrified, it sinks back. We sit down, some distance away from each other. An awfully bad beginning. You get stuck to one spot and then cannot get any closer. I don't know why, but I feel that she isn't comfortable either.

"You've got a new suit," she said.

"Yes, I stole it from someone."

"You must be joking."

"No, I'm not. I've decided to steal whatever I need, since they won't give it to me any other way."

"I can't believe that. You, a Communist! Doing such a thing! I don't believe it."

I had to keep her around here somehow, so I told her, in some detail, the story of Boyo Mumlo and Tsaga, about their niggardliness and their immense wealth, about how they tormented their son Dukan with hard work and bad food. When he fell ill with consumption, Tsaga offered him all sorts of things, but he refused. "It won't go into a dead mouth, Tsaga! Why didn't you feed me when I could eat?"

"That's the way it is," I concluded philosophically. "A man gets what he wants only when he doesn't need it any more."

"Is there any hope for the movement?"

"Yes, there is: we'll win, only I don't know if anyone will be around to witness our victory."

Even if a few people are left they won't be the same. I have already tossed good old Lado to the skunks in the Leper's Cave. Others will do the same. Victory or not, people will still be grabbing and bickering.

To stop this monologue I suddenly thrust my head forward and kissed her. She wanted to slip away, but I had anticipated that with my hands. She tried to turn her head, to the right and then to the left, but when that didn't work her lips suddenly burgeoned forward to meet mine. For a split second I was confused by this sudden change. I almost let her go, and she, in turn, was getting ready to run.

"That's enough for you," she said.

"No, it isn't," I growled, "I'll never have enough."

"Look at you! You'd do anything if one let you."

"Yes, I would."

There is no wall, no fear, no anxiety that will stop me. She'll scream, she says. Let her! Two large fishes glisten in the dark and then hide themselves. I feel they are trying to cheat me. But I am terribly persistent. And sly. I've become very skilled at pursuit. I reach out and I no longer feel the ground under me. One hovers on these strange wings in a simultaneous rising and falling, above the warm dark countryside in whose rivers reflections penetrate into time, trying to preserve an image for the summers and autumns when there will be nothing else left of us on this earth.

The next thing I knew, I thought I had suffocated her. She was so soft, motionless, and limp. I was terrified. In my zeal I must have hurt her. I kissed her to bring her back to life. She didn't move. I wanted to scream for help, but then I felt her limp weightless fingers stroking the back of my head and my hard unshaved neck. Exhausted, I stretched out next to her in a brief respite.

A spring by the forest could be heard in the stillness, and occasionally the barking of the dogs. A rock tumbled down the slopes on the other side of the valley and meteors were falling. Above us the stars were gliding along unknown ways, which my son will perhaps discover.

At dawn we parted and I walked off, empty and spent and transferred into an uncertain dimension. In my sweet drunkenness I weave up and down, back and forth on the road. I am embarrassed, I smile stupidly at the heavens which were kindly disposed to me. I smile at bushes and trees. I feel like winking at a cloud of fog above the stream—I am no longer what I used to be. I've known a woman, and that is a profound discovery and the real root of all celebrated discoveries. After this, come what may! I got my share, and she got hers.

RULES OF THE GAME

THOSE WHO WISH, as I frequently do, to see and yet be unseen, should find a place by a road which passes between a forest and a field. You hide yourself behind the trees, whose branches form a sort of curtain through which you can peer. You lean your rifle on a nearby rock or a tree stump. One such stump was a particularly interesting companion; the shepherds had made fires on it, but it was not dead all the same. Its roots were powerful, straddling the earth like an enormous pair of legs screwed into the ground.

A dull underground sound, like that of a huge snake emerging and uncoiling itself, woke me up. I opened my eyes to see what was going on. The stump had pulled out one of its legs, and was staring at its outstretched claw. It was slightly bent, its face contorted by its exertions, its claws digging up the earth. Then an arm appeared, deformed and asleep. Could it be Yevrem the Leper? He was rubbing his arm with a lump of earth. Should I attack him before he has extricated himself? But my hand didn't move.

"Are you surprised to see me?" he asked in a hollow voice.

"Not very," I said.

"You look exhausted."

"I am."

"Men are always tired after such things."

He said no more. He was digging up the earth at the roots, where his knees should be located. The underground din continued. He pulled out his leg, twisted and covered with earth, felt it, and then pulled out the other one. He sat down Turkish style, and grinned at me. He had a torn cap on his head. Tough gray hairs stuck up through his cap. Above his forehead was a scabby hump from which a stunted old horn, or perhaps the embryo of a new one, was growing. I'd seen him before, but he seemed much younger now: he had a dark beard, like the one I used to wear. He laughed and said in a mocking voice:

"The swallow is a tiny bird, but it'll wear out both the horse and the rider."

"What swallow is that?"

"The one you chased all night long."

I remembered and closed my eyes. Yes, indeed.

"We are partners," he chuckled. "We shouldn't conceal anything from each other."

"I agree, so long as it applies to both sides."

He grinned and licked his lips, as Kacharanda used to do at weddings when, shameless with drinking, he would tease the women and ridicule the teetotalers. Let them watch their health! As for Kacharanda, he would prepare their coffins and escort them, one by one, to their graves. And he would drink over their graves, and sing for them his own special liturgy.

"You are too mixed up, too involved," he said. "You are trading with unclean forces."

"You aren't my conscience, are you?"

"No, but I enjoy poking you."

"Don't, because I'll poke you with a knife, and I'll peel you like a potato."

"I'd rather not quarrel."

He was angry. He began withdrawing into the earth. He flattened out—a burned-out stump I couldn't talk to any more. I was sorry: I should have let him yap as much as he wanted, if only to fill the time. Time is a raven to me: it always finds a new way of gnawing and destroying me, of slicing into me as drops of water bore into a rock. I prefer to deal with unclean powers, even with the devil himself. If only he would appear again. He did.

"You are a thief, a burglar," he said.

"You led me on."

"That's my business."

"Why are you complaining then?"

"Because you should resist me. You are a man."

"You want me to go naked, don't you? But I prefer it this way."

"What will you say to your comrades?"

He knows everything, the bastard! He digs it up from underground and then offers it to me. But I couldn't care less! After all, when will I see my comrades again? And if they harass me, I'll tell them that you have taught me a lesson. I'll explain that I wanted to go to Bosnia, where the fighting is clean, but they wouldn't let me. I don't want to be thought a coward, and I don't want to be pitied and mocked. So here I am at the Wailing Mountain.

"There was a time when you thought you could make an honest living."

"That time will come again," I replied.

"Never! Listen, you're not a child! You know that Michurin's theories of cross-breeding are fairy tales. German tanks ran over it all and found nothing but mud. And Dneprostroj and the canals surrounded by flower gardens and co-operative farms—nothing but fog."

"I don't follow you. People dreamed of flying for ages, quite innocently, and they used wings and wax and stretched linen, and when they fell and broke their necks they provided entertainment for cowards and slaves. Yet now they have taken off and they are flying. There was always that grain of possibility in the imagination."

"Yet, in spite of all that, you've only succeeded in killing off one another more efficiently."

"That's only temporary. It'll pass."

"Can you really be certain that something worse won't follow?"

No, I was not positive, only tired. I am always tired when such questions come up. Perhaps he was exhausted too. I looked at him: again he was a stump with roots screwed into the ground. There was a streak of the sun under the knot that marked his aquiline nose. He looked as though he were grinning, pleased that I had no reply to his taunts. I banged the knot with the butt of my rifle. It crumpled, accompanied by a screeching sound. Black dust spilled out, across the cracked earth. The grin did not disappear, but, rather, broadened out still more.

I turned toward the forest: it was advancing, threatening to trample me underfoot. I looked at the field: it was indifferent, empty, hopeless. No one was on the road; no one ever had been. I stood up with my rifle in front of me. When I feel depressed, such a stance always sets things straight. The trees came to a halt. In the sky above a fleece of clouds sat on the crooked horn of the Wailing Mountain. Everything had ended **well.**

BLOODY HANDS

A TERRIBLE ANXIETY has come over me. Sometimes it lasts for hours. When it goes away it is replaced by a strange joy. I want to scream and jump with senseless exuberance. Between these two extremes there are transitory states of apparent normality. They are short—that's what worries me. The old balance between me and the world has been toppled and I don't know how to restore it. In moments of exultation I can scarcely restrain myself from leaping off cliffs; but that very restraint only accelerates the return of a depression so severe that it will finally force me to blow my brains out.

It's clear to me now that I need support. I thought about Neda, and about Yasha. I chose Yasha: he had more experience in such matters. I went off looking for him. In vain, as always. Still, walking makes life easier for me. Danger diverts my attention, eases my night's sleep. On my way back, in fields lit by the moon, I thought of the sheep with her lamb and I regretted I had given them away. If the sheep were with me now, I wouldn't give it to anyone. I sat down and waited, in the crazy hope that another sheep would turn up. Instead a twisted, forked dark being arose from the shadow: my old friend.

"Don't bother looking," he said in his hollow voice. "Even if a sheep wandered by, it wouldn't come to you."

"Why not?"

"Your hands are bloody."

My friend was dressed in rags, even more pitiful than those I had discarded, and his beard had grown. He was rocking between two branches filled with leaves shiny from the light of the moon. He looked younger than before. He had gained weight; he must have been eating better.

"That ox was mine, you know," he said.

"Well, here's to his health!"

"He was in my territory," he persisted.

"I am here too, yet I don't belong to you."

"In time you will."

He smiled ironically. He has outlived many who thought they might succeed him. There was big Kustrim, whose shaggy hair came down to his shoulders. He used to dwell here, and spent his winters with the sheep along the River Drina, where he had snatched a beautiful girl from the Turks. They hid together in the cave. They had a good time. The Turkish woman screeched with delight when he did that thing to her. But news got around and the Turks stoned them to death at Sitna Luka. Then came Yevrem the Leper. At night he was overcome by such pain and howled so loud that the wolves ran for dear life across the Lim. Doselich was here a short time. He will probably end up under a hail of stones, like big Kustrim. And then it will be somebody else's turn.

"The most extraordinary thing," he said after a short pause, "is that you think you are suffering for humanity."

"Not at all. I am simply suffering."

He grinned and rocked with inaudible laughter. Only the upper portion of his body was visible above the branches. His legs, turned the wrong way around, were hidden behind the bushes. As the moon rose, shifting the illuminated space with it, he too hopped around. He wanted to make sure I didn't notice he had no shadow. Was he ashamed? Or was he afraid? No matter. He went on talking.

"What about your comrades in Bosnia? Do you think they'll come home as innocently as they left?"

"No, I don't. Nor would that be a good thing."

"They'll be more cunning than the devil himself."

"Probably so."

"Then why your good spirits? If you could only see your comrades boasting and competing and struggling with one another! Those who joined the ranks earlier lord it over those who joined later, and so it goes all the way down the line. They own nothing, they are tramps, and yet they have ranks and honors and grades. They quarrel over women, intrigue to get ahead, caress you gently and sneer at you the minute you turn your back. And there are heroes who tell tales and sing songs about themselves, and bootlickers who help them celebrate."

"Is there no end to you?" I yelled. "No way of stopping you?"

"Only my people can do that, and they are too timid."

In that case, I must organize them, I thought. But they'd probably attack me before they would think of helping me.

I can't bear him any longer. He is poisoning me, like the devil in the story who put a harness over a man's head, as thin as hair. He rode him and spurred him and did what he wanted with him. The man thought he was going home, but he was going in quite the opposite direction.

"When do you ever sleep?" I asked him.

"I sleep when it rains. I don't like to get wet."

"I don't either. It's boring. It's enough to drive you wild."

"Only those who plow and dig appreciate the rain, and you and I don't do either."

He's right. We don't. And that's what we've got in common. That may explain his affection for me. If only I had something to do: cut wood, hunt men or rabbits, tend cattle. But I am denied these simple pleasures, and left to quarrel and bore myself with the devil's arguments. Niko probably had the same affliction, and the same arguments. I rose to my feet.

"What's your hurry?" he asked.

"I am exhausted."

"You're running away in vain. We'll get together again!"

I staggered across a series of trenches dug by Albanians and Italians last summer and I was in such a hurry that I had no idea where I was going. I must have entered the Rugovo Mountain chain, where the earth is especially tough and the grass especially tall and thick. At this rate, if I am lucky, I'll soon reach the mountain above Pech. There I'll hear the trains arriving at that eternal last stop. Perhaps I'll find Yasha. He may be there, listening to their sirens. It would be a relief to hear something break the silence other than shooting.

I paused. I am not going to Pech! Why run away from this silly ghost in rags? To do so would be like jumping into a lake to get out of the rain! Besides, the Rugovo Mountain people are rather fond of catching a man who's lost his way. In their infinite shepherd leisure, they break his joints, cut off his ears, and scratch out his eyes. The devil is more civilized. He understands every word you say. I turned around and in the moonlit valley I saw two peaks like two stony wails thrown into the clear sky among the stars. I headed toward them.

THE CHARMED MAN FROM AMERICA

FOR SOME TIME now I've been aware that loneliness is no compensation for what I've lost. Rather, it is an apparent excess of freedom which lures me across frontiers and alternately sharpens and blunts my senses. In relation to the society which has defeated and banished me loneliness is my temporary death, at best some unnatural hibernation. It resembles sleep in that it liquefies, changes, transforms those images of the outside world which within a natural state of affairs (and for a man the natural state is society) seem so different.

I lay in the forest a long time, purposefully quiet, like the old wolf who hides well before he quietly digests his meal. I felt comfortable for a while, hopeful that I had come across an attitude which best reflected my relations with the world. Then I looked back: the sun was setting. The trees on the slope, lit at an angle, glistened like the hips of a woman. The whole forest had become shameless, dancing with its skirts lifted. I growled aloud at this sight and closed my eyes. Then I got up: I must go to Yablan to see Neda and on the way I would think of some pretext for doing so.

The oxhide was dry. I cut out the center piece to make two pairs of sandals: one for her, one for me. It was not exactly the right thing for a gift. But I hadn't got anything else. It was still light when I arrived, and while I waited for the night to fall I walked around in Velko Plechovich's forest. I found the spot where we had sat and the hollow beech and the rock I had slept on. The dreams I had then! And what a strange turn things had taken! At last night fell. Fires and the stars were lit. As I approached, a man's voice burst forth from the cottage, as if punching me in the chest with a fist. I stole up to take a peek: her father-in-law, Obrad, a strong middle-aged rock of a man, was twisting his mustaches and blabbering.

"I don't recall that our trees have ever borne such fruit. They are breaking under the weight."

"Isn't that a good thing?" said Neda.

"Good for the pigs, not so good for us."

"At least there'll be plenty of brandy."

She served him supper and they fell silent. He lapped it up noisily, bent over the dish. His mustaches were in his way, even though he had twisted them and lifted them as high up as he could. They were spotted with sour cream, which made them look freshly whitewashed. From time to time he pressed them between his tongue and his lower lip, wringing them out like a sponge. At first I thought I hated him only because of such behavior. Then I realized that there were other reasons

as well. Perhaps the devil himself brought him here to trick
me and mock me.

"And the Plechovichi," Obrad said, waving his spoon, "they
seem to despise me now."

She lifted a pot of milk to the fire and began twisting the
spindle above the hearth.

"I say 'good day' to them"—he raised his voice—"and they
—not even a word. Do they really think that I informed on
that Communist of theirs, that Velko?"

He lifted his head, waiting for her to say something. She
busied herself with the fire, scorched her fingers and put them
to her mouth to soothe the pain, perhaps deliberately to avoid
answering him. I asked her once if she knew who had betrayed Velko and she said yes, she did. Now she was not
saying anything. This old man was a sly fox, that much was
clear. He could easily have done it. He was a trifle surprised;
his face stretched into a sad reproach.

"You should tell them the truth," he said. "They are your
family, they will believe you. Tell them Choran did it."

"Choran didn't do it. He lay in his cottage all day long."

"You think I did it, don't you? I wouldn't be surprised if you
filled their ears with such nonsense."

"All I know is that Choran was not involved."

"I didn't do it either, Neda! I give you my word of honor!
It's true, I hate Communists, but I wouldn't touch Velko. Because of you, and that's the truth! I could have turned in
Velko a dozen times, but I didn't. Not that I'm afraid of their
vengeance. They can't do a thing to me. They know me—I
was born with a caul and even in great America no one could
do a thing to me. But we've always been friends and we
should be now."

Neda mumbled something which he couldn't quite hear.
She went out to fetch some water. I hurried across the field
after her. She noticed me only when I put my hand on her
shoulder. She was startled and raised her arm to defend herself. She recognized me and her arm dropped obediently next

to her body. I leaned over her pale face, which sought shelter on my chest. A moment of oblivion swiftly passed, and suddenly she stiffened. I had overstepped myself and I let her hand drop.

"Why didn't you tell me about your father-in-law? Are you sure he did it?"

"Yes, I'm sure."

"It could have been an accident."

"No. I know him. He is a crook; he has a greedy soul. He discovered that my sister was helping Velko, and he had her taken off to a prison. Once she was out of the way, he could do what he liked. One morning he went for a walk at the Hollow, and when he spotted Velko sunning himself he ran to the village as fast as his legs would carry him. The patrol arrived soon after. They headed straight for the Hollow."

I reflected a few moments. "I should get rid of him."

"He hasn't done you any harm.

"Velko was a good comrade. I should avenge him."

"They say you are not allowed to do that any more."

"Yes, but that doesn't apply to me."

"You aren't rebelling against your own people, are you?"

I am rebelling against them a little; they are rebelling against me a little. What's wrong with that? I rebel against myself, why can't I rebel against them? I have to do both if I am to survive. I am free to do what I want, regardless of the party line. The party line is far away and can always change. If it is not in accord with what I want, so much the worse for the line. I am tired of this constraint, tottering forever along the line, as if it were the only path in the snows of life. I am going to venture outside of it, at least for a while, to suit my fancy! So what if I get lost? What the hell! Many have lost their way on all sides. I am lost anyway.

The woman lowered the buckets, and pulled me down onto the grass.

"It's not good now," I said. "That bastard's waiting for you there."

"Let him wait, let him rot! I want to have something too. Let him think all he wants! I want to do it because he is here! To spite him."

She knew all my weak spots and she was setting me afire. Even if I had wanted to defend myself, it would have been in vain, for everything was on the offensive: her hair, her mouth, her breasts. So why should I weigh things too carefully? And instantly I abandoned my restraint, suspended as I was and ignited like an evening cloud above the sobbing of the earth and its charms. We finally emerged on the grass and I helped her straighten out her dress and hair.

I filled the buckets with water and urged her to hurry back to the cottage. I hurried off too, afraid that she'd change her mind and follow me. Then I remembered why I'd come here in the first place: to give her the leather for the shoes. So much the better, I thought. It'll be a pretext for my next visit. But why should I fiddle with excuses? It's just as well I didn't give her the leather; that old fox, her father-in-law, would put two and two together instantly. I'll take the leather to Iva. She'll make a pair of shoes for herself, and a pair for me. She's been barefoot for a long time. The thought that I could be of use to my family filled me with joy.

All of my ill-fated ventures begin this way. They are generally followed by periods of depression. And the devil sneaks up to torment me with his talk. He's probably somewhere nearby right now. He is wasting his time. I am not going to stop and rest. I am going to the village, and that's too much for him. I've outwitted him. And I'll outwit him again. The moon shot up between two peaks and the shining earth smelled of green oranges.

IMMORTAL TROBUCK

OF BRANKO TAYOV's old house nothing remains but one thick wall. In the light of the moon the scorched stones are pitch black, giving them a grim look. I am guilty, I know; were it not for me, everything would be in its place. The rooms would smell of soft spreads of fern, grain would foam in the barn, and Dana would be sitting there, knitting socks for her grandson.

After the First War one could see several of those lonely stone walls in our village. We used to call them plots. I was strangely attracted to them. I felt that behind the visible remains I could see something vague and inexpressible; I tried, invariably in vain, to understand what it was. Now I think I understand: It was a premonition of this very experience and the final metamorphosis of my character. The wood and straw went up in smoke and the smoke was carried away by the wind, leaving only these walls to protect me from dogs, rains, and snows.

I pulled myself out of this whirl of memories and made my way once again to Iva's house. She opened the door and was astonished.

"Brother, in God's name, what are you wearing?"

"A shirt, a coat, like everybody else."

"I really didn't think you'd do it."

For a few moments it looked as though she were shaking with laughter. I wanted to ask her what they were saying about my burglary in the village. I wanted to be amused. Then I realized that it was not laughter that was choking her, but tears. Leaning against the doorjamb, she had covered her face with her hands. What was I to do? I wanted to scream at her, but at that moment I couldn't remember her name. In place of her name there was simply a void. I remembered that she was my sister-in-law, that she had a baby son, that she came from Bilo, but her name escaped me entirely. That simply increased my fury.

"Shut up," I finally yelled. "Did I steal from the poor?"

"No, but you shouldn't have done it anyway."

"What should I have done? If I had asked them for clothing, would they have given it to me?"

"No, they wouldn't have, but this is shameful."

"Don't you lecture me on shame! I know what shame is. They've robbed me of everything; why can't I rob them in turn?"

Her tears suddenly stopped. She gazed at me as if she didn't recognize me: has some other man assumed my shape and voice? Yes indeed, I am someone else! While I was taken up with eulogies to freedom, they burned down my house and killed my Dana and Yug. And finally Niko destroyed himself. Well, now, I've turned my skin inside out. We'll see how much harm they do to me. Ah, I remember her name: Iva.

I was cheered up instantly.

"Iva, why did you let the corn burn?"

"They won't give me water. It was my turn yesterday, but Trobuck refuses to give me any. I don't know what to do."

"You go to the field. I am going to turn the water on myself. Go!" I commanded. "And don't leave until our fields are flooded. Let them kill you, but flood our fields. It's your child's bread."

She lifted the cradle with the child to her shoulder, and obediently walked out toward the spring. I followed. We reached the plot with the wall of scorched stones. She paused. She didn't know what to do with the baby. She didn't want to leave him here, where snakes could easily get at him. So I sprinkled the earth with tobacco. A snake would not go anywhere near tobacco and it had no business here at night any-way. Then I turned the water on, flooding our fields. I went over to the baby and watched him frowning at the stars.

The purling of water lulled me to sleep and everything became even, soft, and tranquil. The sound of Iva's hoe, as she broke up the moistened earth, made me think Dana had come back. The baby wasn't crying. I could sleep. An apple in the orchard hit the ground like a bomb and woke me. The moon-light had faded, even before the break of day. I should be going. I'd rested and everything seemed clear in my head. I gave Iva the leather for her sandals. She placed it in the pond to soften it, and put a rock on top to keep it in place. We said good-by to each other and I walked up through the neglected plum orchard where the alder bushes have conquered space by force.

I paused. Why in the world do I have to cope with so many steep hills? I am a free man. I can live where I want to. They think I am in the mountains and perhaps they are now looking for me there. But I am here, and I am going to stay here. I want to observe this small inferno of theirs—the village—lis-ten to their voices and their curses. I found a good observation post behind some bushes, and went to sleep.

In my sleep I heard the baby crying. His father, Branko, used to awaken around this time too, and ask for food. This gave me a strange idea: Time is not always a river that flows in one direction, but a series of whirls and revolutions that often brings back images and voices long since drowned. I lifted my head; Iva was feeding the child. Along the pond, below the wall, Lokar appeared, Trobuck's crippled son, with a hoe over his shoulder. A conversation started, followed by the sound of shrill voices. He hollered: "Iva, you're a bitch." She replied: "Lokar, you are an overgrown monster."

"Your turn was yesterday," he said. "Why didn't you water your fields yesterday?"

"You wouldn't let me."

"I won't let you today either. Communists have no rights."

"Who's asking you? Just leave the water alone."

"Turn it on again, you bitch, and I'll break your ribs."

He was scraping swiftly with his hoe and tossing pebbles into the corn, wounding the stalks. This bitter spite, which hits the weak, can infuriate one more than an open blow. Brandishing her hoe, Iva started toward him. He spotted her at the last second and took to his heels, yelping curses and threats. I could no longer see him, but I heard his voice calling his father. Iva was trembling with fear. She turned the water on again, and squatted in the green thickness of the corn. Trobuck appeared.

"Where are you hiding, widow? Why are you wasting so much water?"

"Whip her, Trobuck," yelled one of the neighbors.

"By God, I will. I'll cool her bottom to save her head."

"Get her! Get her!"

"I will, I will, by God, as soon as I sniff her out."

He was sniffing all right. He looked around the scorched wall, then at the sheepfold overgrown with ivy. It didn't occur to him that at one time there was a house here, and a family. He has no thoughts. He is one of those people who lie in wait for human suffering. He did well in the last war too: men rebelled and lost their lives while he stole their land. Now he is even better off: he receives a stipend from the state on the first of every month. And all the while he pilfers at my expense and eats meat. His view of life proved more correct than others; one look at his red neck is enough to convince you of that.

"What are you doing, Trobuck?" I yelled out.

He started in fear and his voice trembled.

"Who is it over there?"

"You are tormenting the poor, and shaming an honest family."

"Who is it?"

"You must know who it is."

He did. He was off like a gun. Up to that very moment I

had no clear idea of what I intended to do. I had imagined a different conversation, a reasoned debate. But now, if he got away, he'd boast that he'd outdone me. I fired a shot. He toppled over once, and then a second time. He got up and ran off faster than before. Like shooting a snake, I thought, you can never hit it where you should. I fired again, knocking him into a trench by the road. I could see him waving his arms above his head, like a huge beetle turned on its back. Suddenly he turned over and dashed toward the corn. At the edge of the field I managed to hit him once again. But he was not on the ground.

I paused. I was not going to chase him! If he could survive such a blast, let him go! My ears were buzzing from the shooting. Through the buzzing I could hear the baby's cries. I shouldn't have frightened him this way. Someone was calling Trobuck. Getting no reply, he shouted that Trobuck was dead. A woman started wailing, then a second, and then a third. For my ears, accustomed to silence, this crescendo of noise was hell. But that was only the beginning. Kacharanda, who was repairing a barrel, joined the lament; Boyo Mumlo growled like a bear. From the hamlets above, voices cried out. The gunfire started.

A FORMER COMRADE

THE SUN WAS up. It was warm. The patrols started for the mountain. I watched them passing by, I listened to them yelling and was surprised at this sudden change. They used to prepare such expeditions in strict secrecy and carry them out in absolute silence, shooting exclusively at live targets, and singing on their way back from the hunt. But not this time. They acted as if their aim was not to kill me, but merely to frighten me or chase me out of this territory. There must be some explanation, but I could not grasp what it was.

They disappeared behind the hills; the shots and cries were barely audible. Then it was quiet. Only a child's flute was heard from Gluv with a thin pale voice of memories. I put my jacket in my knapsack. I felt warm and stifled in the plains, whose air I was no longer used to. For half an hour I studied a rock that was sprinkled with silver grains; mirrors for ladybirds, and fine caves and valleys for hiding. In the branches above me leaves were turning yellow. To divert my thoughts from autumn and winter I rambled aimlessly around the forest. I approached the house of Vanya Lopa. He was in the sheepfold, in front of the door, sharpening stakes.

These former Communists, now enslaved and domesticated by their families, seem like patients in a convalescent home. No one asks them to participate in anything; in fact, they are not allowed to leave their homes. A perfect recipe for Vanya; he is at peace and asks no more of the world. I approached him stealthily, arranging for my shadow to creep in front of his eyes before I did. He was startled and raised his eyes in horror. I beckoned to him, and he turned around, hiding his face. I asked him about Trobuck.

"He was taken to a hospital. You broke his ribs and one leg."

"Do you feel sorry for him?"

"No, but the Chetniks seem quite pleased."

"Of course, now there's no one to steal their sheep."

"No, that's not it. They can now justify their salaries to the Italians. People get killed, it's dangerous. And just as the salaries were going to be abolished!"

He was looking at me with his yellow eyes, which were saying what his mouth dared not say: You are suffering in vain, you madman, because everything you do is to their advantage! Your activities keep them going, provide them with salaries, canned goods, everything! Without you they would disintegrate, things would calm down, we could live again, and work among the masses. Through indoctrination. Slowly. I recognized this long ago, and yet you've condemned me as an opportunist.

"I want you to go to your father-in-law," I said. "I have a message for him."

"I can't, I can't," he stammered. "I promised, I had to, that I'd kill you if you came here."

"Kill me with what? With a scythe?"

"No. They gave me a pistol."

"Let me see it."

He was sorry he had said anything and bit his lip. With a trembling hand he pulled out a small pistol. He had merely intended to show it to me, but I grabbed it from him. To think that one could kill with such a fine small object! I had never had one in my hand before. It resembled poison and it was made for the faithless: you sit with a man, telling him a story; he thinks you have nothing in your hand, and you just bang him on the forehead. He has nothing more to think about. That's what they've told Vanya to do. Afterward, they bind him and display him to the crowd. I pushed his hand away and shoved the pistol into my pocket.

"Won't you give it back to me?" he said.

"Perhaps I will, but bring me something to eat first."

"I can't, because of the women. They are combing wool in the house and they would see."

"Never mind that; I am going to leave afterward anyway."

"They can do nothing to you, but what about my family?"

He looked at me with open hatred; a senseless power which had suddenly come to destroy an order that he had achieved at no small cost. I replied with a sneer, letting him know that while I understood his position I felt no pity for him. On the contrary, I took a special pleasure in having caught him this way. So he went off looking for some food. He was pale. If they find out, they might very well put him in prison. But he

deserves it. His father-in-law would get him out anyway. It
made no difference to me. My head ached from this stifling
flatland heat.

I looked at Gluv in the distance across the valley. It's a
long time since I was there in daylight! I don't know what it is
that draws me there, but my urge to live now seems concen-
trated in the desire to pass through Gluv's springs and alder
woods once again in the daytime. Vanya interrupted my day-
dreaming. From under his sleeve he fished out some bread
and cheese. I knew that he had cursed his offering a hundred
times over. Besides, I wasn't hungry. Yet I forced myself to
gobble up the damned food: I want to go on living for a while
longer.

"Did Niko ever call on you?" I asked him.

"No, he didn't."

"How can you say that? You pleaded with him in the name
of God and Saint John to get out of your house!"

"I don't remember."

"But I do. And so do the others. Perhaps that'll be the only
memory left of you."

There'll be more to remember me by: Trobuck on crutches,
and that woman Neda, and the people I have frightened to
death. In terms of eternity that isn't much. I should cause
more commotion. Gaining a bad reputation on the Wailing
Mountain is hard work. As I was musing I heard Vanya talking: they are suspicious of him, they ransack his house
and the attic, he is constantly being threatened with impris-
onment. He has ruined his family, his property is falling apart,
he'll have to hang himself, his father has fallen ill with worry,
his mother has a chronic heart condition, his wife, his
children, his cattle . . .

"Tell that bastard," I said, interrupting him, "your father-in-
law, that Iva had nothing to do with Trobuck. Tell him to
leave her alone."

"Why him?"

"He has influence."

"I can't leave the house."

"Send your wife. I'll write a note which she will hand to him personally."

I wrote out a note. My purpose was not so much to achieve anything as to sound important. It said: "You have a lot of possessions: hay, timber, horses, a house. I could do you a lot of harm, and I don't know why I should spare you if you don't spare a child in a cradle. If you don't leave Iva alone and release old Luka Ostoyin from prison, watch out! Take good care of this letter. You'll want something to read at midnight when the whole of Meda is set ablaze." That's it. I folded the letter and gave it to Vanya. He again begged me for the pistol —he wanted a favor for a favor.

"I'll keep the pistol for the time being," I said. "Tell them I disarmed you and tried to kill you."

"They won't believe me."

"And why should they? We don't believe you either, but that doesn't seem to bother you."

"It could cost me my life."

"So what? You were going to kill yourself anyway. Why not die like a man?"

We looked at each other. He lowered his eyes, withdrew his head into his neck, his neck into the collar, his blood into his heart. His face was shriveled up, his body diminished in size. This is the way to greet them! Let them say that I am crazy— perhaps I am. Let them say that I am horrible—it'll gain their respect. If Niko had acted like this he might still be alive. I shouldn't be critical of him; we all used to be like that. In failure, Niko showed me the way.

I kept moving from shadow to shadow. My head ached terribly. My stomach started to churn. Perhaps something was put in that food. Or was the cheese bad? I was terribly thirsty. I kept imagining things. That was ominous! Once before, I thought it was leprosy, and now it was poisoning. In this kind of weather thirst is normal, especially when a man is young and sweats so much. There was a spring somewhere here in the forest. We held a meeting there last year. I found it. But it was dry and the marshes around it were scorched and rusted. I rested a while. Then boredom again. I moved on.

There was some good strong water some distance away. I couldn't bear this any more. I didn't know if it was poison or not, but some devil was working inside, chewing up my intestines. Sweat was boiling over like water in a pot. I kept walking. Perhaps I was near the spring. Perhaps not. I couldn't see very far. My eyes smarted when I tried to look ahead. Finally I heard the bubbling of water, but it sounded like people talking. Now it was the water, then again talk. That was why I slowed down. I got closer and the picture was clear. It was both. Men in shirts, rifles at their sides, were playing cards. One of them was Vuyo Drenkovich. I recognized his voice. I didn't think he'd miss me. I hid behind a bush. I was breathing very quickly.

IN THE FOREST BY THE SPRING

Now AND THEN, like a clearing on a mountainside, there is an easing of my pain. I open my eyes and see a familiar hill flushed with an unwholesome light: remnants of a landscape broken up into swaying islands by the dark waters. I know that there are bridgelike links between them. I search for those links, and I am exhausted. Imperceptibly my fatigue lapses back into pain and into some sweaty oblivion in which

I imagine myself an anthill as huge as the Wailing Mountain
and as hopelessly diseased. Soon I'll no longer exist at all:
nothing but the anthill, ablaze above and flooded below. The
still-live coals are hissing and vapors rise along with the
smoke.

The earth under me, softened by sweat, has turned muddy
and slippery. In vain I search for some firm support. Everything I touch glides away and liquefies. I fancy that when I
keep still the motion diminishes, and that's why I have been
lying here for an eternity. The salt of the marsh, lukewarm
but sometimes boiling, eats through my cracked skin. I sense
that my devilish friend has arrived and I see him: he resembles the dark knot of a cave at night. He's carrying a black
doctor's bag. Now he will torture me with syringes and pincers.

But he said nothing. He pulled out a heap of rags from the
bag, and stood silently for God knows how long.

"What's all this about?" I asked at last, in a weakened voice.

"You're to take off those stolen clothes and put on your
own."

"You want to make an honest man of me? I'm not that
mad."

"You've played your role. The comedy is over."

"Go to hell!"

For a few moments he slipped out of my vision, but I felt
his presence. Everything was confused again, and I no longer
recognized him at all. Who is he? The abyss that is dragging
me down? Or an ancestral fear still echoing within me? I
shouldn't anger him; I can no longer defend myself. He might
give me away to the men sitting by the spring playing cards.
They would tell people that I hadn't defended myself, that I
had asked for mercy, that I was a coward. To comprehend the
variations in a man's strength, from hour to hour, from day to
day, is too difficult for most people.

"They are playing cards down there," he said. "Why don't
we?"

"I haven't got any money; I lost it through a hole in my pocket long ago."

"We don't need money. If I win, you must give up your clothes."

"And if I win?"

"Whatever you wish."

"Let me think it over."

It was like an episode from a story representing a search in the dark that lasts five thousand years. In such a time a steady drop of water can bore through a rock. My search should also bear fruit. I do have one wish. Let's say he puts me in touch with my comrades. They would accuse me of having done everything that Bayto had expressly forbidden. But suppose they allow me to cross the mountains into Bosnia. There I would be treated as a beginner and I am tired of beginning for the hundredth time. The best thing would be a little flying mechanism; not wings like a bird's, but springs which one can attach to one's feet and adjust, to fit each jump to the occasion. That again suggests desolation; everything leads that way.

"It's taking you a long time," he said.

"I don't want to gamble. You've marked the cards anyway. So why play?"

"We'll take a new set, unused."

"I don't believe you."

"You are afraid to lose," he said slyly.

"No," I protested, "let's say I don't need to win. I am all right the way I am."

I said this only to spite him of course. Twisted and uneven bars of rusted metal loomed above me. The iron was peeling, it was scratched and in some spots trimmed with dusty scraps of paper dipped into green paint. Then I realized that I was looking at leaves, lying under an ugly tree with which I had no connection at all. I have been lying here a long time and I don't know what day it is. Perhaps it is the day after tomor-

row or Sunday, when the newspapers come out in big editions.
. . . My friend sighed somewhere behind a tree.

"Why are you sighing?" I asked.

"It upsets me to see you tormenting yourself for no good reason."

"What do you mean? If my way is wrong, that'll soon be known and others will not follow it."

"Your arms are too short," he observed rather abruptly.

My arms are not merely short, they are buried. I am unable to lift either one or the other. I feel as though I were in a cradle, all swaddled and tied. Where are my weapons? If those characters by the spring stop playing cards long enough to look for me, they'll go berserk with joy. When they see my condition they will be in no hurry to kill me. They will make a fire and put the rifle rod on the flame until it turns red. They'll poke me with it, ordering me to tell them stories. And Vanya Lopa will peck at me, and his father-in-law will come, and Trobuck, and Masnik and Mikla: everyone whom I've come to hate.

"You can't change yourself," he said in his cavelike voice.

"How can you say that? Haven't I changed enough?"

"Yes, but it's all wrong. Everyone can do that. And they do."

"The times demand it."

"What makes you think it'll be different later?"

"Because the Revolution will win."

"Win! So what? You'll become powerful, drunk with glory, and you'll put on new trousers. You'll be caught by women from good families who know how to turn your heads. Even now, under the occupation, they are getting valuable experience, learning how to pump men for money to turn into junky jewelry. You'll be so busy making money that you'll forget everything. They'll isolate you, make you quarrel, divide you, and you'll rarely look at one another. You'll grow more and more perplexed. But everything else will remain the same: the forests, the rains, the dark, and the Wailing Mountain."

"Stop it. I've had enough," I shouted. "Is someone paying you for this poison?"

"No, I only want you to see reason."

"All for nothing, friend."

They have brought me to this. You couldn't have done it alone. You've made a bargain with them. They've persecuted me and I have retaliated. And now, I've grown accustomed to it! I've removed my beard (their mark of malice) so it cannot be seen from the outside; it's inside now, and quite black. I've turned my skin inside out. And blood, hot blood straight from the arteries, I can drink like wine! It clears the mind and is generally beneficial to one's health.

"You'll be rejected by your own people first," he said. "That you must know."

"I don't give a damn!"

"They aren't having too good a time of it either. Yet they are taking it."

"That's their problem, not mine."

Suddenly he threw himself at me and in one leap mounted my chest. He was black, bony, dressed in grayish rags with multicolored patches, the very same rags I had tossed into the Leper's Cave. That explained our close resemblance. He was terribly heavy and he was suffocating me. He was moving his clawlike hands closer to my throat. I could not defend myself, for as soon as I gathered my strength he drained it out of me. Suddenly I thrust my head up and hit him on the jaw with my forehead. The ground beneath broke up and crumbled away into the darkness. I found myself hanging in space. To save my skin I grabbed hold of his tough claw and ended up falling with him into the abyss.

There was no bottom or support anywhere: only the two of us. We were sinking. Trying to find support I fell through his shadow as through a sieve. He has finally tricked me, I thought. I woke up in pain and fright. A knotty dry tree stood in front of me, one of its roots was in my hand. Blood streamed down my face. My hand guided one of its trickles to my lips. I got to my feet. It was dark. I could still hear the sound of the spring. I picked up my knapsack and threw it over my shoulder. Using my rifle as a support, I descended into the valley. By the spring, scraps of paper on which the card players had jotted down their winnings glistened on the grass.

The Devil's Signature

You have forgotten your sins and your shame,
you consider neither your souls nor your honor,
you can never have enough of your brothers' blood;
your glory, your honor, your pride and dignity,
your heroism is in your country's war and dissension
in which you find much of your happiness . . .
. . . From now on, leave me out of your affairs. I
shall not get involved, and yet . . . I remain in vain
your unhappy well-wisher.

—BISHOP PETAR (*A Message to the Montenegrins and the Highlanders*)

THE LIZARDS FLEE

EVERYTHING HAS PASSED. And I have slept. I feel better this morning. I mount the ridge of the Klin, holding onto the mane, racing along as though I were on a white horse roaring into the skies. Day breaks slowly. A rebellious pine slants toward the east, resembling a tilted drawbeam over a well, and if I so much as nudge it, the sun will emerge from the abyss. I nudge it. The sun emerges. Trees and bushes, fleeing into the valley for dear life, pause in their tracks. The weak, I say to myself: women and children and a few old men in sheepskin coats. It's a good thing I saved them from calamity.

I can just barely see the villages at the bottom of the valley. In smelly rooms brother humans are sleeping and stretching. They are scratching themselves, blowing their noses, blinking through their bleary eyes. Barefoot and in their underpants, they go behind the bushes to relieve themselves. Before they have even slipped on their trousers, they will put on their cockaded caps and strap on their pistols. This gives them a certain importance before their women, who are angrily scraping cauldrons. They begin calling one another, through the bleating and barking, through the hungry bellowing of the calves, in lamenting pale voices as though from a tomb or from hell itself.

One wail, more distinct than the rest, rose, lingered, and announced that someone in the village was dead.

The sound came from somewhere in the center of the valley —could it mean that Bele Trobuck has finally given up the ghost? If so, there will be speeches and tributes. The calves and goats he has stolen and eaten will be forgotten and never mentioned again. Actually, I hope it's someone else. I should like Trobuck to remain deformed and crippled, to limp and totter around for a long time, as a memorial to me. If it is Trobuck the news will spread quickly. It might reach Ivan and Vasil, and they'll know that I am alive. They'll find out that I am indulging in all sorts of silly things, and they'll look for me and save me.

When my fancy gets hold of such an idea it quickly embellishes it and magnifies it. It was imperative for me to learn who had died. I left my perch, descended through the forest to the crossroads, to lie in wait for someone who might know. I thought of Vanya Lopa: I should let him know I was alive, to worry him a little. I'll write him a note: "Thanks for the pistol and the information." I shall arrange for the Commander to see it before Vanya does. Clever! Vanya will be done for!

Taslach came by, interrupting my train of thought. He had a clean shirt on and new socks were bright on his feet.

"Who's dead?" I asked. "Why the rush to bury him?"

He was startled and his jaw fell open. "Tsaga," he said at last. "Mumlo's wife, that madwoman; she broke her neck."

"Not by herself! Mumlo must have fixed it up."

"It wasn't Mumlo. The devil himself showed her how."

"What do you mean?"

"You know that they used to keep her locked up. Well, there was a trap door in that room, leading to the cellar. They had fastened it so she couldn't open it. But the devil came along and helped her open it, and yesterday she tossed down all the bedding and clothing, as though she had decided to move into the cellar. She threw everything down, and finally she dropped herself down the same way."

"Perhaps she liked the devil," I said, "and she went after him, down the hatch."

"That could be. When old people go crazy they see things they've always wanted."

"They should thank that devil," I added. "He relieved them of a burden."

Taslach shook his head and gave me a sharp look. Perhaps I hadn't been sufficiently cautious in my praise of the devil. But I don't think he's clever enough to suspect me: perhaps it wasn't me, in any case. It's true that I had opened the trap door, and this might have upset something in the deranged mind of this madwoman. But a long time has since passed. Was it my partner?

"It looks like someone gave you a good smack on the forehead," said Taslach, observing me.

"Yes, I ran into a hairy devil too."

"By God, that one didn't pity you much. Let's see." And he reached out to wind off the bandage from my forehead.

"He didn't get off in much better shape," I boasted.

"Did you knock him down?"

"He managed to get away, the bastard, but he won't the next time."

Worst of all, I am not even sure what happened. The devil always appears at times of his own choosing, when I am least able to settle accounts. I must devise some new and clever tactic, such as the revenge I've prepared for Vanya Lopa. But what was it I had in mind for Vanya Lopa? Ah, a letter.

"I have a letter for Vanya Lopa," I told Taslach. "I want you to take it to him."

"I have nothing to do with Lopa," Taslach said. "He's sly. The letter would immediately reach the Commander's hands."

"That's exactly what I have in mind. I don't want you to give it to Lopa, but to the Commander."

"I won't get mixed up in this."

My efforts to explain it to him were in vain. In the history of the Taslach family, and even before, when they had a different name, they have never participated in such intrigues. He has no pity for Vanya Lopa, of course. He would in fact like to shake the sly bastard up a little. But he could take no part.

He sank into deep thought. "No one could help you better than Masnik."

"You warned me not to trust him, and I've decided to take your advice."

"Well, yes, that's why. Ask him not to show the letter to anyone; he will take it straight to the Commander."

A crowd of noisy children appeared from below. Taslach left immediately. At the edge of the forest the children gathered around their leader, who climbed on a stump to give them final instructions before the chase began.

The forest is full of Communists, the leader explained, who are enemies of the king, the fatherland, the church, and everything sacred. Therefore, their heads should be cut off and their sympathizers shot. That's the only way to root out this scum. Those who do not help in this effort will be put to death, their houses burned down along with their stables, cottages, and all their property.

And they were on their way, yelping like bloodhounds. Most of them were barefoot and badly dressed, poor little ruffians, their snouts dirty with fruit. They are not really dangerous and the reds they root out are strawberries. All the same, my head began to swim. So this is the future generation which will finally pass judgment on us! Naked, scabby, scratched, and careless, they have in fact already judged us. Even if the Revolution wins, nothing that subsequently happens can overcome this early judgment.

I was about to leave. But why should I? Perhaps I should have a chat with them. Let them see what we really are! One should be able to reason with the young. However, before I had time to say a word, one of the children recognized me and signaled to the rest to run, run for their lives. To the accompaniment of squeaks and cries, they scattered, knocking down dry leaves from the trees as they ran.

The forest remained bare. A lizard stole up on the stump and looked at me. What is it, you scabby rascal, you hunter of flies? Do I resemble a leper or a devil? He gazed at me another moment or two and then vanished, like an arrow, through a heap of dry leaves. Along the way he stirred up a multitude of lizards and snakes which were lying in wait, and the sharp quick sound continued here and there for a few more moments. Everything was on the run. I found that even my own shadow was trying to break away and hide. Only the trees, lazy and ruminating, stood motionless.

PROPHET JONAH AND HIS JEHOVAH

I DON'T KNOW whether they were frightened by what I'd written to them in that unhealthy state of mind or whether they had quite another reason. At any rate, Luka Ostoyin was released from prison. He came back yesterday, Iva told me. She had cleaned up his house for him. He was so weakened that he could hardly walk. He had seen Niko Saykov in prison every day. Niko was alive, but that just made him suffer more. She asked Uncle Luka to move in with her, but he said he was ill and afraid he might pass his illness on to the child. The fact is he doesn't want to burden anyone.

Be that as it may, Luka's arrival struck me as a resurrection from the grave. It was hard to believe that anyone could emerge alive from the Kolashin prison. I decided to go and see him. I approached the house cautiously because I was sure a trap was set for me. I recognized Luka's cough. It didn't come from the house, but from under the apple tree where the beehives used to be. He had spread his bedding on the ground, and was leaning against the tree, smoking. He was not surprised to see me.

"I knew you'd come," he said. "I've been waiting."

"It's really nice here."

"In prison I had only one wish: to spread out a blanket on this grass and rest here. But I thought: Never again. Yet they let me go. They must be up to some kind of trick."

He offered me some tobacco, and carefully put out his own cigarette. Someone watching from a distance might see the two flames. There was a solitary tree in the prison yard, he said. In the springtime he was given five minutes every day in the yard. The tree began to blossom and reminded him of his own apple tree.

"You have a cough," I said. "It must have been cold there."

"Hot and cold, and never comfortable."

"But you were not alone."

"Yes, bootlickers, informers, and groveling scum of all kinds."

He sighed. He pulled out from under the pillow a flask of brandy, a home-coming gift. He himself had lost his sense of taste, but he wanted me to have some. I took two or three swigs, throwing my head back with each one. Through the branches I saw the spurs of the Wailing Mountain among the stars. Suddenly I felt threatened: perhaps the brandy was poisoned. Luka might not realize it, of course. I sneered at my own fear, but I lost the taste for the brandy all the same. I asked him about Niko.

"Niko Saykov is in fetters, and he is waiting."

"For death?"

"Yes, for death. Why did you let him go down like that?"

"He let himself go. No one else is to blame."

"Don't give me that rot! You *are* to blame."

They were in the same room for a time. Niko told him everything: where he had found us, what we had promised him, how we had betrayed him. He still believed that we had gone to Bosnia, and left him here for punishment. He was cheated by everyone: Mikla, his aunt, and his friends. He was convinced that he was cursed, and he often compared himself to the prophet Jonah, whom God dispatched to the city of Nineveh to preach justice. Jonah, of course, didn't go, and instead boarded a ship for Spain. When the ship was engulfed by great waves, the passengers threw the cursed Jonah into the sea, and a great whale, the Kolashin prison, swallowed him up.

"But the real villain," Luka explained, "was the man who told Niko that the leaders had left for Bosnia without him: Masnik. Niko no longer cared what happened, and then Masnik added: 'If you only dared surrender . . .' Niko had nothing left but courage, and so this idea appealed to him. He rushed headlong into disaster."

"What would you say if I killed Masnik?" I suddenly asked.

"It would be better if someone else did it."

But Luka couldn't think of anyone else. Everyone was dead, or far away. The affair with Trobuck was quite another matter. Luka was pleased with my conduct. But as for killing Masnik, his brothers would certainly avenge him. Such reprisals were unpleasant, and we'd paid enough for them.

"If I don't take care of him soon," I said, "he'll make a lot of trouble for us. I am the only one who can do it."

"What about your friends?"

"I have no friends."

He felt sorry for me. That hurt. I wanted to make him angry; he might stop pitying me. Then I realized that the pity was for himself, not me. He had grown old, his legs were giving way. Why hadn't all this happened a few decades ago, when he was still in his prime? But he'll make out; he is clever. At night rebels are safe, and in the daytime you have to sit still and wait for the enemy at a distance of two paces.

"What have you got in mind, Uncle Luka?"

"I'll go with you. I can't let you go alone. A man alone loses his mind."

"I've already lost my mind. It's too late."

"You mean to say you don't want me?"

"You'd just be in my way! Stay here. It's nice to have someone to whom I can come when I feel like talking. That's enough from you."

"I won't throw myself on you. Luka Ostoyin has never thrown himself on anyone."

I rushed off before he had a chance to change his mind. The night was dark and it smelled of milkweeds. From time to time the faint sounds of a waterfall were heard, then a sleepy dog. A whole river of stars was flowing and foaming between the prongs of the hills. On the rutted space below them, among the paths and caves and the ferns on the abandoned fields, there was nothing to stand in my way. I turned toward Gluv and found a small spring that was still running. I stayed there a long time, draining a thin trickle of water through my teeth.

I am truly sorry I have no voice for singing; I'd make up a song and let it soar so high that it would echo. Instead I lit a cigarette: if someone is looking, let him burst with anguish! I'll disappear from view along with the flame of the cigarette and he'll never know what sort of a devil he saw. Nor where he has gone. Those who wish to have nothing to do with me will pray to God that I leave them alone. But they shouldn't count on it. Nor will I try to comfort them and please them, like Niko, while they play tricks on me. Rather, it will be a trick for a trick, until they scream. It has to be that way, for the sake of entertainment. If they hate me, let them spit under my window.

A TRAP IS SET; SOMETHING WILL BE CAUGHT

THE TIMES OF honest labor have passed, of sowing buckwheat and barley on mountain patches, of careful plots of potatoes and cabbage. Once the Wailing Mountain was adorned by these gentle plots. Now only Masnik and Taslach keep them up. Masnik had anticipated the drought by refilling the pond. All morning long I watched him distributing water and flooding each potato plant.

He was staring at the plants, and on his face there was a blissful expression. My anger suddenly faded and lost meaning. Not out of fear or morality, but out of an unwillingness to kill before I am convinced, I must put him to a test. I wrote out the note to Vanya Lopa: "I've delivered your pistol to Bayto. He thanks you very much. Please try to get one for me too. We meet on Sunday, the same place and time."

I had nothing with which to seal the letter. I found a few drops of pine resin and I glued the ends of the letter with it. If Masnik delivers it to the right address, Vanya will collapse in fright; if he shows it to the Commander, there'll be a lot more work to do. I approached the fence made of stumps and felled trees. Masnik hadn't noticed me; I cleared my throat and he jumped up as though he had stepped on live embers. He recognized me. He was about to curse, but checked himself in time.

"Hey!" he yelled. "You always scare me! I can hear a fox approaching, but not you."

"I am protecting my skin. It's just as valuable as a fox's."

"You've learned your trade well. I was just joking."

He was again in full control of himself. He came up and shook my hand, sat down near the fence. Now we are going to lie to each other; it should be amusing. If perfidiousness has become a way of life, why should I lag behind? My father was Yoko the Sly. That should mean something.

"I have a letter for Vanya Lopa," I said. "I'd like you to take it to him."

"All right," he said. "That'll be no trouble."

"It's important to give it to him personally."

"Don't worry, I understand."

"If you don't find him at home, go there later."

He nodded his head. Had he guessed everything? I was

suddenly afraid of his intuition. But he can't do me any harm. If he decides to blackmail Vanya with the letter, that's none of my business. He pulled a huge tin box out of his pocket and offered me some tobacco.

"Have you heard about Trobuck?" he asked.

"What happened?" I smiled, hoping that he would realize my complicity.

"Someone broke his legs, God save him! They say it was you, but I don't believe it."

"It was me," I confessed. "He had shamed my family."

"There are many who've blessed you for it. I for one. The village was sick of him."

He shook my hand in congratulation, but I let it hang limply. I assumed a worried expression and explained to him that our people were critical of what I did. An inquiry was being conducted. My action was contrary to the line of appeasement. If the punishment is minor, I shall accept it, because I am guilty. But if it is my head they want—I won't give it to them. I'll rebel against them too. They can't do a thing to me!

At first Masnik didn't believe me. Then he pretended surprise. He said that it was not good to be pursued by both sides, with no one to go to for help. One has to be clever about such things. After all, Trobuck is not dead. Not even the regular courts will judge me so strictly. My accusers should come to see him; he would tell them how the village felt about Trobuck.

"Perhaps they will come. But be careful, don't cross me!"

"Me . . . ? You know me! When are they likely to come?"

"On Sunday, but I am not really sure."

"If they come, don't worry! I'll explain the whole matter to them. But you take care of yourself. If you'd like to stay here, food is no problem. And we can always put you up."

"I've got a place to stay," I said.

"Where?"

"At the Leper's Cave. If all the armies of the world were to look for me, they'd be wasting their time."

"That's no good! Everyone knows about the Leper's Cave."

"They know where it is, of course, but what goes on inside that cave I hardly know myself."

He stood there for a moment. I felt that I could penetrate well back into his mind. He was searching for something in the darkness and stench of the cave, something of which he already had a glimpse. I seized the chance to place before him a fanciful image of the main cave: the pit in the center, and the corridors radiating outward, emerging like tunnels on the other side of the hill. The only trouble was that it smelled. Perhaps there was sulphur or some other gas down there. I was surprised at myself! Solitude had indeed twisted me. I'd made exaggeration a habit, and reality had lost all significance. I suddenly fell silent, feigning regret that I had revealed more than I should have. He was about to say something, but restrained himself. In some confusion, he trotted off and turned on the water. He suggested food. Not for me, I said, I've got a bagful.

I started off, leaving Masnik deep in thought. He seemed to have lost interest in his vegetables. A new idea had entered his head and was buzzing around. I had deposited it there. Perhaps I really am evil. Never mind. That's why I've been banished. Not to show them the right way, but to lead them astray and thereby win their gratitude.

My feet started for the Leper's Cave. I don't recall having made a conscious decision to go there. I entered the cave, and a rat or a lizard rustled in the dry leaves and disappeared. My eyes soon accustomed themselves to the darkness. On the floor of the inner cave I came upon my old rags, looking like carrion. I brought in dry twigs and leaves and made a fire to drive out the stench. On a rock, standing nearby like a night table, I put the remains of my English Grammar. To make it appear that I had suddenly run off, I scattered some salt around.

Then I left. Let them think that they've found my traces! At any rate, they'll know where to place ambushes and keep watch on rainy nights. I looked back once again at the cave, whose opening was staring at me with a gloomy eye, like a monster trying to emerge from underground. I hurried to get away and I climbed up to the Byelanov Laz. I don't know whether Byelan was a shepherd or a dog whom wolves tore apart. Now it no longer matters. The sun is warm and the white summer clouds foam at the edge of the horizon. It is quiet. Only shadows and ants move on the ground, and a lone bumblebee is heard and the sound of the fountain on Dorov Yavor.

SECOND TRAP FOR THE CHARMED MAN

SEEN FROM ABOVE, the oval fence surrounding the watering place resembled an eye: a patch of blue in the middle of the forest. At the edge of the pond was a row of pines—the eyelid. Above, a forehead of rock, with eyebrows of deep-green yew trees. It really is an eye, I thought, the eye of the Wailing Mountain, looking up at the bright sky. I walked down and found the juniper whose head was drowned in its own reflection. I climbed up in it and rocked back and forth, myself blue between the water-blue and the sky-blue. Then I stretched out flat on my back and idly gazed at the celestial infinities. They open up, one after another, and branch out ever further, continuously upward, without limits. They are sucking me in, baiting me and absorbing me, and I've become a swarm of flakes which are drifting away from the earth, and from one another, into the infinite ether.

I feel comfortable this way and I've no idea how long this daydream has lasted; I have no fear of men, and no desire to return to them. Whom would I need? Perhaps only Neda. I would build a wooden shack and plant potatoes along the riverbank. If my back should ache I would stretch out here again. I stood up, actually convinced that I would someday fulfill this idle daydream. The excitement carried me across the glade. I saw the shack and the fire at Yablan. The old man was not there, and Neda was glad to see me.

"You haven't been here in a long time," she said. "I thought you'd found another woman."

"Why should I look for another? I have you."

"I'm not yours. I'm only temporary."

"Everything is temporary except you."

"Wait a minute." She pushed my hand back. "You don't mean to do it here. . . ."

"Yes, right here! I want to see how it feels."

If it is a sin, let it occur where it is the blackest sin of all! On this property, in the smell of wool and milk, with the curious calves and cows eavesdropping from the fold and interrupting their digestion to nod their heads mockingly. Later we'll try other places: by the water which roars like eternity; in the forest between two layers of leaves; on a rock lit by the moon. At each spot it will be beautiful in a different way. This earth, over which we fight so much, should give us some reason for loving it as we do.

"What an idea!" she reproached me. "What an idea!"

"Do I remind you of the devil?"

"Much worse! But never mind, I have a good time with you."

"You had a good time with the other one too. With your husband." I finally got it off my chest.

"No, not as good."

"You've forgotten. You'll forget this too."

"Stop it! You knew I wasn't a virgin."

I knew it and I was not angry with her husband. In fact, I felt sorry for him. He had always lived under the shadow of his father. Now he was behind bars in Italy, cut off from his home. They would have released him, but the uprising changed all that. He and others like him are probably cursing us now. They've done us no harm, yet we are punishing them, and we take their wives too. There was a time when I thought that only a scoundrel would take advantage of wives of war prisoners. I've surpassed these scoundrels, and I've never felt better.

"I am sleepy," I said. "But I don't want to fall asleep here."

"Why don't we go out into the fields? You can sleep there. I'll sleep with you."

"Fine."

She brought out a rug, a pillow, and a sheet. She was naked under the sheet and her skin was smooth, her backbone supple. Her ears were small. Her hair smelled better than any grass. We were lying face to face. The sound of our breathing made me drowsy. My old comrade Ivan broke into my consciousness, and said in a sharp whisper:

"What are you doing here?"

I was indignant. "Can't you see?"

"Who set you to this task?" he asked, and I replied:

"Are you my keeper?"

I woke up, but only long enough to assure myself that I was dreaming. Neda's arms, which have joined somewhere in the dark, enclose me and defend me against the unfriendly world. We are surrounded by dark straight-edged hills which stand like the walls of a spacious cradle in which we two children are rocking. The cradle is not on the ground. There is no ground. It is suspended against the sky, against a few of its golden bolts, rocking us to sleep again.

The swaying is gentle, and in the sky directly above us there is a whirlwind of stars. Sometimes the cradle sways in a different direction, revealing a piece of the road, the bank of the river, a half-familiar village, and the caves in the hill above. On the edge of a precipice, in front of one of those caves, squats Niko Saykov, looking at me in silent reproach.

"Why are you looking at me like that?" I said at last. "I never interfered with you and Anya."

And Niko said: "What makes you think there was something between us?"

"I didn't think there was, but that's your problem. No one was in your way," I said.

"Lado, why are you jumping about?" said Neda. "Wake up!"

"How can I know what I do when I sleep?" I said in a drowsy voice. "No one has ever watched me."

"If I were with you all the time you would know."

"Then we wouldn't want each other the way we do now."

"I don't want to want you. I want to be with you. I have your child. I've conceived! But that's no shame."

"What!" I said, and jumped into a sitting position. She put her head on my chest; I don't know whether she was laughing or crying. Perhaps both. She had no regrets. In fact, she was quite pleased. For two years with her husband she hadn't conceived. They reproached her constantly. Her husband was the only son, and the family's future depended on her. They had even threatened to send her back to her family. Were it not for the war they would have done so. Now the fault is clear. She will bear my child to spite them all! She wouldn't have stayed in that house anyway. And now she no longer can. She has to find a new place to live.

"We'll arrange something," I said, moved at the thought of this new life.

"I can't wait: the old dog is bothering me and asking for things that don't belong to him."

"Don't worry," I said. "I'll give him his due."

"You can't touch him. He is a sly fox. He was born with a caul."

"I am something of a charmed man myself."

This may work out. Neda and Iva will live together as sisters. It's not their house, but the smoke will rise straight to the heavens, as if it were their own. Of course, they'll quarrel with each other, but against an outside enemy they will always unite. However, we must take care of the old man first. I'm rather pleased that he is a good hunter, and not merely some old bastard who wouldn't be worth wasting a bullet on.

"If only I could turn into a fox and bait him to the cave, that would be the best arrangement," I said.

"Someone is always with him," Neda explained.

"Suppose you stir up the chickens, as though a fox has been here. Tell him you saw a fox running toward the cave. He'll probably follow."

If that doesn't work, I'll think of some better scheme. There's plenty of time. It's not urgent. No one else will take him away in the meantime.

The stars have thinned out. They are disappearing into the heights and growing pale. The chickens are beginning to stir. Day will break soon. Everything must be put back in its place, as though nothing has happened. I stopped at the cottage to drink some milk. The calves stared through the fence, like prisoners. I stroked their damp snouts, I patted my woman on the back, I felt somewhat like the master of the house. That's it. Now I can go. So much has changed, and yet one goes on the same way as before. On one's legs. Step by step.

It's lovely in the forest. The early morning murmurs in the leaves and the dry twigs crackle under my feet. I am not sad, but I am not cheerful either. There's no reason to be. My child, if it comes, will be born at the foot of the Wailing Mountain and it will have to cry a long time: because of the dogs by night, and because of the people both by day and by night. It'll cry until it learns to defend itself and to attack, and after that it will no longer have to shed a single tear. But that isn't so bad either. When everyone else betrays him, he will find, in his solitude, that the bright sky is vast enough to drown in. There's no need for me to tell him these things. From the trees he will learn to stand straight, from the rock to be firm; the rest will come by itself.

A VOICE FROM THE LEPER'S CAVE

IN MY SLEEP I felt the clouds massing and the shadow that preceded them stirring up the dry leaves on the ground. I woke up and looked at the sky. It had turned into a gray quarry and was dropping lower and lower until it touched the unmowed fields. A fierce wind turned against the trees, mixing the dead leaves with the green. For a moment the mountain became a roaring reflection of the celestial chaos. All boundaries were erased and everything was fused in the ensuing haze. I closed my eyes and the earth seemed like an abandoned ship.

It started to rain. I was forced to take shelter in the Leper's Cave. It no longer seemed repulsive, for the whole world had become an endless chain of caves, expanding and contracting. I entered; inside, there was a dreadful silence. The wind had pushed the odor of skunks back into the depths, so that the cave smelled of rain and scattered dust. The din outside reached me only in distorted echoes: sometimes screams and calls, sometimes the trot of a herd looking for shelter. I was full of anxiety, waiting for the mob to appear at the entrance. Finally, I ceased waiting. I grew listless, callous, and drowsy. That same dull voice startled me from my sleep.

"Ah, you've come," he said boastfully.

"For the time being," I said, "until this calamity is over."

"Why leave? It's not bad here."

"And what about you?" I asked.

"I am tired and, as you know, I don't like the rain."

"Why don't you leave!" I shouted. "Things would be better for both of us."

He was silent. I could no longer see him. Perhaps he was lying somewhere, quietly giving up the ghost. The rain grew heavier, beating down both sides of the cave. A flash of lightning struck against a mountain peak, echoing across the valley. Hazelnuts, walnuts, and chestnuts were split open— everything that was in a hard shell. I turned pale, like wine losing color in barrels. The same old fear. I jumped to my feet and picked up my belongings. This cave is no good, I thought; it's a hard shell and its walls will collapse the next time lightning strikes.

"I see you're leaving," he said in his flat voice. "Why don't you wait until the rain stops?"

"I want to get away from you. You smell again."

He laughed despondently. "That's not it. They are after you."

"I'm afraid that's true. What of it? I don't want to be caught here like a badger in a hole."

"And what would you lose if they caught you here?"

"Perhaps not much, and yet I don't want to stay just because you want me to. Or because they do, for that matter."

"You're going to have to face them sooner or later; of that you may be sure. You think you'll be able to squeeze between the drops and survive, but you can't. As for death itself, it's not so terrible. Like having a tooth pulled: it hurts a little, but later on there's relief. If you'd done it last summer, how much suffering and disgrace you would have spared yourself, how clean your memory would have remained! That's why I urge you to stay."

"Thank you for your advice, but keep it for yourself."

"There's no need to hurry. They surely won't be here till dawn."

"I'm not made of sugar, like you! Or of salt. I'm not afraid of the rain. It won't dissolve me."

I went out and stood under the trees, getting soaked. I thought about Masnik. He reminded me of a childhood friend who wanted a diplomatic career and prepared himself accordingly. He got a post with the Ministry of Foreign Affairs and he would have done very well, as Masnik would have become rich, if the war had not intervened. During the uprising he took refuge in the mountains and dug out a shelter and covered it with oak beams and branches and earth. He survived: now he negotiates between the Italians and the Chetniks, working his way up, aiming at a comfortable position in the diplomatic corps. His shelter also survived the winter, and it's not uncomfortable; perhaps I can find it again. I staggered along and finally stumbled on it. I lit a match. Centipedes and earthworms and reddish bugs with tails crept on the ground. Perhaps there are scorpions here too, I thought, but never mind! They are certainly less poisonous than I am. I'll keep my mouth shut and thereby keep them out; that'll do the trick. I spread my blanket and stretched out on it.

For a time I thought about the enormous distance between these red bugs and the clear skies. Only the trees touch both extremes, and I. . . . Upon awakening I ran my fingers over my ears and my neck. Everything was in its place. Nothing had stung me, nothing itched. I was at peace with that world of underground creatures who are afraid of light. Either my skin is thick or I am drenched with some substance that keeps them away. There was a leak in the shelter; a puddle had formed and I heard the raindrops falling into it. I counted seconds to find out if there was a regular interval between each drop. This pastime was interrupted by the sound of voices and shooting from the Leper's Cave. I left my new shelter and concealed myself under the wet branches. Once the drumming in my ears died down I could hear them calling to one another.

"What are you waiting for?"

"We've given him five minutes to think it over."

"I wouldn't give him a second. To think what over?"

It is me they are talking about! They think I am inside. Perhaps I am, and this is only a wandering scrap of my soul hanging around and listening to what is going on. That scrap is secretly hoping to hear a conciliatory voice, something gentle and warm, even a sign of pity, from neighbors and acquaintances. Nothing. I hear no such voice. Instead, bombs go off and a new wave of shouting arises, and a sharp pain pierces me. It separates me from the ground and carries me into a greenish darkness where I am to remain alone forever. For a few moments I am deadened by it. Again I recognize voices.

"Has he paid at last, that wild son of Yoko?"

"Yes, unless his limbs are made of steel."

"Haven't you brought him out yet?"

"How can we do that? He's gone back into the cave like a skunk. The devil himself wouldn't be able to find him."

"Some heroes you are! You'll let him get away again."

Now I feel better. I know I am alive and I've cleared up one important matter. An insignificant link was obstructing me, but now I am free. I feel that I've been purged by a fire that was meant for me. A man who survives a thing like that can push ahead for a long time. I don't hate them, and therefore I can consider the question of revenge with complete patience. I can see the man on the hill quite clearly; I could remove him from this world with one bullet. But I don't want to. There are worse bastards. There's plenty of time. The rain has stopped. The leaves are dripping and the puddles are slowly disappearing. The full sails of a clear blue sky are poking through broken clouds. The man from the hill calls down again impatiently:

"Are there any traces? Why are you all silent like old women?"

"Just rags and books, and a little blood."

"He's wounded! We should finish him off with smoke!"

"What are you mumbling about?"

"With smoke! With smoke! Smoke him out. He'll cough everything up."

"It's easy for you to yelp! With your fat bottom in safety up there!"

They made a fire in the cave and the smoke burst out like grime and dragged itself along the ground in front of the cave. In the intensified light of the rainy day I could see them standing around, leaning against trees. A tuft of smoke arose and shrouded them; later it thinned out and made them seem like ghosts. They were arguing bitterly about something and the noise was growing. Suddenly a dull howl gushed forth from the earth: a scream and a laugh at one and the same time, coiled and two-sided, all suffering and guffaw. It continued, martyred and ominous, for some time. I stopped up my ears so as not to hear it and to forget it as soon as possible.

The men nearest the cave took to their heels; they paused and then returned to find out what had made those strange howls. The fear abated, and was replaced by laughter. They began singing the song "The Red Flag Will Never Flutter." Others came down from the hill to join the festivities. One man was propelled higher than the rest and, like a madman, began ejaculating a speech full of the word "anathema." He was often interrupted by cries. They finished with another song, and then went down the hill. I could no longer see them in the steep valley, but the singing and shooting continued for some time. The fire in the cave had died, the smoke emerged in thinned-out coils.

I sat down and studied the mutilated leaves scattered around. They are still green, and no different from the ones on the branches. And yet they are dead. They are dead although they may not know it, and their effort to vibrate and turn toward the sun is in vain. My case is similar: everyone says I am dead, and I have no proof that it isn't so. I am tired, trampled. I don't feel like smoking. I don't feel hunger. I don't hate anyone. Nor do I love. I am merely moving my hand, or I think I am. I haven't even got a shadow to convince me that this is so.

Then I remembered the pond, and with a great deal of effort I got to my feet. I walked, step by step, and finally reached the pond. I bent over it. Surly and hairy, with an aquiline nose, a black devil stared at me from the troubled mirror.

SAVO SAW THE DEVIL

UNDER THE JUNIPERS there were circles of dry earth, covered by a soft spread of needles. For an hour or so I sat under one of these junipers, then I moved on to another, and sat there for a while. The view varied from place to place. Above the stream two rainbows had crossed and tufts of fog wandered under their arches. The bright fields beyond glistened with raindrops. Little by little the skies brightened and cleared. At the end of the day the sun itself appeared. The huge shadow of the peak filled the the valley and began creeping up the other side, looking like a black horse, with a mane and a head, and I was in the saddle. The shadow of my outstretched arm reached the house of Marko Ogriya on the other side of the hill, and roamed among the wild plum trees.

The sun had gone down. I descended into the valley in the dark. One could see nothing but the hills turned toward the sky, and I could tell by the smell of the earth that the torrents had forged new ruts and grooves in the land. The road was broken up. The River Meda was humming in a husky voice. It had knocked down dikes and run into the cornfields: the river's reply to the industriousness of men. I approached the house of Luka Ostoyin. I heard him coughing under the apple tree. He was quarreling with someone. He noticed me and yelled out in surprise:

"Is that you, Yoko?"

"Yoko's son," I said reproachfully. "Yoko hasn't been bothering you for a long time."

He chuckled with joy. "Yoko's son, you devil! How did you ever get out of that cave?"

"I wasn't in it."

"And they think you are still inside! Burned to a crisp! That's what I thought myself."

He stank of brandy, his tongue was thick, he was incoherent. Finally he confessed: misery drove him to drink. He knew of no other cure. They had told him that I was torn to shreds. He had been looking for someone to help gather together my pieces so that the skunks would not gnaw at them. He found no one: some didn't want to, others didn't dare. There were no friends left, no men. The men had gone. Only the rabble were left. Luka was no longer a man either! As he talked, he grew angry. He started to shout. I tried to calm him.

"Don't worry," he said. "They won't hear us. Not tonight. Everyone is asleep. Drunk as lords."

"In honor of my departed soul?"

"Yes. They've been singing their heads off. They've deafened me."

"They'll soon regret it."

"Don't do anything right now," he said in a soft voice. "Let them think you are dead for a while."

He offered me some brandy. Deceive them, he said; they'd do the same to you. Once Sayko Doselich deliberately spread the news that he had been killed. They even dug up his grave and found a corpse inside, the body of a man who had been beaten to death. They were fooled, and for a year or two they forgot about Sayko. He breathed easily again, and everyone felt free to give him refuge.

I promised Luka that I'd be careful, and then I went to see Iva. She opened the door and embraced me. Her head, pale and very light, fell on my chest and she listened: Was a heart beating or was it just an illusion? She said she hadn't really been scared. Somehow she had felt that I was alive. The Vuko-lichi sing "Sly Lado is no more. . . ." But instinct told her not to lose hope.

"If a woman should come here, Iva, take her in to live with you."

"What woman?"

"A woman as dark as I am, since she's mine. Actually, I have no idea what she looks like, but take her in anyway."

"Did you get married without telling anyone, Lado?"

"I didn't pick the right time, I admit. Our men always get married in their own way."

Her eyes were moist. She approved of my action. She would no longer be alone, she would have someone to talk to. But something bothered her. Is this woman educated, accustomed to a better life? No, she is not. Ah, that's good. Is she tall? What color are her eyes? She must be beautiful. . . . Iva will put a bed by the window, and she herself will move into the baby's room. The baby mustn't wake her up with his cries. She'll scrub the floors until they are as yellow as wax, and she'll put apples on the shelves for freshness. Her daydreams of a more genteel life seemed already half realized.

"When will she come?"

"I don't know. She must finish up a few things. Perhaps not until autumn."

"That's too long, Lado! Can't she come sooner?"

"There'll be plenty of time for you two to quarrel. Sisters-in-law always quarrel."

"We won't. You'll see."

The late moonlight cast a golden light over the rocky contours of Zelin. I hurried to get through the village while it was still dark. I knocked on Trobuck's door and bleated like a sheep. I retreated into the bushes, and when Lokar opened the door, I tried to bait him out with the bleating. He hesitated and then, suddenly changing his mind, ran back into the house and locked the door. Passing by Kacharanda's house I put a shell between my teeth to disguise my voice. I knocked and knocked. At last his wife appeared, drunk as a piper, and asked peevishly:

"Who the devil is it at this time of night?"

"I've come for the coffin," I said in a terrible voice. "Is my coffin ready for me?"

"There's no coffin here; Kacharanda's forgotten all about it. He forgets everything when there's brandy around."

"I don't want to be buried without a coffin. Tell him that! Wake him up and tell him to start work right now."

"In the name of the Father and the Son!" she cried, stumbling somewhere in the hall, knocking down several chairs.

I set off for Boyo Mumlo, to give him his dead wife's regards, but on the way I stopped to gather some apples and the whole idea slipped my mind. I ate apples until my teeth grew numb and I filled my knapsack with the rest. Then I started across the fields. Passing by the cemetery, I saw something that made my hair stand on end: half a man, the head and the chest, lying in the brushwood above the road. I jumped aside, then plucked up enough courage to take a careful look. How extraordinary! It wasn't half a man at all, but a whole one, old Savo. The moonlight had cut him in half and his legs were lying in the shadow of a bush where his drunken head had misled them. His mustaches were moving, as though by deliberate effort. I shook him.

"Leave me alone, you devil! Get away from me, I tell you!"

"Why don't we have a drink?" I asked. "I've got some good plum brandy."

He raised his head and opened his dopey eyes, suddenly aghast with surprise. He had recognized me! He slouched back and covered his face with his hands.

"What is it?" I yelled. "Don't you want a drink?"

"I can't," he groaned. "Let me be! I haven't done you any harm."

This was true. He'd done no one any harm or any good for a long time. When I was a child, however, the shepherds were afraid of his broomlike mustaches and his green eyes. It was said that before the Balkan Wars he had been quite a brave fellow. At the time of the first election in Montenegro, he was given a rubber ball and told which box to deposit it in. However, he put it in neither one box nor in the other, and instead hurled the ball out of the window.

But since then he has consistently avoided places where courage was required. And now he was watching me askance.

"You are Yoko's son," he said. "They killed you today at the Leper's Cave."

"Yes," I said. "They did. If they hadn't, you'd never've been able to get so drunk."

"They heard you moaning and they suffocated you with smoke. That means you're not alive, doesn't it?"

"How could I be alive if they've suffocated me?"

"What are you doing here then?"

"Where else should I be?" I asked him. "This is the grave-yard, isn't it? I am doomed to wander around the cemetery until they bury me. I had a Christian soul once. I'll never have peace among devils and skunks. The coffin will have to be buried empty, mind you, because they can't find my remains. And I hope Masnik himself digs the grave. It was he who informed on me. Have you got it straight? Here it is: Masnik, the coffin, and I don't want to be buried near the cemetery, but *in* it! Come on now, get up and get going! Walk fast and don't turn around!"

He felt for his stick, got to his feet and stumbled off. He couldn't find the road. He tripped over some stones, but he made damned sure not to turn around. He left his cap behind in the brushwood. I kicked it over the cemetery fence. This detail will make his story all the more convincing. He fell once more and I heard him groaning. He mumbled something. Probably the Lord's Prayer. And he vanished. The oak trees in the graveyard, the carrions, all lit by the moon, are swaying, drunken from the buried flesh and the spilled plum brandy.

THE CHARMED MAN AND THE DEVIL

ON THE ROAD across Breza a convoy of Italian trucks is moving along. Every day they bring food for the army, which is idling, and ammunition for the Chetniks, who are defending themselves even though no one is attacking them. In the afternoon the trucks return, empty and much faster. From where I am sitting they are inaudible, which makes them appear timid before the abyss into which they are descending. Not until they turn around the hill does their threatening roar reach me. Perhaps most things in life are like that: you understand them only after they have happened, if at all.

I am sick and tired of these empty meditations. I can justify anything, and in such circumstances a man may just as well cross his arms and die. I don't want to die. I still have half of the summer before me and possibly part of the autumn as well. And I have a wife. But one that I barely know. Nor does she know me. We've seen each other only by the light of the hearth or the stars. Never by daylight. Perhaps we'll never see each other in the daytime; it'll always be a night affair, cursed and clandestine. All the same, I can't live without her for very

long. Everything around me—the forests, the clouds and the
rivers—loses its taste when I remember her voice and her
laughter.

I had hurried needlessly. It was still daylight when I arrived
at Yablan, green after the rain. I could see the saltworks, like
scabs and dung, and the posts to which the horses were tied.
Sheeps' bells were heard from the other side of the valley.
Perhaps Neda is with the sheep. I'll cross over tonight, and
tomorrow I'll see what she looks like in the daytime. Out of
boredom I went over to take a look at the cave. Actually it
was quite a spacious place. In some spots there were level
areas as wide as rooms, full of pits and broken rock. In one
place the wall of the cave had eroded away, and through the
opening, as if through huge binoculars, one could see the sky,
bluer and clearer than anywhere else.

The mustiness and deadly buzzing, which penetrated my skin
rather than my ears, soon grew tiresome. I left for the forest to
wait for Neda, who will come here to gather leaves for the
calves. I didn't have to wait long. Across the field came a tall
man with a hunting rifle. He seemed strong, his bearing was
upright, his temples were gray and so were his mustaches. It
must be Obrad. I hope he decides to lie in wait for a rabbit
until the sun sets. I watched him from behind a tree, but he
changed his course and soon reached the top of the hill. He
sat down on a felled tree, rested his rifle against it, and pulled
out his tobacco pouch. I approached him stealthily and leaped
out in front of him, my pistol in hand. His face contorted, his
cap rose, his black brows stood on end.

"Don't budge, old man," I said. "Just lift up your hands!"

His pouch dropped to the ground, the piece of paper flew
off. But his hands didn't move. His mouth twisted into a sneer.
He regained his voice.

"Who are you to order me around?"

"Lift up your hands before I chop you to pieces!" I pulled
the Colt from his belt and placed his hunting rifle out of his
reach.

"Do you realize what you're doing?"

"Yes, of course. Now get moving!"

He realized that he couldn't argue with me. Hesitantly he rose to his feet. I shoved him with the butt of the rifle and shouted. He shook his head threateningly, but moved along. We entered the cave, his eyes searching desperately here and there.

"What is this?" he bellowed.

"You have a debt to pay." I tossed his hunting rifle to the ground.

"You're wrong. I owe nothing to anyone."

"Who was it who informed on Velko Plechovich and got all that money?"

He squeezed his lips together as though they were full of poison, and paused to think.

"I did," Obrad roared. "Not for money, but . . . because he was living with my daughter-in-law, Neda."

I forgot where I was and felt dizzy, as if he had hit me a hard blow on the head. He did in fact strike me. He hit me on the chin with a blow that I didn't even see coming. It felt like a horseshoe rather than a fist. He was a boxer, I remembered; he had learned that too in America. The pistol slipped out of my hand. I fell on my back, on the knapsack filled with apples. Everything was surely at an end. Masnik will live, and Mikla will go on robbing her neighbors, and this foul dirt, this shit, will continue to contaminate the earth. Through the darkness I saw him preparing to strike again. I thrust my head aside and with my legs, as with a pitchfork, flung him over me. He must have landed on his head. He groaned.

"Have you had enough?" I yelled even before I got back on my feet.

"You'll soon see."

I reached for his hunting rifle and struck him on the head with all my strength. The rifle broke. He swayed. I grabbed his arm and twisted it behind his back. He hit me hard. I let him go. To avoid a new onslaught I buried my head in his ribs. I felt his sweat and heartbeat. Our fingers got entangled and we looked at each other, disheveled and crazy with fury and fear. He was worse off: his face was running with blood, blood was dripping from his left eye. But his hands were terribly strong. He was stronger in every way, and he knew it. If I let him strike me just one more time it would be the end. He'd break my fingers . . . ! The coffin I ordered from Kacharanda in jest . . . I must have had some foreboding. . . .

"Don't you see? Don't you see?" he screamed. "I was born with a caul. Do you know what that means?"

"And I am the devil," I yelled.

"I'll kill you like a snake, you son of a bitch!"

My mother was not a bitch, I thought, and with a sudden jerk I pulled my sweaty fingers out from his. I ducked my head to avoid a blow, grabbed him by the hips, and shoved him onto a pile of rocks. To keep him from getting up again, I stepped on his right hand. I made a knot of his arms around his neck and began tightening it. He howled. Was it in fear or for help? Or just to scare me? He howled for some time, interrupting it only to gather energy for another attack, thus warning me inadvertently to protect my head. Finally his voice grew weak and dwindled off into a death groan. I should let him go, I thought, and interrogate him while he can still talk. I want him to tell me about Velko and Neda. . . . Then I felt a sharp pain below my belly: he had grabbed me and was pressing tight.

"And now what do you say?" he thundered in a wild voice which echoed sharply in the cave.

I was bent over to the ground in pain. Without thinking, I picked up a pointed rock.

"Who are you to match your balls against mine, you bastard son of a whore?" And he kept on gripping.

I beat him with the rock, on his back. Blows without anything behind them. No force. He didn't even notice them.

"This is how I castrate the devil," he croaked. "This is how! This is how! This is how!"

With a last look, almost unconscious, I caught sight of the nape of his neck in the distance. That was where I wanted to hit him. I think I did swing my arm. Then I forgot everything.

I was lying on my back; a long time had passed and the pain had moved from down below up to my head and teeth. I couldn't see a thing. It was dark both inside and outside. He was still here. I could hear him crawling toward me. My knapsack was under me. His Colt was in it. But that was as distant as the mountain across the valley. I remembered Vanya Lopa's little pistol and I shoved my hand in my pocket. It was there! Perhaps it couldn't kill a man born with a caul, but it would scorch his skin. Somehow he sensed the pistol, halted, and turned away.

"Here I am," I yelled. "Where are you going?"

He paused. He moved away again. A rock in front of him rolled off into a large pit.

"Don't you want to go on?" I asked him. "We must finish this thing."

Two or three pebbles tumbled into the pit, followed by the sound of something falling, perhaps a sack. I was frightened: had he some new idea? He had had more time than I to think of something.

"I think I've squashed one of your eyes," I said, hoping to lash him into a fury. "I'll work on the other one too."

There was no response. I couldn't even hear him creeping. We were silent. When it came to silence he was even stronger than I was. I'll give way, I thought; we can't wait all night! I lit a match, the tiny flame flickered and created another cave within the cave, lighting the trembling walls of darkness. He was not within these walls; just rocks, apples, and pools of blood as black as tar. The apples must have spilled out when I first fell on the ground. Nor did the blood surprise me; it didn't matter whether it was his or mine. But I didn't know why he had run away, or why I was still alive.

I felt my swollen jaw; a tooth or two must be out of place. My bones were numb but intact. I got to my feet; I could barely stand up. I dragged myself along, practically on all fours. I came upon my rifle and was surprised that he hadn't taken it away with him. He must have been frightened, and run for his life. I had no idea what could have scared him; I didn't even want to think about it. I was tired. I took off my knapsack—a few smashed apples were in it, the Colt, and a candle damp with the juice of the apples. I lit it with difficulty. I resumed my search.

A trail of blood, like a fragmented snake, dragged across the rocks. Following it, I reached a slope that descends sharply into a pit. On the edge of the slope I caught sight of two enormous feet with peasant sandals. A battered head lay at the bottom, quiet, as if listening to the pulse of the earth. I called to him, I nudged him with my foot. No answer. I felt his hand. It was cold. Well, I said, I had better luck! But luck or no luck, I'm glad you're staying here, and not me. You wanted a rabbit, you ran into a bear. Today it's you, Obrad. Tomorrow it may be me.

For some ten minutes I looked for my pistol. Finally I found it between some rocks, crushed and dusty. While I was dragging myself out of the cave, I saw people approaching from the village with torches: a man and two women. One of them was Neda. They paused and called out for their man. They waited a long time for his answer. This waiting, as stupid as hope, made me furious. I let out a dull wounded cry from the hilltop. I hurried to get away before they got any closer. Again, from another spot, I let go the same stifled cry. They paused in confusion. They were waving their torches but no longer calling.

JUNIPER, MOTHER

WHEN I COME across a valley that I haven't seen in a long time, a familiar rock, a path, or an old water trough, these objects flicker in a double light—one emanating from the sun, the other from memory. The joy I feel is neither as crazy nor as senseless as it may seem. In these objects I find that constancy I've searched for in vain among men. Even more important, they serve as affirmation of the lasting quality of recollection. Like reflections on the water's surface. And as durable as the hills and rocks.

On the other hand, there are times when this recognition makes me feel dreadful. For instance: I find myself on a nameless street lined with rotted walls and closed shutters. The act of recognition makes the vision even more painful than necessary, for it destroys an old hope that I had escaped it and would never see it again. Two rows of putrid houses draw near and recede, and surge up again under the low skies, convulsively, like a wounded snake. Gradually I realize that it is indeed a snake. And that I am that snake! And that I am looking at it from the inside. I don't know where it ends, and I totter through the liquid mud of her undigested meals, without hope that I shall ever reach the end.

I wiggle this way and that, and finally realize that its head and tail are joined, forming a hollow, endless circle. This is a dungeon from which no one has ever escaped. Let it digest me! To prolong my suffering, it transforms itself back into a street, crowded with butchers' hooks, flies, and people calling out to each other. Somehow it's clear that they represent two belligerent groups: the right and the left. With trumpets blowing, they are each asserting their sovereignty over the future. The winner is the party that can talk longest; the score is carefully being kept. Since neither side will yield, not even out of exhaustion, the loser will be the party that can no longer bear the stink.

Sometimes the walls recede altogether. There is grass. It is night. I am on a field. I bury my head in the turf and sleep a while. But a gray corridor again rises on both sides. They've spotted me; they're shouting again. I seem to have alienated both sides. They're after me with a dogcatcher's net. It falls right in front of me and scrapes me up in one pull, along with the mud and the scum, and my crumpled shadow, which kicks and struggles for a few moments, then drops quietly to the bottom of the net and vanishes across the wall. The chase is over. I surmise that it was my shadow that provoked them, not me, and that now everything is settled and paid for.

Both sides have quieted down in the hope of cheating and tricking each other the better. They are entertaining themselves with cards, lice, and propaganda. That's how they pass their time, which is, in fact, a great wooden beam that gets heavier and heavier, so heavy that only many shoulders can keep it aloft. They've discovered that I carry my beam alone; they are shouting that I am an isolationist and a damned leper. I take off my shirt and show them that my wounds are only an ordinary case of impetigo. But it's of no use. They've made up their minds it's leprosy and in the midst of their din I cannot even hear my own voice.

The dawn finally broke through; I felt the sun on the nape of my neck. I peeked through the dust in my eyes and licked several glistening dewdrops. I revived, and vaguely understood that it would not be wise for me to stay in an exposed place. To conceal myself, I pulled my cap down to my brows. But I was still afraid that I might be recognized, and started up the hill. I leaned on the branch of a tree, and it stepped aside to open a door for me. Inside, there was shade and a different kind of foliage, untouched by light and wind, filled with the sweet smell of plant oil and an ancient tranquillity in which there was no humankind on earth.

I stretched out on a brown rug of pine needles. Everything swayed quietly. In some spots the pain had diminished, in others it was still strong, bristling and almost pleasurable. Especially when it ran into waves of strange softness, drowned in it, and disappeared.

Dana had soaked the clean cold sheets under me with a balm of lavender. Everything had been taken care of, and I slept as peacefully as an uninhabited valley in some deaf mountain range. Suddenly, human voices began rolling down the valley, like an avalanche of sooty rocks. Another dream, I thought. They want to torment me again. And I woke up. The voices hardened and, linked in chains, resounded around me.

"See, there's nothing here," said one; "you've been dragging me through this damned country for nothing."

"Maybe," the other admitted. "But he was lying here. You can tell; the grass is pressed down."

"What of it? It's like that all over the place."

"I saw him, I tell you! He lay here, like a dead man. Head down, at an angle. A healthy man doesn't lie like that."

"Did the devil take him then?"

Yes, I thought, the devil! I arranged my three guns: I'll try to defend myself somehow. The day is long and they are sly. It's not likely that I'll make it. Perhaps they'll stick together; that would make things easier. But they won't. One will stand guard while the other runs off to fetch a patrol. The same old fear was lifting me off the ground; it pulled me up and let me fall. It cleared my sight, reminding me that I was merely a wounded heap of flesh. Then it muddled my brain and shook my ankles so that I was no longer in control. I buried my elbows in the ground and my knees and my toes, and I clenched my teeth to keep them from chattering.

Now I hear them again: they are standing in the same

place, mumbling to each other. They seem frightened. One of them in particular: he warned his friend not to touch the pressed grass lest his mind grow feeble. He lowered his voice to an ominous whisper, and explained that men born with cauls always die a strange death. As a rule their bodies are never found. When two of them happen to meet they challenge each other to combat and they fight with thunder or whatever is at hand. Sometimes they are both cut down and never come back.

"Shall I call him?"

"Don't bother. They called him and each time he answered from a different spot. To trick them."

"So they say. I don't believe a word of it. Velko's people killed him in revenge."

"But they were down there in the village when it happened."

"Then it was someone else—to take his money."

They were looking for Obrad. They had forgotten me, as if I never existed. For a moment I felt angry: the old bastard had pushed me into the background again. He wanted to take my woman from me, and now he is lying in the pit and pressing on his wallet with all his weight. I should have taken the money from him and bought a soul or two with it. Now it's too late. Perhaps it's better this way. Let them think that he was done in by that devil—who, as everyone knows, has no use for paper money! A new voice began calling from the ridge: something dark fell over the meadow and the valley.

They went off to look and their voices grew weaker and then died out altogether. The air was finally free of their stench. I breathed it in with both lungs and my eyes were wet. I looked at the branches. They were slender and spread wide as if for an embrace. Their tiny eyes, golden and green, looked at me with a quiet sadness: you've wandered too much, it's time to rest! Gentle arches vaulted one above the other, heaven above heaven unto eternity. Sleep overcame me and I was slowly forgetting. But while I forgot with one portion of my being, I remembered with the other: Gluv, the summers, and my mother at harvest time spreading alder branches above my cradle to protect me from the sun.

Now too the branches are suspended between me and the high sun. My mother is somewhere nearby. I hear her sighing as she stoops in the shade to rest. I move a branch in the mad hope that I may see her before she disappears, but she is no longer there. As usual. But this doesn't surprise me any more. In her place is the Wailing Mountain, lit by the sun, buried up to its shoulders in the green sheaves of the spurs. You are not a good mother, I said bitterly to her face. You are evil: you sow too late, you reap too early—nothing to boast about! Your children fight over a bone or they loaf through the world. Under strange roofs they serve the rabble and every fool makes fools of them.

There is silence. It has pacified me. The mountain seems to be growing. It trembles slightly. There is something alive, something passionate in this trembling. It would like to fly up and merge with the clear empty blue of the sky. In the process it screams with inaudible cries. It has been burgeoning and preparing for this merger with the sea bottom for a long time. It has sharpened and turned everything upward. Trees grow up straight, eagles fly toward the sun, and men go mad dreaming about the happiness they cannot find down on the earth.

There is a time around the equinox when even snakes climb up the trees, climaxing their desire for madness and glory. Then comes the autumn and oppression: leaves fall and rocks break off from the cliffs. Rebels go home, flags are folded up. Old age and fear come with the frost. Eagles annihilate their young in caves. Snakes find holes. The chiefs of the wailing valleys seek out the lord of the land, to bow before him and receive in return some furs and ready money.

That's how it goes: when my mind, incensed by this lazy wind, seizes upon something, my thoughts wander off I don't know where or why. And I pause in astonishment to ask myself if I've gone mad. Why do I feel I have to justify these mercenaries and crooks by citing the laws of nature or ancient precedent? Do I owe them anything? The Christian Bishop

Njegoš seduced them with furs and with faith, and destroyed them on the sly. Later he would put on his bishop's robes, sing the liturgies, and his soul would seem as clear and sunny as a spring morning.

What was it about us, Niko, that made us stay so hopelessly green and soft, so childlike and virginal? In those gay swarms of ours we prepared ourselves for everything except for what was going to happen. Out of every trifle, out of the shadow of a sound and a pale memory . . .

I am not going to think about it any more! It always leads me astray, and there's no one around to show me the right path. I've covered my eyes with my hands and I've hidden my head under the low branches. It's better this way. I am adjusting my breathing to their swaying. I wish it were slower, though, quite slow. Compared to eternity, what does it amount to? And there will be time after that too.

MIKLA TRANSFORMED

HUNGER REACHED ME in my sleep; but I was still too weak to do anything about it. It first interrupted my sleep yesterday, and I deliberated for some time what to do next. The world around me was full of terror. I finally got to my feet. Nothing happened. I took off; no one shot at me. The trees stood and watched me go by as if I were a stranger heading for the unknown. I was sure that the trees could walk too: if only they could cross the threshold of fear which binds them to the earth. I carefully washed my hands in the stream and rinsed off my bruised cheeks.

Whenever I stand up my body aches. That's why I haven't taken the trouble to look around. It doesn't matter where I

am. Later on I'll be somewhere else, and then somewhere else
again. The odors of food tempt me, like an apparition. Fear
has gone, leaving only a drunken desire, unaware of anything
but itself. Steep hills drop behind me like days of the week. I
spotted the village of Bilo and I thought with anxiety: This
must be my destiny! In the sunny oak forests above me I spied
several capricious black dots: people. They were gathering
leaves. They didn't notice me. I sat on the ground and waited
for the women to turn up with food for the workers.

I waited for a long time. At last, on the lower path, a group
appeared carrying baskets. As I was deciding what course to
take, I noticed a dumpy woman scurrying behind them. Her
sprightly gait reminded me of Mikla. Perhaps it *was* Mikla,
with whom I had an account to settle. I slid down to the path.
Instead of being frightened, she averted her eyes and pretended not to see me. I knew it was Mikla. Her detachment
infuriated me. I yelled louder than I intended to:

"Hold it, woman! That's no way to greet a man!"

"I am late with lunch as it is. My workers are dying of
hunger."

"You know me, don't you?" I bellowed, in the hope of fright-
ening her.

She looked at me and instantly cooked up a lie. "Not me, by
God! Who are you?"

"Give me that basket."

She paused in confusion; she looked at me with her green
eyes, nervously wondering whether I would really rob her.
She came closer. I broke off a large hunk of bread from the
basket. She looked at me as though I had broken her arm. I
yanked out a chunk of cheese wrapped in cabbage leaves. She
sighed as though I had wrenched her heart. She glanced at
my rifle, obviously tempted to grab it and strike me with it. I
poked her under the ribs, and she looked at me with respect
for the first time.

"You owe Niko Saykov some money," I said, my mouth still
full of her cheese. "In payment for a meadow."

"Should I take the money to him in prison and let them jail me too?"

"No, not the money: the sack of flour he asked for. In fact, I want you to bring three sacks; and leave them here. That'll be less trouble."

She sneered. "You won't be able to carry it all."

"In that case, load it on a horse. By tomorrow evening! That'll give you time to grind the wheat and bring it over."

I banged a rock with the butt of the rifle, indicating exactly what I meant by "here." It was a good move: a prisoner should always be kept in a state of fear with a bit of noise and an exaggerated precision. She bit her lip. She realized that I was serious. Her face, flushed with the heat and young for its years, suddenly turned ashen. Her eyes looked greener than ever; she blinked as she watched me eat, trying to decide whether to follow a policy of open resistance or of sly obedience. I watched her with malicious pleasure. Finally I said:

"If you dawdle, it'll cost you more."

"Now, that's not nice of you," she whined.

"I can do better. Your house could burn brightly, giving off light for the neighbors. They'd like that. Do you understand?"

She understood. She suddenly changed her attitude, her voice. She knows, she said, how difficult it is to live in the mountains. The mountain is hungry and thirsty, a cruel and tough foe. She cannot sleep when she thinks about our suffering in the mountains. Some people don't even give it a thought, like that Grivich who mocked people who didn't have salt. He called them from the hilltops to come and get salt from the leaves on which he had urinated.

She was practically in tears. She thought I was the same naïve fellow I was last year, like Niko, who would melt as soon as he saw a tear. But since then more blood has been spilled than in the last hundred years, and I am a good ten years older. I am a sly devil who believes no one. That Grivich is no good and I'll get hold of him one of these days, but I am not crazy enough to let her go in order to catch him. It's her turn now,

and we'll see about the others later. I looked her straight in
the eyes until she understood, and she was quiet. I showed her
again where she should bring the flour. She trotted off.

That was yesterday, time enough for her to have given
warning. No patrols have come this way. She hasn't said anything. That's fair. She hasn't been fair for a long time, that's
why she feels so uncomfortable. I slept for a while and was
hungry all over again. When I am hungry everything irritates
me: the day because it's too long, the Lim because it twists,
the sun because it's so bright.

The shadows have stretched down along the path that leads
into the valley. From below, walking in the shadows, Mikla
appeared, trudging behind a tired horse loaded with sacks of
flour. Misery and humiliation had aged her. I was on the
verge of pity, and thought of sending her back home, along
with the flour. But she would lose respect for me, earned at no
little cost.

"It would have been easier if you'd paid Niko directly," I
said.

"Easier, yes, but I had nothing to give him then."

"Tell the truth. You thought you were going to get the land
for nothing. You were too mean to light one candle for a saint.
Well, now you are lighting two for the devil."

She looked at me incredulously and said nothing. She was
wearing an old dress, probably borrowed from a scarecrow.
She had no stockings on, and her heels had gone through her
sandals and were stained with blood. This must be deliberate:
to evoke pity. It's a disguise. She halted the horse and then
stood motionless. She was still hoping for mercy. She sighed
and waited a little longer. Finally she started to untie the
rope, at first indecisively and awkwardly, as though her fingers
were numb.

"What are you doing?" I asked.

"I must take the horse back with me," she replied.

"And you want me to lug the sacks up the mountain on my
back? Are you mad?"

"I can't let the horse go," she choked.

"We must get the sacks up there. Either the horse carries them or you do. Take your choice."

"You have no soul, do you?"

"No, I don't. I left it on the trail among the rocks, as a snake sheds its skin. I feel a lot better without it."

She spurred the horse and waited for me to go in front, as is the custom here. But I let her go ahead to save her from the temptation of attacking me from behind. We climbed up in silence, the only sound that of hoofs. My hunger was painful, making my thoughts bitter and poisonous. At dusk we reached the upper slope. From the valley the voices of people heading home from work reached us. They are too loud, I thought; I should silence them. I could simply dislodge a boulder and let it roll down the hill. But that's an old trick! I'll get more satisfaction hearing Mikla scream.

"You once had a billy goat," I said, "and I was told that you set a fee for every goat he mounted. How much did you make off him?"

"I earned a lot," she said. "The state is richer than I am and they charge for the services of their bull."

"Their bull is pure-blooded. Besides, you used to tie up the billy goat's thing down there. The first time he'd always bungle it. So you were able to charge twice for the same thing."

"We all try to get what we can."

"And now I want you to bleat like that billy goat of yours. But louder, so that they can hear you down in the valley. If you don't know how to do it, I'll show you."

I cut off a slender bough from the birch tree and showed it to her. She wailed in fear, and after the first blows her wailing turned into a series of fragmented shrieks interrupted by several attempts at bleating. I kept telling her to bleat louder, and not make it continuous. When she lowered her voice, I hit her harder, which produced a sound between the howl of a dog and the siren of a fire engine. After that I no longer listened. Nor did she, I believe. She was too busy defending herself, protecting her head, hiding behind the horse, diving into the bushes. At last I let her go, and there was not a peep from her.

I spurred the horse and it struck a handful of sparks with its hoof. I was worn out, as I always am after a good time. If Vasil knew what I was doing he would grind his teeth in pain and Ivan would shudder . . . ! In time they will surely find out. Mikla will talk. And Vasil and Ivan will come to interrogate me and punish me, and they will be late as usual. It's too late even now, for I've already grown accustomed to these things and I enjoy them. My conflict with the world has resolved itself into a mutually satisfactory impasse. I have no regrets. My conscience does not gnaw at me. Morality is a fictitious thing anyway; in fact, nothing really matters under this starry sky.

I passed through an oak forest and emerged in the fields by the river. The road was soft here and I let the horse get well ahead of me. I heard a splashing sound to the rear. I turned around. Mikla paused like a shadow. I made a move toward her; she inched backward. She still wanted her horse and would trail after me to hell's very door. I let her follow me for a while longer. At the top of the hill I untied the rope and brought down the sacks. I let the horse go. She grabbed it by the halter and dragged it into the darkness. She didn't say a word. But I knew she respected me and would remember me until her dying day.

THE RECEIPT

ALL NIGHT LONG, in a fever, two women tormented me with a new game whose rules they made up at random to suit their whims. They pinched the cap off my head, flung it back and forth and hid it in the darkness under their dresses. The game started in the open. Later we penetrated ever deeper into the thorny thickets of hawthorn and sweetbrier. Somehow I caught one of them—I had her hanging and screeching on the thorns. The other one giggled. I recognized her by the tone of her voice: Neda! It was she who started the whole thing. And Mikla is suffering on her account. Now I think I am awake. I can see the mountains strain and shiver before daybreak.

Perhaps it was not Neda's game, I thought, anxious to make excuses for her. That bastard from America, her sly old father-in-law, concocted the story about Velko only to throw me off balance! He made it up on the spur of the moment, as we were approaching the cave, and made use of it at exactly the right moment. I shall no longer think about it, or poison myself with suspicion. He made it up out of the clear blue sky, out of doubt and envy. He is dead now, and it would be ridiculous for those doubts, transferred to me, to continue gnawing away like worms. It's ridiculous, I repeated, but they were there all the same. They multiply and regenerate even as I pray that they vanish. After all, Velko needed a woman, Neda wanted a child. And the child which is supposed to be mine could be a mere deception.

How would it be if I were to tell her all these things openly? But doing so would merely be an excuse to see her: and I'd fall again. I rose to my feet to flee from such thoughts. I started off in the opposite direction, so my legs wouldn't by chance bring me closer to her. I walked at a tilt, leaning to one side, but that didn't matter. Suddenly I heard people yelling like poisoned animals. I took shelter. They continued to yell, but they didn't get any nearer. They wouldn't come this way. They were not thinking about me. They had climbed high up into the trees, like snakes, each in his own grove. They were lopping off branches. Occasionally they paused to rest and called to each other from hill to hill.

"Oh, Markelez . . . look and see why Masnik is so quiet!"

"You'd be silent too, Grivich, if you were busy lifting loads and turning beams over all night long. . . ."

"What beams, for God's sake?"

"Heavy ones. Women are draining him dry; his bones have gnawed right through his skin."

"Hey, Masnik, you old devil, answer us! Don't you hear what Markelez says about you?"

"Not me, by God!" Masnik finally answered from a distance. "I don't listen to Markelez barking, or to you either for that matter."

This hollow, morose voice drew me to it even before I had the remotest idea that something was going to happen that would not be forgotten for a long time. I passed above Markelez and through untouched forest until I reached Masnik's grove. He must have started working before dawn; the trees had already been reduced to naked skeletons; the sharply pointed stumps of the branches resembled hooks. I spotted him high up in an oak, in a net of pruning hooks and clippers. I hissed like a snake, a big one, like Masnik himself. He leaned over, looked at me, and understood everything at once.

"You've done a lot of work," I said. "You should take a little rest now and then."

"I will," he said mockingly, "if you'll free me."

"That's why I've come back from the cave. It's high time someone was liberated by me."

"You've all talked enough about freedom, by God, and yet everything seems to be going wrong somehow."

He swung himself behind the trunk. With one hand he was holding onto the stump of the branch, and the other reached for the scythe, to throw it at my head. I stepped back. Inside I am cold and I don't hate him any more than I hate rain, heat, snow, or any other natural element. He belongs here. He is right and he knows it, and I am a crazy stranger who has disturbed the natural course of events. I can't kill him. I don't feel like it. Nor do I have the energy. That's the way it always works out. I'll let him live. I've grown accustomed to his tricks

and I'd feel lost without them. But I'll throw a scare into him.
Let his pants tremble a little.

"Why did they take Vanya Lopa to prison?" I asked.

"I don't know. Someone ordered it, someone else carried it
out."

"It's not your fault, I suppose. You merely delivered the
letter to the wrong address. Why don't you come out of that
tree?"

"No," he said through his teeth. "Can't you see that I'm
busy?"

I aimed and fired, not at him but at the branch he was
standing on. Weakened by the bullet, the branch broke under
Masnik's weight and left him groping in empty space. One of
his hips got caught against a pruning hook, slowing down his
fall. He slipped down to a branch beneath him, and screamed.
He could have stopped himself there, but his long legs were
kicking back and forth, almost as though he didn't want to
regain his balance. He began falling again, but more slowly
this time, like a huge spider spinning the very thread which is
holding him up. His shadow scared me at first. Then I realized
that he had a rope, and that the rope was unfolding from his
belly like a snake which was simultaneously stretching and
unfolding. He reached the lowest branch, clutched it passionately and draped his chest over it. He was groaning, and
the ball of his intestines continued to unfold from his torn
trousers in a circle about his feet. A stench spread. I felt sick.
If I had fired a shot into his skull I could have ended his
torture. I aimed, but then I put down my rifle: Why should I?
Let him suffer! He was not fated to die by gunfire—he isn't
worthy of that honor. He would have done the same thing to
me if he had had the opportunity. That's what he did to Niko,
and now let him suffer.

His strength failed him. He slipped off the branch. He fell
on his knees and turned on his back to glance at the tree
entangled in his intestines. He was looking at it with hatred as
at a horse who has tossed a rider from his back. He swung his

arms about in pain. Agitated by these motions, the long purple snake splattered me with filth and stench. I wiped my face
off with a twist of dry leaves. His friends began calling to him.
I responded with cries which couldn't be deciphered and
meant nothing. He turned around and looked at me. His face
was sallow and shiny with sweat. He moved his jaws, trying to
swallow something or spit something out.

"Kill me," he mumbled at last.

"I am not that foolish. I don't want to have blood on my
hands. You'll die anyway.

"Kill me, kill me; I'd kill you . . . !"

"Yes, you would, with somebody else's hand. I know you."

He tried to spit at me, then closed his eyes.

He had calmed down. His effort to reduce the pain by not
moving kept reminding me that he was still conscious. It was
quiet now. A breeze rustled in the leaves of the fallen
branches. In the trees themselves there was nothing left to
rustle, except for the bluish band of Masnik's intestines. He
looked again as if he were asleep. He was scattered all over:
in the air, on the trees, and on the ground, as if he wished to
cover as much territory as possible and bind it to himself and
take it with him on a journey he was not eager to make. Even
that wasn't enough: he was grabbing the earth and the leaves
and clasping them passionately.

"You'll pay for this," he groaned.

"You fell of your own accord. Why should I pay?"

"Someone will avenge me."

"But the bullet didn't even touch you."

"I'll tell them what happened."

"Go ahead. I don't give a damn."

He hoped his threats would make me angry enough to finish
him off. When this last hope fell through, he ground his teeth
and covered his eyes with the palms of his hands. The sun was
in his eyes, and he tried to chase it away like a fly. He began
mumbling softly, unintelligibly. I couldn't tell whether he was
praying or enumerating his sins. The blood and foam thick-

ened about his mouth. His breath stank. I couldn't get near
enough to hear what he was saying. Nor was there much left
to hear. From the distant groves there was noise and confusion, and Grivich called over to Markelez:

"Run over and look! I don't think that was Masnik's voice."

"Why don't you, if you really want to look."

"Go! You lost soul! Perhaps he's injured himself."

"I don't want to get mixed up; I've got enough troubles of
my own."

"I heard a shot, Markelez. It must be something evil."

"I'm not going to take a scythe against a rifle. You go, if
you're so brave."

They would go on like this for an hour or two. Masnik
straightened the upper part of his body and fell back. He sat
up again and looked around. He was searching for something.
He could no longer find peace. He was groaning and rattling,
and pushed himself on his back toward a heap of clipped
branches. He reached it, buried his head and chest in it. Only
his legs stuck out. The branches above him rose and shook,
then lay still. I uncovered him and looked: his eyes were
glassy. He had paid up.

I should have been on my way, but I'd forgotten something.
I didn't know what it was. I thrust my head into his stench
and pulled out his wallet. There were a few coins. Not worth
taking. I pulled out his Italian identity card and his Chetnik
papers. They might come in useful some day. I thought I
should give him a receipt, and I wrote on a piece of paper: "I
received the soul of the faithful Masnik—signed/ The Devil."
I shoved the paper into his wallet and back into his chest. Let
them wonder!

The Summer Is Over

The twittering of birds scattered
a hell of worries,
announced a glorious dawn.
I thought then
how the dawn would scatter the darkness.
And I didn't know
if it meant good luck or bad.

—MARKO MILJANOV

YASHA'S SUDDEN APPEARANCE

THERE WAS CONSTANT shooting in the Donyokraiske Mountains. At first it was dull and infrequent, making me think it was either the usual plunder or the usual border dispute with the Moslems. By noon it had developed into a chase, growing ever closer and more vigorous. As I watched the wind-swept Strmoglavats, its ridges grew lively with black swarms, the gulleys resembling worm-eaten meat. Then the pursuit formed itself into a semicircular chain, and started off again. At times the shooting thickened, as if they had all spotted the common target and torn it apart with lead. I felt sadness and fear: it'll happen to me one of these days too. But then lone shots rang out, reviving hope that the persecuted animal was still alive, and had perhaps managed to get away. . . .

Before sunset, pale in the shaded valley, the shots died down. I was about to find shelter from the wind when, quite by chance, I glanced across at the clearing and saw a man with a rifle. I crouched down and crawled back into the forest in fear. I felt better. He was approaching slowly. He had something in his hand. A cauldron! He looked like a gypsy who has stolen a chicken. He had a cap on—it was Yasha! I called out his name. The cauldron fell to the ground and tumbled away, and he went after it. He reached the trees and called out in a grumpy voice:

"Who are you?"

I told him. I felt uneasy pronouncing my own name. Any old lie would have made me feel better. I felt naked, as if admitting my guilt.

"Step into the clearing," he said, "so I can see you."

197

"Don't you believe me?" I asked in order to hear his voice again.

"No! I don't believe anyone."

I stepped out. I didn't see him. He was in a better position. I was frightened: he might kill me if only to get my clothes. Or for my ten bullets. He's been alone for a long time and is perhaps wilder and crazier than I. I should run away while my bones are still intact. And I would have fled, but he finally stood up. He leaned against his rifle and looked at me in perplexity. His face was thin and wizened, and across his nose was soot from the cauldron. All the same I was happy to see him. I wanted to embrace him, but his cold suspicious look held me back. He still doubted me, or he might have heard bad things about me. I didn't give a damn!

"I've looked for you several times," I said, "but couldn't find you. Just places where you'd made fires."

"All sorts of people have been looking for me. Those characters today almost found me."

"So they were chasing you?"

"That's their job."

"Good thing too, otherwise we'd never have found each other."

He waved his hand. He didn't care much for me or my talk. His cauldron had rolled down into the forest and his chief concern was to find it. He was walking at an angle, looking at me askance to make sure I didn't get behind his back. I wanted to help him and was quite obliging, but he didn't appreciate it. I found the little cauldron next to a tree. He grabbed it from my hand and looked it over to see if it was damaged. Fortunately it wasn't, otherwise there would have been a quarrel and I don't know how it would have ended. We sat down under a tree and we no longer had anything to say to each other. After the war, I thought, the survivors will have many similar encounters.

"Why are you looking at me like that?" he growled.

"You are as shabby as a gypsy and you haven't washed the soot off your face since God knows when."

"If Mr. Comrade is so sensitive, he shouldn't bother to stay. I haven't asked for your company."

"You should get a pair of trousers, and not be going around like a wild beast."

"Do you have any food?"

I should have offered him food before he asked me, but I was no longer in the habit of offering things. I pulled out my knapsack and offered him what was there. As I stretched out my hand I felt a certain relief: the custom of salt and bread had not left me. I was not what I'd become, after all.

Later on, by the river, while we were gathering twigs for a fire, Yasha no longer looked at me quite so suspiciously. He lit the fire. It crackled cheerfully. There is a special skill in this, which Vasil had too. I'd lit fires a hundred times, and they always looked sorrowful. The flame would buzz ominously and its shadows would vibrate with evil forebodings: I could hardly wait for the miserable supper to cook, to put the fire out and get away.

Yasha is silent. It's better that way: there's plenty of time to talk and even to annoy each other. Why hurry? Having saved our own skins, there is nothing much to say. Nor is there any good in bemoaning our senseless fate and abandonment. In fact, we should forget it. Across the trees and rocks we can hear the sound of the river, an interminable song in the desert. We also listen to the rustling of the leaves and bones; all that sinks into the earth and, carried away, is transformed into nothing.

The alder trees by the river stand like black cows next to a watering place. They are lashing their tails. In times past such scenes roused all my suspicions, as if the whole gloomy forest were advancing on me. I used to be afraid of shadows too. Loneliness is continuous fear and frenzy. It was loneliness that prevented me from grasping the song of the water in its entir-

ety, and led me into that futile round of encounters in the
valley, the folly with Neda, and the apparitions. These things
will never happen again. There is no loneliness. The world is
pacified. I am no longer bent on my destruction.

Yasha finished eating and wiped his hands.

"Now we should get some sleep," he said.

"Would you like some tobacco?"

"Give me a little, since you've got it."

"We'll get some more when we run out," I explained.

"You seem to have good connections."

It was still too early to tell Yasha what sort of connections
they were. He is straight. He wouldn't like it. We finished the
cigarettes and started toward my precious juniper on the hill.
We walked past stumps and fallen trees which resembled
corpses, rotted out and hairy with moss. The devils who once
used to play here, jumping from carrion to carrion, had vanished. The day was fading away over the shady water, blacker
than ink. We came across clearings and paths I had never seen
before. It seemed as if they had been created the previous day
and would vanish tomorrow. One rock resembled a cottage.
Perhaps it was a cottage. Some day we might settle here.

"How come you're so well dressed?" Yasha asked suddenly.

"All stolen. I'll find some for you too."

"I don't need any. We are not exactly on parade."

Yasha liked my juniper. It was on a hill and by the road: if
a patrol should come by, we could easily hear them. Inside, it
was like a room, but he didn't like rooms and he didn't want
to be inside. He went out from under the tree and lay down. I
really think he did it to save me from his lice. In my dreams I
got entangled in a story about gains which are easily lost,
about a carbine belonging to one Vuyo Drenkovich, and God
knows what else. At sunrise I was awakened by the grinding
of teeth and a terrible jolt. I looked through the branches:
Yasha was standing up and turning around. The palms of his
hands were over his ears as he pivoted on his heel, occa-

sionally pausing as in a mad dance. I barely had the courage to ask him what it was all about.

"They," he said, pointing toward the Donyokraiske Mountains. "They are still going."

"I don't hear a thing. You are dreaming."

"No, no! They are nearby. And they stink horribly. Let's get going, and don't argue."

He grabbed the cauldron and the rifle, and was off! I caught up with him by the road and listened. Still, I heard nothing. He was mad. We crossed the road and the field, and then I heard it: the stamping of feet and the soft sounds of movement. I could see them at the clearing. They were carrying branches or long brooms in their hands. But no, it was a small forest, silently climbing up the crags. Nothing human: no cigarettes burning, no talk, no coughing. I didn't even notice the stink which had awakened Yasha. Nothing but waves of darkness following one another.

In this dull motion there was superhuman energy enticing and mesmerizing us like a whirlpool. I had forgotten the danger. I was merely looking at it and growing dizzy. Yasha yanked me by the sleeve and we started off again. We descended to the river and climbed into the Donyokraiske wastelands. Above us a cliff glistened like a summer cloud. We came upon a crevice, which let us through, and then steps of stone to pull us into the heights.

If they kill us here, we'll have a permanent and conspicuous tombstone.

A LITTLE PLUNDER TO PASS THE TIME

I LISTENED AS the noise and the commotion on the slopes below receded. I was so cheered that I smiled inadvertently. I thought Yasha had smiled too, but he gave me a surprised look, almost scornful, and spoiled my good cheer. I didn't know what could be bothering him. Perhaps he was feeling sorry for humanity. I expected him to say something along those lines. I had a reply ready, but silently he turned over on his stomach and rested his forehead on a rock. He turned his back on me—deliberately, I thought, to avoid conversation and to insult me. I was angry.

It was more than anger. I was disappointed. I had hoped I had found a friend, a companion. But he represents a new loneliness in addition to my own—a dumb emptiness which, by exposing itself to the sun, allows lice to creep on its back. They emerge from all the holes, they scramble on top of the patches and on flat surfaces, two or three tottering in the same direction. They resemble patrols, searching and sniffing out fugitives, like us, who were also crawling on this living relief. I moved away to avoid the lice. The world regained its form.

Down below a valley opens up, yellow with stubble, cut up with ravines. Blotches of autumn are at its edges. Past the willow thickets and the sooty cornfields I can see the Lim branchy with tributaries, like a huge tree felled in the groves. I seem to recall that at one time those trees stood straight and that I climbed one of them and was exhilarated. Now it's lying flat. The sun is rising and the pond under the rock reflects a light which changes from blue to mother-of-pearl, like tears and smiles. Once upon a time a maiden drowned there. She is calling me as she used to do in summers past. Everything was soft and bearable thereafter: mists, snows, and a few mad loves.

I cleared my throat to awaken Yasha. "What would you think if we took a swim in the pond down there?"

"Out of the question," he replied.

"I've bathed there every summer, even last year. If I pass up this summer, I may as well let my youth go."

"If they catch you there you'll let it go for sure."

"At least we'll be clean."

He lifted his head and wiped off the sweat with his crumpled cap. His glance was fixed on the bottom of the valley. He was pensive. Suddenly he arose and signaled me with his hand and started down toward the pond. I don't know what prompted him to change his mind. Perhaps nothing: a simple lack of resistance, the toppling of a deep indifference by the slight breath of another will—my own. Yet I think what really appealed to him was the idea of mutual death. For a person who has anticipated a lonesome end, like a rabbit, or a viper, such a thing would have great appeal. I felt that way myself. The pale echoes of the shooting were still heard, like a huge bellows behind the hill.

"We'll make them pay for this," I said.

"What do you mean?"

"I don't know yet, but I'll think of something clever."

"We'll see," he mumbled.

By the tone of his voice I could tell that he was tired and bad-tempered again. I had better go slowly in explaining my scheme to him. I am destined to make evil seem tempting. Why not? They are trampling on my clearings, and spitting into the pond that was once my mirror. They will infest the whole mountain. They will find Neda and mistreat her. But I don't want to think about her any more. They will sniff out the meat and the sack of flour we have hung on the branches. So why shouldn't I take from them in turn?

"How about killing someone?" Yasha asked suddenly.

"Why not?"

"Yanko, for example?"

"I don't know him, but I have no objections."

"He was the first to kill one of us."

A good thing Yasha knows nothing about Bayto's orders. And I'd be crazy to mention it. But should we begin with Yanko? They'd surely see our hand in it. I'd much prefer a scheme that would cast suspicion on one of their own people.

We descended into the valley. We heard the sound of trucks approaching the town. The Lim was muttering in the distance and my pond glistened through the branches like a naked woman. I laid my rifle against a rock. A childlike impatience seized me as I was undressing. I plunged in among some round blue rocks, next to a surprised fish.

Then it was Yasha's turn. He placed his rags on an anthill. But he was fooling himself; to get rid of his rich supply of lice would require more than an anthill. The sand was hot. Shots continued in the distance, as if someone were stepping on twigs. From time to time anxiety returned like a shadow, but I pushed it away. No one knew where we were and perhaps a week would pass before someone came this way. We took turns: one kept watch, the other swam. Our lips had turned blue. The sun was going down. We should be getting dressed, but we didn't feel like it. Particularly Yasha, who was sadly looking at his rags.

"Tonight," I said, "we should break into some rich man's house, like a patrol. We'll make a search—let him complain later."

"Good idea."

"We'll pilfer a thing or two, not because we want anything, but to make them howl louder."

"Then we should rob my uncle. He'll howl louder than anyone."

"But they'd recognize you. You stay outside, and I'll go in alone."

We walked along the warm sand on the banks of the pond.
The shadow of the hill had spread over the valley and was
climbing up the slope along with the houses and the plum
orchards. Yasha's uncle was a rich miser who didn't smoke or
drink or lend money, and was always on the side of the law.
His only son, an idle artillery officer, lived in Kolashin, spent
everything he had on women, and was not really bad. We
waited until it was pitch dark and we approached the isolated
stone house through the plum orchard. A frightened servant
came to the door. Then Yasha's uncle appeared—a suspicious
creature with a hole in his mouth where several teeth were
missing.

"How many people live here?" I asked.

"The family, who else! Who are you?"

"And your nephew, Yasha, where are you hiding him?"

"Yasha is not here. I have nothing to do with Yasha. Don't
look for him here."

"I've been ordered to look for him. So move along." And I
gave him a shove.

That surprised him. Automatically he grew tame and ordered his women to be quiet. He reached for a candle and
took me to the attic, filled with old trunks, tools, and smoked
meat. While we were rummaging through the junk, he told
me about his envious neighbors, how much they hated and
cheated him. Even now they'd set a trap. Everyone knew that
Yasha hadn't been here in three years. His brother, Zaro, was
here, but Zaro was not a Communist. . . . We came down
from the attic. I shuffled through their bedding. An officer's
uniform in the trunk caught my eye, as well as a heap of
beautifully ironed shirts. I looked at them as though I had
come across definite evidence of some kind.

"You've prepared these things for Yasha," I said. "You might
just as well tell me where you are hiding him."

"Leave those things alone," the old man hissed. "They
belong to my son."

"No one admits the truth at first. But if you are right, come to the Command tomorrow. You'll get more than you need."

"You're not going to rob my house! Not while I'm alive!"

"I'll do it then over your dead body," I said, pushing him onto the bed. "I am doing my duty and you're getting in my way."

I pulled out my pistol, as though I intended to kill him right there, on the bed. Perhaps I would have, but the women shielded him with their bodies, pleading with him to remain calm. While they were crying, I crammed clothing into my knapsack. Then I gave the old man a lesson: don't think that you can cheat us; we know your heart only too well! You've joined the Chetniks, but you co-operate with the Communists. Why haven't you turned in your nephew? And what of your son? Chasing whores all over Kolashin! He has hardly ever used his rifle, with the exception of that one down there, and that one is in constant service. And trying to cure syphilis! He drifts around with an Englishman from the Mission! The two of them have made life insufferable for the Kolashin doctors.

They were stunned by the last charge, resembling, as it did, the truth, which had caused them a lot of concern before. I quickly looked around to see if there was anything else I could grab. No tobacco, no brandy, nothing. A razor and a bar of soap were lying on the shelf under the mirror. I pinched them with one sweep of my hand and put them in my pocket. In a corner I spotted a pair of shiny black boots. When I discovered that they didn't fit me, I kicked one of them across the room in anger. I ordered the old man to come to headquarters tomorrow and threatened a little more.

In front of the house I pretended that I had caught one of my patrol stealing apples. I yelled at him ferociously. A pack of thieves can put the whole Chetnik army to shame! I banged the barrels with the butt of my rifle, but they were full and didn't resound as I wanted them to. A dog barked in the middle of the village, but the rest were silent. The men were silent too. Spreading fear is an instructive experience: by taking pleasure in their fear you can forget your own. I should

like to sing for joy, but my voice isn't good enough. Then I
thought of Kacharanda, who drank like a fish at feasts. And I
let go in a hoarse voice: "I drink and I drink, but the brandy
is bitter, and my wife is still a virgin. . . ." Two more dogs
barked and one star sparkled over Turiya.

AMBUSHES AROUND YABLAN

IN FRONT OF the cave there was a mound of yellow shells.
Obviously the siege had been carefully planned: a circle that
was tightened foot by foot. After extended preparations, the
settlement of skunks was conquered in one bold move, without any losses. Inside, the stench of animal glands had gone,
having been replaced by the more perfect stink of ammunition
gases. Thus the world is constantly improving and advancing.
There were no other traces of the pursuit. On the slopes there
were some bones, picked clean, and some empty cans. The
grass was upright again and had swallowed the traces of the
struggle as if nothing had happened. In time the ground will
swallow up the bones and the empty cans; all our human
confusion will be absorbed by this huge green sponge that
sops up everything.

We reached the pond. The water showed no signs of the
struggle either. It was clear blue, warmed by the sun. I offered
Yasha some soap. He should wash himself, and then shave.
What else was there to do? Loafing had become something of
a bore. He undressed behind the bushes, went down to the
bank, and dove in. I cut off a long branch, hung his lousy rags
on it and dragged them over to the brook which drains this

little pond. I watched the water crumpling them up, unfolding them and taking them away. I pulled the officer's uniform and fresh underwear out of my knapsack, put it behind the bushes, and retreated to look at the skies. Finally Yasha came out, saw the uniform, and was stunned.

"What's this?"

"Your uncle sent it to you."

"He sent it to me? That's rot! You mean you stole it."

"It was your idea. But it doesn't matter: to kiss the young and take from the rich is neither sin nor shame, as the saying goes."

"Still, I can't accept it. Where are my rags?"

"I don't know." I waved my hand. "Look around! Perhaps they grew a pair of feet. Or the lice have taken them to the cave."

He was not amused by my jokes and started looking around. He went down to the brook and came back.

"Have a drink of water," I recommended; "it calms the nerves."

He said nothing. He'd wait until my jovial mood passed. He finally grew tired of waiting. He approached the uniform, and I thought that he would put it on. The lining must have kept a smell that reminded him of something. He kicked it with his foot and started toward me, his fists clenched.

"I've had enough joking! You've got no shame left. You can't do this!"

"Why not?" I said. "It's the only way to stay alive."

"Is that so damned important?"

"Yes," I shouted. "Right now it's more important to me than anything else. Out of spite alone. To spite those who left me here to die like an idiot, and to spite those who'd kill me for money. If you think I am here to do good deeds, to be helpful, to beg for each morsel of bread, you're wrong! I am something else. If you don't like it, look for better company. Your rags have gone down the stream. You can catch them if you hurry up. They've even been washed. And send the uniform to your uncle! I don't need it! Tell him that it was all my fault. That'll show him what a fool you are."

"It's better to be a fool than a thief."

"And what are you now? They made me a thief before I ever attempted to steal anything. The same is true of Niko, and he was more honest than all the saints put together."

"No one believed what they said about Niko."

"Did that help him any? I wouldn't want to be in his place."

"Talk as much as you like, Lado, nothing will save you from being kicked out of the Party. If no one else reports you, I will. You might just as well know it."

"I don't give a damn," I said. "Haven't I been expelled as it is? And if by some miracle Niko were released from prison, he'd be expelled too. He, because he didn't do it, I because I did. So what? Why shouldn't I act in the spirit of this greedy place anyway? The people of the Wailing Mountain do. The mountain took this lust from the land around it. Even when the wind brings a tame seed, it either turns wild or dies. Why should I resist it? I'm not here to become a saint. I don't feel like it. And even those saints! God knows what they were really like."

I felt bored. I undressed and descended to the bank of the pond. The water was warm only on the surface, and a very thin layer at that. Below, it was ice cold. I splashed about for a while, then came out. Yasha had put on my clothes and was waiting to see how I'd react. I understood immediately. I pulled on the officer's trousers and smiled. They are much more comfortable and soft. I am ahead. I make gains even when I don't want to. What can a man do when luck is smiling at him?

We made a check of our stock. The sacks of flour stood untouched on the branches where I'd left them. That surprised me. Mikla hadn't betrayed me. Perhaps she didn't want to give her neighbors the pleasure of knowing of her humiliation. But the meat was gone. Their carnivorous sense is much more developed. We ate something. We lay in the sun. I thought about Neda. I should have called on her. To find out the truth. If she's a close relative of Velko's, the old man told lies; but if she isn't, anything could have happened. I don't want to think about it, but the thought, like a fly, won't leave the wound alone.

I resisted the thought for an hour or two, then rose to my feet.

"I want some milk," I said to Yasha, "and I know where I can find some."

He stood up too. Perhaps I'd finally won him over. Some of my evil spirit had passed on to him with my clothes. We crossed the meadow, on which sheep were grazing. There must be a curse on Neda! She can never be seen in the daytime. Perhaps she doesn't even exist in the daytime. On the ridge the oak trees grew denser. Yasha studied them with particular care. He said at last:

"Summer's gone!"

"It's gone, and here we are, still alone. No one remembers us."

"A caravan doesn't stop to pick up trifles that've fallen by the wayside," Yasha added philosophically.

"Some caravan!"

"We won't see another one for some time. We're not on the overland route."

True enough. Even the richest earth is finally exhausted, and afterward it's put to rest, useless and scorned. And a lot of water must flow before another generation is raised with enough courage to go back to the old fields. However, even this is doubtful. Tired of the long journey, the new generation will settle in the valleys like a sediment and will flood the cities and the rich plains. The desert through which it has passed will remain as barren as ever. The dams, the hydroelectric plants, the bridges, the Michurian orchards will fade away like wild boyish dreams.

"There should be a lot of rabbits here," said Yasha.

"There are. And foxes and badgers—everything. A paradise on earth."

"They come out toward the evening; we should wait for them."

"They avoid me. Our temperaments don't quite match."

Never mind the rabbits; I had other things to worry about. I went forward to take a look at the village where Neda lived. The fields around it were mottled with shadows and sheep. It seemed that, like a fortuneteller, the mountain had spilled the tea leaves on a green scarf and was reading my fortune. Next to the sheepfold were two women dressed in black; neither resembled Neda. My eyes were beginning to smart, yet I hadn't discovered anything. The dusk was thickening and fires could clearly be seen in the cottages. One of them, like a cursed star, had a particularly strong appeal to me. I could hardly restrain myself from running. We approached the fields. Suddenly Yasha grabbed me by the arm.

"Shhh. Let's go back."

"Why, Yasha?"

"There's an ambush here. Ten men for sure."

"Why don't you count again?" I mocked him.

"Don't be a fool. Here, listen!"

He squatted on the ground and broke a twig with his hands. A huge animal in front of us awakened and hissed. A shot rang out. Then silence, and tension. We crawled noiselessly a while, until we were some distance away. Then we went across the valley. We pushed through the forest, and Yasha didn't notice that we were going in a semicircle around the same village. But as we crossed the ridge he again became aware of the stench of live flesh, grabbed me by the hand and pulled me back. I didn't resist, and my desire to see Neda suddenly seemed senseless. Why should I go to such effort when, like me, she is cursed and constantly surrounded by misfortune?

We moved along the quiet dry river, and then up a path

through the alders. On the slopes above us, the oak trees and
junipers were engaged in a struggle whose outcome was uncertain. We sat down to rest. In the silence a leaf broke off and
rustled as it fell. That was like a signal, and as soon as the
rustle died down, two more shots were heard and the whisper-
ing continued. There was no wind; autumn was stealing upon
us. The summer had gone, and we would go with it. We
should leave something behind as a personal memorial. I don't
know what would be best. People will forget whatever you
say; they will destroy whatever you create. Death is the only
safe thing. If we knock someone off his feet, nothing in the
world will make him stand upright again.

LET HIM SUE AT THE CEMETERY

AT DAYBREAK we found ourselves at the edge of a village
damp with dew. In front of us was a cluster of houses with
barns, a well, and under each window a wreath of peppers.
The last house on the right must belong to Yanko. We were
waiting for him and peering left and right: the shutters were
closed. The house was old and run down; one wall had fallen
in. Awakened by the dawn, the chickens were filing out, one
after another, stumbling as they reached the ground after a
short flight. One fell over and, scared by its own screech, fled
under the barn. Everything was strange. I would hide under
the barn myself if I could.

The day was breaking slowly. The ears of corn looked like
rusted knives. I was surrounded with knives that stabbed me

from all sides. I simply couldn't find a comfortable spot. My view was limited to the house and the walnut tree. There was no forest and no sky. I felt that we had come here in vain and that we would go back the wrong way. This evil premonition was in fact only fear. It had to be repressed. Finally the sun reached the crown of the walnut tree and coils of smoke began to rise above the roofs. We could hear bees buzzing and the voices of women. This quiet life, which had excluded us, continued its daily course like a gentle river.

An old woman opened the shutters and paused a moment, her eyes scanning the meadows. She didn't see us. Perhaps Yanko would appear now. We raised our rifles. Minutes passed slowly and aimlessly. They'd driven the cows out of the barn. Women were milking them. A huge old man staggered into the sheepfold, scratching himself as he gazed at the sky. The children had come together. They were kicking empty cans back and forth. I feared them too. They might come to pick corn, and uncover us too soon. And we would flee, and they would always remember that we had fled.

"Yanko isn't at home," I said. "If he were around he'd be with the men. God knows where he is."

"You're afraid."

"Not yet," I said. "I feel like smoking."

"So do the Chetniks when they wait for us. Yet they stick it out."

"I'll stick it out too. Until tomorrow. But that's the end."

The sweet smell of ripening corn and dry silk thickened the air, along with the smell of sties, chicken coops, and wine barrels and the dust from the straw mattresses lined up against the fence. Breathing was difficult and I was constantly coughing and sneezing. The murmur of talk, the animal grunts and screeches, the sudden laughter which sounded as though it were directed at us, was chopping my nerves to pieces. They must know where we were. They were watching us in our confusion and entanglement. Swarms of flies buzzed dully and ominously over the hay and rotten fruit.

"It's noon," said Yasha. "Yanko must have spent the night in town. There's no point in waiting for him any longer."

"Now you're afraid," I said to avenge myself.

"Never mind that. My feet and hands are numb."

"Rub them a little. It'll pass."

"It'll be over when we get out of here. Come on, let's run."

That was easy to say. In fact, we had to waddle through the long curved tunnels between the rows of corn, our rifles and knapsacks entangling us in the stalks and pumpkin vines. The sounds grew dimmer, finally thinning out to one continuous furrow of sound. The murmur and buzzing were no longer heard. Everything had fallen silent and turned its attention to us. They must have noticed us! It was crazy to assume they hadn't. We should get up and run, but I'd let Yasha be the one to start. If he didn't, why should I? This episode resembled those fearful dreams in which your knees grow weak and you sink into the mud up to your belly. At long last we reached the stream with blackberries, leading into the forest. I flopped in the shade to catch my breath, but Yasha wouldn't let me.

"Not here, let's go down the road!"

"I've had enough of roads. I want a smoke."

"I feel like smoking too. But what if Yanko's at the road now? It would save us another morning in that damned cornfield."

"To hell with it! Why should I kill him anyway? He doesn't deserve to die by a rifle."

"There's a spring there, Lado. We'll wash our faces like human beings."

That got me. The thin stream and the clear purling of water refreshed me a little. Above the spring there was a thicket of alders and hawthorns. We crawled into them and I closed my eyes. Let Yasha keep guard, if he likes! I forgot him instantly. I am alone again, and I am standing in a deserted street, in front of a house from which the smell of barbecued beef oozes out. I enter the house with the vague intention of stealing something. But I am confused: there's no one to serve me, only an infinite white sheet on which chunks of raw meat go past. I move closer to pick out a really nice piece. Some brains pass by, followed by a liver, some human ribs and a hand with a ring which I know from somewhere.

The hand frightens me. I turn to run away and in my haste I start in the wrong direction. Running down a narrow corridor is another conveyor belt with meat, descending the steps at an angle into the cellars where mills hum quietly. I rush frantically toward the doors, right and left; they keep opening. Yet there's no way out. Just meat. Someone shakes me. I've been caught. I practically dissolve in fear. I only have my eyes left. I open them. I have emerged from water; I see the forest, the skies above the trees.

Yasha was pushing me and pointing at something on the road. Two men: one had a rifle over his shoulder, the other one an ax.

"The one with a rifle," Yasha said, "is Yanko's closest friend."

"Shall we take care of him now, or shall we leave it until later?"

"Later. If we get him now, God Almighty won't be able to catch Yanko. And he's the chief here."

There are so many chiefs. We'll never get them all. We kept saying the same thing last autumn: let's not begin from the tail. But that was evasion. So we never got started. I don't know what to think. My brain is too small for such thoughts. It's too late anyway.

The two men were approaching, talking loudly about a debt and a time limit. One of them owed some money and refused to pay it.

"Let him sue me."

"Where would he sue you? In the cemetery?"

"Why not?" The man with the rifle smiled. "Is it my fault that there's no other place?"

"When there were courts he certainly used them enough."

There used to be people, two or three in each village, who couldn't wait to sue and take things to court. I didn't like

them either. They are in a difficult position now; this is an era
of robbers. This particular robber was young, and he was
handsome. He washed his hands and wiped them with his
handkerchief.

Yet if I don't kill him, Yasha will drag me into that cornfield
again. I'll have to crawl on my stomach and suffocate and risk
being caught like a badger. I prefer to stay alive. As for him,
let him carry on his lawsuits in the cemetery! I aimed at his
chest. He crouched down as if trying to avoid my bullet.

"I certainly drank a lot of milk at this spot," he said.

"How did you get milk here?" the other one asked him, and
sat down too.

"I used to tend goats not far from here. I would sleep, then
I would whittle a cup out of alder wood. I would milk the
goats and have a drink. . . ."

I thought of old Yug. Perhaps this fellow is poor too. I can't
kill him, I decided. And I wouldn't have done so, but his
friend started singing "Here's dawn, here's day," to which he
added in a stronger voice and quite cheerfully the refrain,
"There are no Partisans."

I didn't even let him finish this refrain. I pulled the trigger
and the butt shoved me under the throat like a fist. His chest
rose, and an inner voice, like an internal cough, reached us
from the other side. I slipped another bullet into the rifle. By
that time he was blindly waving his arms on the ground. The
earth under him was turning soft and sticky. The kicking suddenly slackened. Yasha rose and started toward the spring. I
followed him.

The other man had disappeared like a shadow, leaving his
ax behind him. Yasha called out to him several times, but got
no response. The dead man lay crouched by the water, which
sprinkled his colorless face. I pulled a tobacco pouch from his
waistcoat pocket. He had some good cigarette paper. I took
his ammunition too. I wanted to take his money as well, but
Yasha wouldn't let me. It's shameful, he said. I didn't see why

it should be shameful. Someone else would take his wallet and put the blame on us anyway.

His rifle lay by the bush where he had been sitting. Yasha looked at it pensively. Perhaps it was with this rifle that his good friend was killed. I could take it to Uncle Luka, but he was too far away. I pulled out the bolt and buried the shaft in the ground. We moved the dead man. A chirping bird hovered above us. We took off, but I kept thinking there was something important we had forgotten.

AN IMAGE FROM A DREAM

WHILE WE WERE crossing the ridge we saw an unfamiliar mountain spread before us. It was a long, strange mountain, like an old decayed wall which concealed a secret land. It was flat at the top and its sides were covered with heaps of rock and stone, as if some creature, infinitely stronger than any man, had stored these materials for some sort of construction. Between us and the mountain lay a spacious valley. The bottom of the valley couldn't be seen, just a plain that hovered above the void like a balcony, bordered with wreaths of pine.

I paused in amazement: it was out of one of my dreams. At the time I had wanted to escape from everyone. And this was exactly what I was after: grass-topped cliffs and a brook flowing into a little lake that was clear down to the very bottom. I took a few steps and was sad to find that this spot was already occupied. The grass had been mowed, the hay gathered. There were paths, and a field of potatoes, and behind it the

sheepfolds, huts, and a small house with windows. The lawn
in front was well kept. Someone lived here, and lived well.
They had dogs: quiet dogs, well-fed and as big as calves.
There was a haystack by the rock and scythes hanging nearby.

"These are prosperous people," I said to Yasha. "They have
spread out all over and are enjoying themselves."

"I think you know this man, Lado."

"I doubt it. I never had much to do with such men."

"But he was one of our people. He wanted us to come here
with him, and then left us."

"Vranovich, you mean. By God, he knew how to select a
good spot!"

Yasha nodded. He didn't like talking about Vranovich. A
year ago I would have been reluctant to bring him up myself,
but a lot has happened since then and customs have changed.
It had not been easy for our people to do away with him.
They tried to negotiate, but Vranovich was a stubborn man.
Perhaps this paradise played a role in his decision. For a long
time this old Communist had dreamed about an intelligent
world system, while organizing his own little world by these
cliffs.

"I've never been here," I said. "Let's look around."

"It's a village like any other: rennet bags and dung."

"Are we in danger of ambush?"

"The whole village is an ambush. You can imagine how they
feel about us. He was a saint for them!"

"I haven't met anyone for a long time who wishes me well."

Perhaps it's just as well if we don't look around. I'd like to
believe that it's as clean and pretty as it looks from a distance,
to enjoy it as one would a painting. To see a thing is the same
as owning it for a moment, and anyway one cannot really own
anything. It would get boring. I'll keep this moment, em-
bellished by memory, for future times. And who knows? If
men can create a miracle such as this, they may be able to
organize the world as well.

"But we can't go away hungry, can we, Lado?"

"You may have a point there. Let's go down and ask them for some food."

"Ask them? What do you mean?" Yasha exclaimed in astonishment.

"I don't expect them to offer us any."

"Something's wrong with you. You just don't think."

It's true. I don't. Sly, that's what I want to be. There was a time when I went into everything deeply, coming up with obstacles and problems: don't do this, don't do that. It turned out that everything was forbidden, except for the right to perish dismally. I've had enough of that! I'll take nothing with me anyway. I'll leave the forests and plum trees, and the sun and the moon and the sheep and the women. But until then I want to eat, to be warm, and to look at what pleases me.

The cliffs stood above us. They were looking at themselves in the lake, lit by the setting sun, swaying gently along with the clouds set in the blue beneath. Men hadn't done very much here—only retaining walls, bridges, and fences to enclose their wooden cottages. The dogs noticed us. A woman came out and looked at us suspiciously. Two children were playing on a seesaw, and stopped when they saw us. Another woman appeared. Visitors were rare here and were received gladly.

They asked us to come in, but we would have suffocated inside. To protect our backs we moved the bench next to the fence. They watched us carefully; we were a strange sort of guest. I was right on one point: only women and children live in this village. The shepherds are up with the cattle. The youngest brother, a former Marxist, is at Chetnik headquarters giving instruction on how to maintain links with the people. The women offered us a glass of sour milk as thick as porridge. We drank it slowly. We wanted to find out all we could about the village. The women relaxed and started talking.

They have mowed plenty of hay, but you never know when you have enough. The corn is good. The fruit too. Worms are at the potato crop. The village used to belong to some Turks.

Old Vranovich had been here recuperating from a lung disease. The Italians came by last summer, but didn't burn down
anything. All this was merely in the way of an introduction.
Soon they'd start asking us questions. To forestall them, I
said:

"If you've got any food, would you give us some? We are
pretty hungry and hunger has no soul."

"We'll find something. Come inside."

"Could you bring it out here? The air is better and the view
is excellent."

They brought some bread and a dish of milk. The women
fell silent. They watched us and wondered where we were
putting it all away. When we were through, one of the two
women said:

"You two shouldn't be seen around in the daytime. Someone
will denounce you."

"Let them denounce us as much as they like," I said. I had a
sudden impulse to lie, and I added. "We're on our way to
Bosnia. Let them look for us."

"To Bosnia?" The woman sounded surprised. "And what
will you eat on the way?"

"No problem. We go from sheepfold to sheepfold. In some
places people will give us food, in others we can pick fruit."

"Not many will give you food willingly. You've set everyone
against you."

I looked at her. She was determined to make us pay for
what we'd eaten. We'd set the people against us! If we had
listened to her brother-in-law, that saint and martyr, everything would have been all right. I was quick to change the
subject. Now that we were on our way, we were sorry to leave
everything: mountains and forests, rocks, fields. The war in
Bosnia was serious. Perhaps we would never return. And even
those who did return would be different men.

My speech saddened the women. In this wasteland, so barren of speech, words did not lose their original freshness, and
still sounded true.

"We are counting on your silence," I said.

"Don't worry, we don't spy on anyone."

"They would ambush us at the Tara. They don't know what they are doing."

"They never know," said the older woman. "Dust to dust, and ashes to ashes; that's what men are and that's what they are doing."

"Yes," I said, "and it's too early to bury us. Not a word."

They repeated their promise of silence. They certainly meant it, but women cannot keep secrets. They'll tell everyone we are going to Bosnia, and that's just what I want them to do. Let the Chetniks sweat it out up the Tara, and let them wait for us until they drop with exhaustion. When we don't turn up, they'll think that we've already crossed into Bosnia and they'll give us a little rest.

We heard a sheep bell sound from behind a ridge. We would have to go. The younger woman went to gather some leaves and washed them at the fountain. She wrapped two chunks of cheese in the leaves, and gave them to us for a happy journey.

I glanced once again at the lake, strangely lit by the setting sun and the reflections of the lower sky. It looked like a mirror which could vanish in an instant. Hard to give it up. We climbed on the ferry and rowed across the lake, hovering above the world, turned upside down. The sheep were bleating. The shepherds were watching us from the hill. One shepherd had a rifle. If he kills me . . . bless him! I could hardly stretch out on a more beautiful spot. And in years to come, when our new Communist bourgeoisie take their fat bellies for a ride in helicopters, they'll be able to say that they visited the graves of fallen fighters and paid them due respect.

MIRACLES OF VUKOLA TASLACH

BRANCH AFTER BRANCH, tree after tree, the forests are emerging in the early morning light. Beneath the yellow haze, which burgeons like rust from the dark and the cold, a continuous whisper of sorrow passes from valley to valley, from mountain to mountain. Nor is the sky as deep as it used to be; it gets smudgy and pale as the day advances. Clouds float by in the afternoon, unfold and cover the skies, and linger until morning. A good thing. Otherwise there would be frost every morning. And I fear the frost: it's extremely beautiful, the last beautiful event of the year, followed by an onslaught of rain, darkness, and snow. Snow means telltale tracks and dogs to gnaw at our bones. The devil himself will not be able to help us any more.

For the time being it's quiet and deserted. Between the village and the mountain there isn't a soul. My cunning, or, rather, that accidental lie, at the village of Vranovichi seems to have worked. They think we've gone. And they're no longer looking for us. In our idleness we search for rabbits, but they don't turn up either. In the troubled moonlight we descend into the plum orchard to pick plums. We feel heavy and our teeth grow numb. But no patrols. In the villages they are thinking only about badgers: making fires, turning noisy rattles, tossing live coals about to scare them off. All in vain. The freckled animals do their job. They gain weight, store up winter provisions, and keep up the species as usual.

Sometimes I think we should do the same: we should find a

hole and accumulate some food. Yasha is against it. We are not beasts yet, he says, and he keeps hoping for a change. We had been looking for Vukola Taslach, who could tell us what was new. There had been no sound of his ax in a long time, and that made us think he had been mobilized and taken to the Tara to wait for us in an ambush.

But he came by this morning, pale and limping. He was astonished to see us and squinted his eyes in disbelief. He looked at me as if he had me confused with someone else, as if he were trying to disentangle us. Ah, it's the uniform. I let him get his fill of surprise, and then I asked him:

"Did you acquire this limp at the Tara?"

"The Tara?" he said, aghast. "I haven't been anywhere near the Tara. Why should I go to the Tara?"

"To catch us when we came by. You must have heard that we were on our way to Bosnia."

"No one has heard anything. When are you leaving?"

"There you are," Yasha said, and looked at me in anger. "They obeyed you. They said nothing! Women always do things wrong, don't they?"

They wanted to help us, but they really played a trick on us. Never mind; the next women we meet will not keep secrets so well. Vukola sat down carefully. A falling tree had grazed him. It could have flattened him altogether. This time he had more luck than usual. Two days before the accident a doctor had fled the municipal hospital. It couldn't have happened at a better time. They say he is crazy. He probably is. Who in his right mind would leave a good job for this damned wasteland, and trade white bread for hominy? But he knows how to bind wounds and set bones. And he had saved Taslach!

"Where is he now?" Yasha asked.

"Near Bilo. He's got relatives there. They're hiding him."

"Either he's done something wrong," I said, "or he is imagining things. People do these days. What else is new?"

"There really isn't much," he said. "Old Savo died the other day."

"From brandy, I suppose. He really got his share this time."

"Well, they thought they'd killed you at the Leper's Cave. So Savo got drunk, and on his way home he was mounted by the devils—or so he said. Well now, something must have happened, for his cap was later found in the middle of the graveyard, and his skin was torn to shreds, as if he had been spurred and forced to jump fences. In the morning they found him in the pond, neither dead nor alive, raving like a maniac. Before the leaves fall, he said, Masnik will go too. And that's exactly what happened."

"What happened to Masnik?" Yasha asked him.

"Masnik slipped from an oak and broke his neck. Some say they heard a shot, but not a bullet scratched him. People think the devil did it. And that's not the only strange case. In Bilo they heard the devil bleating like a billy goat skinned alive. And above Yablan a hunter was found in a cave with his head battered in and his brains spilled out all over. Traces of the devil's paws were clearly seen in his brain. And his money wasn't touched."

There are all sorts of miracles these days, he said. A man who escaped from a camp at Scadar walked the whole way home on foot through strange country, but when he got home, where he knew every bush, he grew tired of hiding and reported himself. To make matters even more mysterious, he was not handed over to the Italians, not even put in prison. He was now sitting at home and crossing himself.

"Are there fewer patrols around," Yasha asked, "or are we just imagining things?"

"There are fewer. They've grown tired."

"We're getting tired too."

"They are sick to death of rifles," Vukola said. "They use clubs now."

"I guess they are no longer afraid of us," said Yasha.

"That's true," Taslach said, "but that's not the only reason. The wounded carry canes and limp. Others are envious of their glory, so they now limp and lean on canes too. It's easy enough to do. And a man looks important, especially where they don't know him. He can get ahead in queues and get his business done; and the Italians will take him in their trucks; and women prefer a man who is likely to stay in the back yard to some bastard who slings a rifle over his shoulder and doesn't know where he'll spend the night."

"It's strange," said Yasha. "It seems that carrying a rifle these days is a form of punishment."

"They say," added Taslach, "that when an army replaces rifles with clubs disaster will follow. The same happened in the last war. When the Austrians took to carrying canes, the old men prophesied their end and it came true. And Mlado Radoshich, who is a hundred years old, says that the confusion came about because of the fear of an evil year. People are afraid of hunger, he explained, the population has been reduced, and when the famine is over, one party will fall. He won't say which party because he'd get arrested."

Vukola smoked away to his heart's content. Finally he left, his ax over his shoulder. As he disappeared, I could see his broad back swaying, now to one side, now to the other. I felt as if old Taslach had brought us something. Something very important: human scale. We missed this, this salt without which the nerves grow weak. We needed it, so as not to grow dizzy from loneliness and not to drive each other mad.

Taslach had reached his clearing and was at work again. The rhythmic blows of the ax echoed beyond the mountains. Yasha glanced up and his face stretched into a smile.

THERE WILL BE PLENTY OF SUN . . .

THE TIRED WATERS are still. There is no wind and no sound. The calm of autumn is in the air and on the earth. Each day is like the next. A deafening silence. The mountains have exposed their ribs and their shoulders, scraped bare in past slaughters. The ferment is over. Everything has found its place. No more questions are asked. Perhaps we should do the same.

For my part, I was dreaming about good times to come: weddings and reconciliations when this turmoil was over. My daydream was interrupted by a rifle shot somewhere near the Lim. Another shot followed immediately, confirming the first. Their echoes met. Yasha, who was lying on his back, jumped up and looked down into the valley. There was nothing in sight except for the second crop of grass and the silvery willows by the river. Silence again, torn and mocking this time, and I realized that it was much too early and quite ridiculous to think about peace.

"The shots seemed muffled, didn't they?" asked Yasha. "What do you think?"

"They hit flesh."

"Rotten flesh. Probably a fox."

"A fox, definitely. One of those two-legged foxes."

"They'll say, of course, that we did it," said Yasha. "There are no witnesses to prove the opposite."

I don't give a damn about witnesses! Even if there were a dozen of them, I should not try to vindicate myself: my account has long since been settled. They can kill me only once, and this one head cannot make up for theirs. But it's different with Yasha. His doubt is like a wound. He believes that his brother Zaro bled instead of him, and that an unjust revenge will continue to pursue his innocent young brothers. That's why he chose that grass-eating life from which I snatched him.

"Well," he said, "it's quiet again. Perhaps it was nothing."

"It was something all right. Why do you fool yourself?"

"All right, if you insist. But maybe they killed a mad dog."

"The maddest dog these days is a man."

If it's one of our men, I am not sorry for him. What was he looking for down there anyway? Why try to live both here and there, sitting on two stools at once? I don't care much for those who provide for their future by sleeping in bed. If he is one of our men, he should join us here, bide his time as I do, and bathe in the sun. The day is going by very slowly. Lit up from the west, the cliffs look like the ruins of a castle. One might find interesting stuff there. I'll take a look one of these days. We separate to search for rabbits in two different clearings. In fact, I don't care much for rabbits. I know they won't come out. But if Yasha wants to go his way, let him go! It's easier to part this way.

He came back at sundown. I'd forgotten those two shots, but he was at it again. It's constantly on his mind, and he'll make himself ill if he doesn't find out what happened. We descended to an orchard at Meda and picked plums. We found Luka Ostoyin lying in bed under his apple tree! He was glad to see that I was not alone. Apples and brandy with gentian had cured his cough. He pulled out a bottle from under his pillow. It's pleasant here. He listens to the leaves as they fall, one by one. That puts him to sleep. The weather is good too, a nice long summer, perhaps his last, so he might just as well make the most of it.

"We heard a couple of shots from down here," said Yasha. "What was it all about?"

"A man was killed. The oil dealer; no great loss. He was neither fish nor fowl."

"The one with the beautiful daughters," I said to Yasha.

"Do you know who killed him?" Yasha persisted.

"Who knows?" said Uncle Luka. "It's been in the making for some time now. He used to sue his neighbors and take people to court for nothing. This is as good a time as any to make him pay for it."

"Good crop of corn this year," Yasha declared.

"Yes, but it won't do me any good," answered Luka. "It's a lot of work, and I can't do it alone."

"Can Iva help?" I asked.

"How could she? She can't get her own work done."

I should have taken the money from Neda's father-in-law. It wasn't his money anyway. Iva and Luka could have hired dayworkers. Next time I won't leave any pockets empty. Uncle Luka continued to blabber about the need for extra help. He seemed to think I knew someone who could help him. I got bored listening to him. He is crazy, and so is Yasha, and so am I.

We crossed the river and the mowed fields, and reached Iva's. She came out. Her face was round again. I asked Yasha if he liked my sister-in-law, but he was embarrassed, and couldn't even look at her. I felt sorry for him. He knows women only from books, whatever else he may say.

"When will your woman come?" she asked me. "We've been waiting for her."

"Oh, is that it? Why did you have to tell Luka? Anyway, I can't bring her. I have no wedding guests."

"But the best man is here already," and she pointed at Yasha. "He'll bring her."

"Something went wrong, Iva. It's best not to talk about it."

"I'm sure someone has been telling you lies and filling your ears with nonsense. That always happens, and I wouldn't listen."

She covered her face with her hands. She had hoped for company and made plans. I shouldn't have demolished them

just like that. And why all this fuss? Because of two words the
old bastard spit out.

"You shouldn't abandon her,'" Iva said. "There's nothing
more sinful."

"You just mind your child, Iva. Leave the rest to me."

She looked at me as if I had slapped her on the wrists. And
on that note we parted. She'd feel better after she'd had a
good cry. I quickened my pace to avoid Yasha's questions. He
didn't know the terrain. He stumbled now and then and had
to hurry to catch up with me. I hoped he'd ask no questions—
let everyone go his own way. He knew enough. But I was not
afraid and I had no regrets. We reached Gluv. I sat down
under a wild plum tree to have a smoke. Yasha seated himself
under another plum tree and dozed off.

The bitter smell of autumn alders arose from the ravine.
Once upon a time girls used to gather there to amuse themselves with a strange game: "A dead man, a dead man! Where
shall we take him? To the Fairy's graveyard . . ." And they
bury him, help themselves to some fruit from a basket, and
sing: "Hey, why did you leave me, Lado, Lado?" I closed my
eyes and listened once again to those voices soaring upward
into the clear sky above Turiya.

RAIN

DURING THE NIGHT a cold rain came down, penning us in a dry
circle under a juniper. The rain was continuous. We left our
circle only once: to bring the flour in. We should never have
done it: the gray smell of the mill, the cellar, the larder now

replaced the scent of the summer, resin, and pine needles. Hours went by slowly. A black day brings black thoughts. In my despair I tried to read *The Theory of Heredity*, in which a sly bearded academician convincingly argued that our struggle was hopeless. Genes were immutable and along with them races and classes—everything we wanted to clean up with one stroke. Finally I tossed the book away. I was miserable enough without it.

Sleep seemed more spacious and clean, but then I kept hearing a black goat, wounded and scared to death, bleating sadly somewhere in the clouds. I woke up. It was the rain drumming against the puddles and into the swollen streams. The smell of flour, mold, and wet shoes was choking me. I closed my eyes, wanting to creep back into my sleep again. But then, from above, from the clouds or the hill, a voice was calling out: "Shar, my little one, Shar!" It was a woman's voice, Neda's; and the Shar she was looking for was me! No other ox or devil would dare get lost in such weather. Her voice was mournful. Perhaps they'd beaten her and brought her here to bait me out of my hiding.

"I don't think she is looking for a bull," Yasha said suddenly. "It's you. Call her!"

"And the patrol too?" I asked belligerently.

"Not on a night like this!"

I don't believe anyone. Why not on a night like this? Their Italian shoes and raincoats will keep them dry. They've won a lot of people over, why not Neda? Out of revenge. So many rebels have lost their lives because of women. Some good-looking Chetnik may have promised to marry her in return for her help. He may fool her, yet he may not. As for Neda, she is pregnant, she wants to bear a child and keep it at all costs.

"What's the matter?" asked Yasha.

"It's too dark. If you're so bold, why don't you call?"

"My voice would frighten her. Come on, get going! We'll see if she's got a patrol with her."

He shoved me out of the shelter and we set off. The rain

grew heavier. The territory I knew so well suddenly appeared different. Fast streams and ravines on all sides. We waded through cold puddles up to our ankles and bumped into trees. I went headlong into a thorny juniper bush. The voice had vanished like an apparition. Perhaps it was an apparition, or Obrad's soul, in search of revenge. We climbed up the hill, through a forest, and straight into a cloud. I paused: we should be at the spot where the voice had come from.

We waited for a while and listened to the deep roar from the valleys. Our eyes had partially adjusted to the dark. We could see each other at a distance of three paces, like monsters. We'd never be able to find our way back to the shelter. There was no need to go back anyway. We were wet through. It would be best to go back down into the trees and make a fire. While we were heading down we heard that pale, hopeless voice again. We were in a field of burned-down stumps, which resembled an advancing army. I got scared. I would have fled if Yasha hadn't been with me. A stooping shadow singled itself out and staggered across the field. Alone. I called out her name. She was startled and stood up.

"Thank God," she cried out. "I thought the earth had swallowed you up."

"There's plenty of time for that," I said. "What's the trouble?"

"Vasil is looking for you," she replied. She noticed Yasha and shuddered.

"That's Yasha. He is on our side. Why isn't Vasil here himself? Why did he send you?"

"He couldn't come. He's sprained his leg. We must move him from the cave; that's why I'm here."

Was that the only reason? I'd much prefer it to be an excuse. Well, it didn't matter. Her hand was small and warm. I lit a match, she squinted bashfully. A wisp of black hair fell across her face. With a swift movement she pushed it back. The match went out and everything sank into darkness. I grabbed her and pressed her to my chest as if she could save me from the troubled waters swelling up in the valleys. Now I saw her again, with my skin and muscles, and I was not going to let her get away. She was still slender, her lips were as fresh as rain-washed plums. She resisted me and she yielded. Her breathing was rough.

She slipped from my hands like a fish. I looked back. Yasha had discreetly vanished. I called him. There was nothing to conceal here. There were so few beautiful things in life. Why should we renounce them? All my doubts had vanished. Her father-in-law lied in order to confuse me and poison me, and in my idleness I had made up ridiculous stories. Even if, like a beautiful book, she had been touched by other hands, she was mine now.

I thought of Vasil. I was ashamed that I'd let him slip my mind.

"He moves too rapidly," I said, "that's why something is always happening to him. What is it this time?"

"They drove him into the cliffs. He stumbled and fell. They thought he was done for and that saved his life."

"How on earth did you find him?"

She had heard the shots and the following day seen the Chetniks searching for his body under the cliffs. They couldn't believe that a man could survive such a fall. She had assumed they were looking for me, and she had set out to find me. She had finally come across Vasil yesterday, and had been caring for him since.

Ah, my Neda exists in the daytime too! Lucky Vasil! I envy him a little, and I resent him a little. I can see Vasil leaning on her arm as they made their way up to the cave.

We slipped down the slope on the wet grass, I holding her by the hand and around the waist, as in a dance. The mole-hills had turned into springs and gurgled with underground voices. The river, which was almost dry yesterday, had risen, depositing bushes and stumps over the fields. It was constantly choking itself with new drifts, murmuring and mumbling as if a hundred mills were going at once. Cheering, wailing, roaring and savage laughter—all sounded together in a rising din. That's the way we are: everything at once and without restraint. Neda waded into the river. We followed her.

"It's a good thing you didn't come back to the village," she said.

"I wanted to, but I felt something was wrong."

"Something was. They were constantly poking around."

Her mother-in-law egged them on, suspecting that Obrad had been sleeping with Neda. She also believed that it was Neda who had betrayed him to that Partisan. A typical story of the times: everyone is suspicious and everyone is suspected. Men are ambushed every day and all that's left the next morning are a few cigarette butts on the trampled earth.

"Go to my people," I told Neda. "Iva expects you."

"You mean it?"

"Of course I do! Tell that monster you're through with her!"

"I can't enter a strange house just like that."

"Why not? The house is strange to them too. Our own burned down. Anyway, most people live in strange houses these days."

She will go. One has to go somewhere. When she married Obrad's son, there was a big wedding, singing, cheering, and speechmaking. She entered a prosperous house, but an unhappy one. Now she is going into a strange borrowed home as an uninvited guest. Perhaps things will improve.

In the forest the branches fluttered and shook off the rain. We didn't notice that it had stopped raining until we got to a clearing. We looked at one another in bewilderment: The rain has stopped! The water murmured and the mist rose in large patches like rocks. The clouds broke up, exposing patches of clear sky with a sprinkling of stars. We were soaking wet. But that was of no consequence. One morning of sun will dry us out. We must move the flour again. I didn't want to be reminded of winter and mice. It was too early for winter and its despairs. Perhaps we would have another week or two of warm weather, even a month. By then the situation might have changed for the better. Perhaps a change had already occurred, but we knew nothing about it. How could such news have reached us in our isolation? It didn't matter. I was full of senseless joy. I wanted to cheer, and had I been alone I would have done so: Hurrah, we are still alive!

VASIL AND THE FIRE

WE REACHED THE entrance to the cave, which looked exactly like a pig's snout, its tongue, coarse with wet gravel, sticking out. Accustomed to open spaces, I grew alarmed. Beset by memories, I wanted to retreat. In one of my dreams I had arranged for someone to be murdered and I buried him in the sand by the riverbank. He would never have been discovered except that the river itself unearthed my secret, exposing the bones through the slushy flesh of mud, and a face with eyes wide open. . . . The dream had come back, suggesting some imminent reality. The corpse had extricated itself, and they were taking me to it.

I hoped they hadn't noticed how shaken I was. It lasted only an instant, and I cursed aloud as if I had hurt myself. Yasha took a candle out of his bag. I lit it and went inside. My footsteps echoed as if a ghost were sealing the entrance behind me. The ceiling of the cave hung low, like a cloud; moisture dripped from it and gurgled in the puddles and on the rocks. Whole regions seemed to be locked in an eternally dead autumn. Shadows were dancing and a mountain loomed up in the distance, then a valley and a human settlement with a red fire in its midst. I clung to a rock for protection and yelled:

"Vasil! Don't fire, you idiot!"

"I'll spare you. But I shouldn't. It's all your fault."

He knows everything. That's why he's come back. Still, it's too soon to yield. I must be resourceful.

"Everyone knows who is to blame," I said. "You and Kacharanda."

"That's true," he said. "But you won't get away with it, you know that."

He must be joking. There's no real danger. I approached him. He had let his mustache grow and it dominated his elongated bony face. He started to press my hand, but changed his mind, and our handshake turned into something limp and lifeless. He pricked me with his mustache in the name of a kiss. He was dressed in the same old rags, but new holes had come to life among the coagulated heap of patches. Through the holes I could see pieces of his flesh, like artificial limbs of skin and dry oak. And he stank! He hadn't had a bath, nor had he changed clothes since we last saw each other. He shook hands with Yasha, and gazed at him in surprise.

"I don't know this one," he said. "Is he a newcomer?"

"You don't know Yasha? Remember the bum with the cauldron in the forest . . . ?"

"He's no bum now. I wouldn't have recognized you either. . . . Where did you get that uniform? And an officer's at that!"

"It was a gift," I said, winking at Yasha.

"No one ever gives me gifts. It's a strange thing."

If he is mocking me, let him! That's the way I was born. An aristocrat of the Nemanyichi blood, and blood is not water. Besides, genes, as you know, are immutable. One day without lice is preferable to three days of honesty and atonement. What can he do to me? At the most he'll take Yasha away from me, and that would be a good thing: get him out of my way! I can do as I please! In a month I'll become a genuine folk hero:

rascal and bandit. Perhaps that's my destiny. I'll steal horses, change women, and when my name is brought up in conversation, they'll scratch behind their ears in wonderment.

"Your ankle is swollen," said Yasha, examining Vasil. "It must hurt badly."

Ah! Yasha wants to flatter Vasil. Next it'll be Neda's turn. Never mind! I can manage on my own. I'll show them.

"If the bone isn't broken," I said belligerently, "it'll heal in a month or so."

"What do you mean?" Vasil was aghast. "If I can get out of this damned cave and into the sun, it'll pass in a day."

"There may be no sun until the spring, and that's a pretty long wait."

They all looked at me in surprise. What's bothering him? To smooth matters over, Neda spread out the sailcloth with which we planned to fashion a stretcher for Vasil. For slings we used the straps from our rifles. We placed Vasil on the stretcher. Yasha scattered the burning coals and the remaining pile of wood. Neda swept up the coals. We left no traces. When misfortune strikes again we can make use of this spot. Perhaps it'll be of use to me personally: to amass my booty and lead lost souls astray.

We lifted the stretcher. Vasil was not heavy, but it felt as if the cave had suddenly grown bigger. We just barely managed to get out. Entangled somewhere in the clouds the moon burned like an ember in the ashes. It had thinned out the night and clearly defined the boundaries of the forests and pastures. Vasil took leave of Neda. In the past we used to promise golden mountains for such favors, but he refrained from doing so. I liked that. The future was too far off. I walked a few paces with Neda, to thank her myself. She must join Iva, but she mustn't quarrel with her. Perhaps we would see each other again. As we shook hands our fingers became enlaced. A tiny dull cry. I jerked my hand away.

We waded across the ford and through fields, going around the forest to avoid the dampness of the dripping branches.

The trip was longer that way, but we were in no hurry. We had plenty of time. The more time we lose, the more we have won. The clouds were amassing and scattering alternately, followed by a breeze which dried our clothing. We unbuttoned our coats and pulled out our shirts so they too could get dry. We paused on several well-drained plateaus where there were no molehills and no springs. We watched the sawlike cliffs of fog rising from the valleys and disintegrating as the mountains emerged from the sea. The din had subsided.

The dawn chased us from the crags into the forest. I thought I saw Vasil smiling to himself. He must be feverish. I asked him what amused him. It was better to laugh, he said, than to cry. By now we were quite warm. Finally we reached our shelter under the juniper. We separated the branches and entered. It was dry inside. Not a drop of rain had fallen on the soft brown layer of pine needles. It felt as though it had been dry like that for ages. The air was a bit moldy. Vasil smelled the flour immediately, like a rat.

"Look at that! Sacks of flour!" he cried. "You seem to have quite a household here. Not bad, not bad."

"Folks give," I said.

"I know folks, and how they give. It's like the story of Voyo the Driver."

And he told us the story. Voyo was sent out to make an important investigation. He came upon a lamb, slaughtered it, and roasted it on a spit. He divided it up among the comrades, and they had a feast. Subsequently, their consciences began to bother them and they decided to expel Voyo from the Party for his bad behavior. He was damned angry. He went straight to Chetnik Headquarters. Instead of throwing him in prison, they gave him a bagful of lire as down payment for the murder of Ivan Vidrich. Off Voyo went, with the money, straight to Ivan. Now they are sitting together and biding their time, and with the Chetnik money they buy a little wheat now and then.

"Any other news?" I asked him.

"Goyan was here. He demanded your immediate expulsion from the Party."

"Really? Why not? But let's start with him."

"A good idea," said Vasil. "But all the same you shouldn't have said that his gun was infested with lice. He is a party leader, he leads. . . ."

Yes, unfortunately, that's why we are having such a time. He was in charge at Kolashin and generally he displayed a superior ability to mess things up. That's why they sent him to us. I don't know what it's all about—perhaps we are still paying some ancestral debt—but we are always blessed with some such Jehovah. I insulted this character, and now why don't you throw me overboard, as you did Niko and others? But I am a different kind of Jonah: the whale will have a tough time swallowing me.

"Forget it," said Vasil. "There's plenty of time. What do you think, will it clear today?"

"No, and not tomorrow either. But I have other faults, ten times as many as Voyo the Driver."

"Why should you boast so much? We all have faults. If it doesn't clear today, we're in trouble."

"Don't you care at all what I did during the summer?"

"Not in the least. You tell Ivan Vidrich about it, if you're so anxious for a quarrel. Or Goyan! He's been looking for someone to shoot for a long time now. To build up his prestige. But leave me alone. I am not going to be your confessor."

He sounded as if he had been alone longer than I. But if he doesn't know what a crime is, he certainly knows a lot about punishment. He'll drag me into the mountains to bicker with him, to watch him making fires and Ivan extinguishing them, to rear a family of lice and to live in fear of patrols until doomsday. It could be amusing, though, at least in the beginning: company, people, a few jokes, and the usual chatter about everything from the Chinese to the co-operative farms. If I get bored I can always look for Voyo the Driver. We have so much in common, why shouldn't we loaf together? We could work on a number of interesting projects.

My soul is precipitous, cut with peaks and abysses, like the Wailing Mountain. There are no other directions in it except up and down. Not long ago I tumbled without reason into the darkness, now I am soaring without support into the clear blue sky of a freedom that doesn't exist. There's no middle ground, no pause or rest so long as one is alive, or thereafter. Others must feel much the same, for we seem to be like hazy mirrors of that space and time which has been assigned us. We are climbing slowly, like the mists. And we are coming to leaf. We fall as quickly as water. We surpass each other in good and evil.

FOG

THE SUNLIT HILL rocked for a few moments, a golden castle hovering between the sky and the earth. Its banners of pine trees suddenly vanished along with the crystal towers of dew that glistened on its translucent rocks. The waves of fog were subsiding: the ugly polyp from the troubled waters below, which had spent the night gathering together scattered limbs and tails, was digesting the filth and beauty of the old Earth in its intestines. The only sound was the constant humming of the jaws of this sea beast as it grazed the branches, chewed up the leaves, melted away the hills stone by stone.

Only we were left: the last victims, our heads lowered. With our cauldron, our flour, our books, and our superfluous memories we seemed helpless and quite ridiculous. Vasil felt like having a fire, and Yasha made one for him. Out of felled stumps we constructed benches to stretch out on whenever we wanted. The pine crackled in the fire, foreboding imminent battle. The tall flames danced in front of our eyes, throwing up red knives and sparks to defend us against the fog. I was watching it. I was dreaming. Finally I got bored. I felt hopelessly ill; to save myself I had to climb above the fog and clouds and reach the sun again.

"This could last a long time," Vasil said. "If I had a horse I'd gallop over to the other side of the Lim."

"Of course," I said, to goad him on, "there's a brilliant sun shining on the other side. And as for a horse, there're plenty of them in the fields. Why waste time? I'll fetch you one right now. No problem."

"Wait a minute," Vasil said. "The fog might suddenly clear, and then what would I do with a stolen horse?"

If he doesn't need one, I don't either. So, I am not going to steal horses and lead people astray. They're wrong in thinking that theft is my passion. Besides, who wants to go down there anyway, and dive into that damn fog? I can barely breathe here.

I collected eighteen pebbles, nine white and nine black. I carved three squares in the stump, one enclosed within the other, and Vasil and I played Mitsa, the backwoods ancestor of chess. I won often; that didn't make the fog any thinner. Then I lost; that didn't give me pleasure either. Finally Vasil got bored; we were too old for this game.

"We might try that doctor from Bilo," Yasha said. "Perhaps he can fix your ankle."

"Why not? If he is really a doctor," Vasil said. "But what's a doctor doing there?"

"He's fleeing from something."

"Let's find out about him. Maybe he's one of us. Or just an honest man."

"I don't know if he is one of us," I said, "but honest he is, because they say he's crazy."

We gathered a heap of branches and roots for Vasil. He could amuse himself by throwing them into the fire. Then we set off in search of the mad doctor. Let's hope the doctor hasn't regained his senses.

In the fields it was a little clearer. I could see Yasha three paces away. He looked like a sea demon. There were other ghosts around: one vanished only to be replaced by another. On the Devil's Table several devils were quarreling over their dinner; they fled in front of us, leaving the spout running. We washed our faces and drank a little water. I wiped my mouth with my handkerchief.

Miracle water: our eyes were able to penetrate the fog, and in the middle of it we spotted a small valley, like a deep well. At first I thought it was an illusion—nature playing with us again and showing off its imagination. We descended into the well, its sides hairy with pine. Below, a stream flowed through a deep crack in the pines. A big rabbit, his ears up, darted out and hopped along the bank in front of us. He hid himself among the alders and, just as I thought he had gone away, emerged to show me his rear end again. He kept repeating this performance. Finally I lifted my rifle.

"Don't," Yasha said. "Vasil might think we are being pursued."

"Only one shot! Can't you see that the damned rabbit is taunting me?"

"Rabbits bring bad luck. To hell with him!"

"All right, but if he makes a fool of me once again, he's done for."

No such luck. He was gone. While we were engaged with the rabbit, an avalanche of fog tumbled down and quietly buried us in the valley. The sound of the brook suddenly seemed remote, and its murmur was drowned out by the soft, almost inaudible humming which accompanied the fog. We

rushed back toward the hillside, lest we forget our route
down. After a few steps I realized that I had already forgotten it. But I continued in the same direction to conceal from
Yasha that we were in fact lost. We pushed ahead. Still no
sign of the hill. It was as though the fog had destroyed it and
swallowed it up. Only the pits were left and white stones that
looked like bones picked clean.

The air I was inhaling was in fact nothing but muck. It
smelled of swamps and urine, of raw clay. My hair was full of
this smell. It was in my clothing and on my tongue. It had
penetrated into my lungs and I felt it in my blood. It had
made me stupid. How else could I explain my ridiculous condition? A dream? A painless disease? Everything was soft and
vague and damp. A firmament of gray dough, limitless and
formless. I was diving into it, falling through it, searching in
vain for support, for focus. Wherever I turned caves opened
up in front of me: winding corridors, rising and falling.

"You don't know where you are," Yasha said. "You've lost
your way."

"Yes, I have. How did you know?"

"We've passed this rock once already. Perhaps twice."

"That means nothing. There are many such rocks. They're
fog anyway."

"That's no fog. Touch it. You'll see."

I touched it and felt as if I were awakening from a stupid
dream. Thank God! We'd come across someting solid at last!
In vain I tried to figure out where we were. This rock was
different from any other I'd come across. Perhaps it was a new
one, or an old rib of the Wailing Mountain, once covered with
soft flesh, now decomposed by the fog. It didn't matter. I
patted it with my hand, on the neck, as if it were a horse,
taking some odd pleasure in its solidity. The world had not
yet vanished and one could still distinguish up from down. I
was walking alongside the cliff, and I was almost sad at the
thought that I'd have to leave it soon and that perhaps I'd
never know where it was.

I picked up a pebble at the foot of the cliff, and put it in my pocket. A good-luck charm. I felt more secure already. We started uphill again. We couldn't find a path. Even if there were one, the rains would have washed it away. We frequently stumbled upon thick roots, indicating that there were forests around. The smell of resin, diluted and altered, reminded us sorrowfully of a summer which was at times beautiful. The air was somewhat clearer. My head too. We were getting to the top. In the midst of the continuous humming one could feel the wind in the branches, and in the distance a dull sound was being repeated at regular intervals.

"Do you hear what I hear?" asked Yasha. "Sounds like an ax."

"It must be Taslach. The man is building a house."

"If we follow the sound of his ax, we'll get back where we started from."

"That won't work either. As soon as we drop down into the valley the sound'll vanish."

"All right, then let's keep going. If worst comes to worst, we'll run into the Lim, or perhaps the Tara, and we'll know where we are."

The smell of squashed blueberries followed us up the grubby hillside. Concealed behind burned stumps, ghosts were squinting out at us. I paused on a plateau. I smelled something familiar in the air, and I was sure that I'd been here before. On that occasion I couldn't see very much either, but I heard voices of tired men from the valley. To frighten them I had forced Mikla to bleat like a billy goat. The wind was driving toward the valley as it did then, brushing my forehead and temples. It must be the same spot. I yelled and waited for an echo to confirm my memory. Yes. It was the place.

Yasha was startled. "What in hell are you doing, Lado?"

"I know where we are. We are getting closer."

"Closer to what?"

"Bilo is below us, and the road is somewhere over there behind those bushes. Let's take a look."

"Perhaps we are on the road right now."

I bent down to get a better look, and in disbelief I touched the ground with my hands. Yes, it was the road. It had stolen upon us and silently offered itself as a guide. It was almost playing around our feet—yellow, wet, with its ribs sticking out. I stroked it. I felt like kissing it. Uneven and rocky, trampled with feet and hoofs, it was tough and it cut effortlessly through the fog. I was walking along it and wiping away my perspiration. I hadn't felt so good in a long time: we knew where we were, we knew where we were going, and I was full of joy at the thought that there was some purpose in our wandering.

It was late in the afternoon and night would fall soon. Suddenly it began to clear above the valley. Here and there trees appeared, yellow with an occasional green leaf, shaking the remaining tufts of fog from their branches. I looked toward the mountains. The huge polyp of mist was breaking up. Its fragmented limbs and tails wandered above the valleys, searching for one another in vain. Their rocking made the mountain sway. Waves of green hillside emerged, rocky ribs strewn across their shoulders. The cliffs were lit by the invisible sun, golden and red.